The Michigan Humanities Council

The Michigan Humanities Council connects people and communities by fostering and creating quality cultural programs. It is Michigan's nonprofit affiliate of the National Endowment for the Humanities. Since 1974, the Michigan Humanities Council has supported communities through family literacy programs, special cultural and historical exhibits, book discussions, author tours, scholarly lectures, films, cultural celebrations, and school programs and performances that have reached millions of people.

The Great Michigan Read

The Michigan Humanities Council's Great Michigan Read is a book club for the entire state with a focus on a single book—*X: A Novel* by Ilyasah Shabazz and Kekla Magoon. The program is intended for young adults to senior citizens, with broad goals of making literature more accessible and appealing while also encouraging residents to learn more about our state and individual identities.

GREAT MICHIGAN READ

The 2017–2018 Great Michigan Read is presented by:

MichiganHumanitiesCouncil
our stories, our lives

Made possible through the generous support of:

The National Endowment for the Humanities
Meijer

The Historic Ford Estates

Charles H. Wright Museum of African American History

Library of Michigan

Detroit Public Library Foundation

Zingerman's Community of Businesses

Sarah Jury

MSU Federal Credit Union

Michigan Radio

X

a novel

Ilyasah Shabazz

with

Kekla Magoon

CANDLEWICK PRESS

Copyright © 2015 by Ilyasah Shabazz

Photograph of Malcolm Little on p. 350 courtesy of
Rodnell P. Collins/Ella L. Little-Collins Estate

First paperback edition 2016

This edition published specially for the Michigan Humanities
Council 2017 by Candlewick Press

Library of Congress Catalog Card Number 2014931838
ISBN 978-0-7636-6967-6 (trade hardcover edition)
ISBN 978-0-7636-9092-2 (trade paperback editon)
ISBN 978-1-5362-0000-3 (Michigan Humanities Council edition)

17 BVG 1

Printed in Berryville, VA, U.S.A.

This book was typeset in Berkeley Old Style.

Candlewick Press
99 Dover Street
Somerville, Massachusetts 02144

visit us at www.candlewick.com

Dedicated to my nephew, Malcolm, in loving memory. And to the far too many young people who seek a father figure: You alone have the power to accomplish what you will. To accomplish every goal. Clear every obstacle. Win every challenge. You have the gift of an indomitable Spirit. Stay strong, focused, and determined.
With love, Ilyasah Shabazz

For my dad
K. M.

Harlem, New York, 1945

Friends tell me trouble's coming. I ease out of the restaurant onto the sidewalk, gun in my pocket. Hand in there, too, keeping it close for good measure. I gotta get back to my pad, and quick now. One foot in front of the other. Keep my head down, hope no one sees me.

"Hey, Red," someone says, out of the shadows. I flinch, flick my fingers on the metal. Detroit Red, they call me, though Michigan seems far behind me now. "Hey, Red, I heard Archie's looking for you."

West Indian Archie. The numbers runner I work for. My pulse beats firmer under my skin. "Oh, yeah?" I play it cool. Keep moving.

Half strangers know? Hell. Rumors don't lie. West Indian Archie's mad. He says I wronged him, but I didn't. You'd have to be out of your mind to try to cheat a guy like Archie.

A door slams somewhere along the block, and I jump about a mile. A voice calls out, but not to me. I clutch the gun in my coat and scurry on.

How did it all go so wrong? When I first set foot in Harlem, I was a step ahead of everything. I could blend in with the jive cats, swirl the Lindy ladies, let my feet groove, think of nothing but the now. I could close my eyes, and in closing them not be seen. Slip into the seams of the streets and let them swallow me. It was a glorious fit, so seemingly warm.

The slick, savvy streets of Harlem welcomed me. I've made friends here, a life here, a whole world opening up.

But now I've messed it all up, in a big-time way. No going back.

Cop car comes rolling around the corner, real slow. Damn. Got to keep outta sight.

In the middle of the block, there's a bar I know. Might be best to get inside now.

"Hey, Red," the bartender says first off. "Archie's looking for you. He's good and steamed. Watch out."

"So I heard," I say, hand in my pocket.

Bartender looks me up and down. "Well, well. You fixing to fight?"

"I don't know," I say. "I don't know."

Sitting at the bar is an old man from the islands. He moves himself in that wise, wrinkled way. His warm, open expression gives me the out-of-place feeling that he can help me somehow, maybe even save me. I want to lean into it, but when he speaks, it's to send me away: "You should get outta town, son. And I mean today."

The door bangs open. Our three heads turn. A beat cop from the neighborhood strolls in.

My hand is still on the gun. I ease it out of my pocket, up onto the bar, behind the old islander's back. The bartender slips it out of sight behind some bottles, but I still can't breathe.

"Detroit Red," the cop says. "You been causing trouble?"

"No, sir," I mutter, summoning a layer of polite. I raise my arms for the pat-down. The bartender meets my eye, wipes the counter. *You owe me one,* he's thinking. And I know he'll collect.

"You're clean," the cop says, which is a strange piece of fortune. No reefer, no joint, no stray bag of powder. I place my hands in my pockets, real casual. The cop stands close. I've seen him around, patrolling the neighborhood. I wouldn't have guessed he would know me by name. "I would've thought you'd be carrying," he adds. "Rumor is you've got a gun."

"Maybe I had one," I answer. "Maybe I threw it in the river."

The cop breathes peppermint inches from my face.

"Watch your back, now," he says, a little bit pleased. I remain stuck there, unmoving, as he strolls out.

It's hard to breathe, to think.

"Get outta here, Red," the bartender says. "I don't want any trouble."

I leave the bar the back way. All that's left is to run. If there's one thing I can do, it's run. I've already been running for so long.

The avenues are alive with people, late afternoon. Stretch your legs and shoot the breeze. Let your throat loose and holler. Blow off steam. An everyday scene.

Not for me. Not today. I run.

People try to stop me. Try to warn me. "Watch out—"

I can't make it home. Not like this.

I race up to my friend Sammy's pad. Sammy's stretched out on the bed, floating high. He lifts his head. Sees me standing there, panting, fists clenched. "My man," he says. "You bringing trouble up in here?"

"I'll just be here a minute." I shut myself in the bathroom, splash some water on my face.

"Red?" Sammy calls. "You OK?"

I'm not. I'm not OK.

My skin is flushed hot. I let the water run, dip my cheek into the ice-cool flow. It feels good.

"Red," Sammy calls. "Archie's down front. His guys say he's coming up. They say he's got a gun."

My knees buckle. My body bumps down onto the tile, back against the door, tucked as small as I can. I close my

4

sweat-stung eyes. And there are tears now, salty and hot. What have I done?

"Red!" Sammy shouts. He bangs on the bathroom door. "You gotta go, man. You gotta go now!"

I curl against the cold tiles. I never imagined I'd be brought so low. Archie's here to kill me, and there's nothing I can do.

My life flashes before my eyes. Every place I've ever known. Every face I've ever loved. Everything I've ever done . . . And it all seems like a dream now, as if any minute I'll wake up in my childhood bed in Lansing, Michigan, and I'll be five years old, with Papa still alive and Mom home and smiling, her arms open wide to hold me.

But Sammy's voice is what's real. "Red! You hear me? Red!"

Here and now, I don't want to be Detroit Red. I want to slip the skin of this life, to be new and clean again. Just start over. I've done it before. I slide my hands over my smooth conk, down to my neck bone, fingers locking tight. It isn't me they're after. It isn't me who's here.

"Red! Red!"

No, no, no. Not Red.

I am Malcolm.

I am Malcolm Little.

I am my father's son. But to be my father's son means that they will always come for me.

They will always come for me, and I will always succumb.

Chapter One

Lansing, Michigan, 1940

I steady my suitcase against the backseat as the car thumps over the streetcar tracks. My eyes drift closed, but I force them open. Don't think of Papa. Not now. Not today. Not when everything's about to be brand-new.

It's four in the morning. Too early for anything, except to catch a one-way bus out of town. Half an hour from now, Lansing will be nothing but a blur in the rearview mirror. I can't wait.

Mr. Swerlin parks the car next to the bus station. I'm out like a flash, up to the ticket counter with the money I've saved. "Boston, Massachusetts," I say.

It's fast. Faster than I expect. And so easy. The clerk slaps a piece of paper in my palm: my ticket. Turns out it takes less than a minute to buy a new life.

The bus pulls into the station. The exhaust clouds up around us like steam, the fuel smell piercing the predawn blackness. The sharp stench brings it home to me. I'm leaving. This big coughing machine is going to carry me away.

The bus door swings open on hinges that creak and groan. The driver emerges, a round white man in a green coat and cap. "Toledo, Cleveland, Erie, Buffalo, Albany, Boston," he announces. He hikes up his pants and stretches his arms. "All aboard."

Around us families stir and mingle, tangling one another in arms. My guardians, Mr. and Mrs. Swerlin, stand by me, calmly watching the proceedings. We're a group, not a family. But it doesn't seem right to just walk away.

I look over my shoulder, toward the road. My real family is supposed to be meeting us here. All my brothers and sisters. I thought there'd be enough time to say good-bye.

A glance at my watch says the bus is early. Eight whole minutes until it's scheduled to leave. A few passengers disembark as the Lansing folks line up. The driver rolls his shoulders and lights up a cigarette, breathing a gray cloud out through his nostrils like fog in the cool morning air. He's in no apparent hurry.

A large black car comes rolling up. I recognize it from the driveway of the home where my youngest siblings—Yvonne, Wesley, and Robert—stay. The doors pop open, and half my family comes pouring out. I'm glad to see the crowd includes my closest brothers, Philbert and Reginald, even though they live in a different home. Wilfred and Hilda, the oldest of us all, still live at our old house. I don't see them yet.

Reginald's familiar voice cries out, "There he is!" My siblings descend, and the distant stillness around me becomes a warm, chattering flurry.

"We made it."

"Are you ready?"

"Are you excited?"

"We're going to miss you, Malcolm."

They cluster around me, sort of hugging, sort of jostling. All speaking at once. I laugh out loud because it feels so normal, compared to the solitude I endure at the Swerlins'.

"Do you have to go, Malcolm?" My nine-year-old sister, Yvonne, wraps her arms around my waist. "Don't you want to come over for breakfast?"

I pat the top of her head. I'll miss those breakfasts, true enough. Getting together once a week with all my brothers and sisters? Yeah, that's the one thing I'll miss about Lansing. I'm used to missing everyone, though. Now that we all live in separate foster homes, that breakfast is the only time of the week all eight of us can be together. Yvonne's foster family is real decent about hosting all of us so often.

"It's gonna be pancakes," Yvonne whispers. As if that would inspire me to stay.

Behind her, my brother Philbert snorts loudly. "Yeah, and there might be enough to go around for once, without this bonehead hogging the butter and syrup."

"Stop it," Hilda snaps. As she arrives alongside us, our older sister smacks Philbert lightly on the back of the head.

"Ow!" Philbert staggers around the lot, pretending a serious head injury.

"Who's the bonehead now?" I quip. Philbert's moaning only grows louder.

Hilda glances around the parking lot as if looking for something to throw at the two of us. "I should have known you all couldn't be serious long enough to say good-bye." Her voice catches.

"Serious is overrated." I grin to cover the twinge of sorrow in my chest right then. Sorrow mixed with a strange glad feeling that, for a minute, things are back to almost normal. The way it's supposed to be, with all of us together, laughing and teasing one another and whatnot.

Wilfred's here now, too, shaking hands with Mr. Swerlin, looking very adult and official. All the Little children, present and accounted for. Won't be this way again for a while.

I turn back to Philbert, who's always good for a joke to keep the mood light, but he's stopped his staggering theatrics. He stands quietly beside me now, out of character for him. I slug him in the arm—not that hard—just to wake him up. He slugs me back. Hard. Then he turns away.

"All aboard," the bus driver calls. He returns to the entry well and starts tearing passengers' tickets.

I pry Yvonne's arms from around my waist, to make room for hugs from Reginald, Wesley, and Robert. Philbert stands off to the side with his head low, looking at everything but me.

I move away from the younger ones, toward him. "That hurt, you know." I rub my arm.

Philbert doesn't react.

"What's your problem?" I ask him.

He crosses his arms tight. He's trying not to look at me, but I recognize his expression.

This isn't how Philbert looks when he's mad. It's how he looks when he's sad, but mad about it. Which is not the same. Like at Papa's funeral. Or when they took Mom away. But this is different. It isn't so awful. This is just . . . me. Leaving.

I don't know how to explain why I have to go. Why the giant weight on my chest suddenly lifts when I think about moving to Boston. When our half-sister Ella invited me to visit, it gave me the first glimpse of happiness, of hopefulness, I've felt since Mom went away. But a visit isn't enough for what I need—I'm going there to stay. All I seem to be able to do around here is get myself in trouble. I've been expelled from school and shipped out to the Swerlins' all alone, causing my brothers and sisters to worry. In Boston, Hilda says, at least I'll be with family.

"Look—" I begin, trying to explain.

Philbert flinches to the side, real dramatic. "Hey," he cries, rubbing his arm in the spot where I punched him a minute ago.

I narrow my eyes at him. He grins. "Your punch just landed."

Philbert is forever teasing me about how slow I am in a fistfight. He, on the other hand, is a really good boxer. My arm still smarts for real.

"No," I say, "that was a new one. I moved so fast, you didn't even see me. Just call me Lightning Little."

Philbert straightens his shoulders, leaning into the banter. "Oh, I've got a better name for you. . . ." But whatever affectionate insult he offers is lost in the cloth of my suit as I circle him into my arms.

It's easier, I guess, to laugh and joke and pretend that tomorrow won't be any different from any of the days before. Easier than trying to talk about how strange it is to be part of a family and still be all alone.

"All aboard. Last call," the driver shouts.

Mr. Swerlin claps me on the shoulder. "Here you go, now," he says. He picks up my suitcase and carries it to the open cargo compartment in the base of the bus. Mrs. Swerlin hands me a paper sack of sandwiches for the road. "Thank you," I tell them.

Hilda fusses with the collar on my jacket, smoothing and tucking and pressing it. Such a Mom-like thing to do. She throws her arms around me. "Oh, Malcolm."

From her purse, she extracts a folded paper map and hands it to me. "You'll want to see where you're going," she says. "Won't you?"

"It's from all of us," Wilfred adds.

"Right. Thanks." I tuck the map into my jacket pocket. It's too dark to read anything anyway.

I get in line behind the others. There's no one my age in line. Older folks mostly. People with the weary look I know well enough.

"You alone?" the driver says, taking the paper ticket from my outstretched hand.

"Yes, sir."

"You sixteen?"

"Yes, sir," I lie, stretching to my full height. Trying to look a year older.

He tears the ticket and hands it back. "Go on to the back, you hear?"

"Yes, sir."

For the first time in forever, my feet are coming up off Michigan soil. Walking up those stairs is like walking into the mouth of the beast, and yet it doesn't scare me. Not even a little.

I should be scared, probably. In fact, as I sit by the window, looking down at the faces of my siblings and my foster parents, what starts to scare me a little is how afraid I'm *not*. They wave up at me all at once, as if someone in the crowd said, "One, two, three." I lift my hand as if the whole thing has been choreographed. The youngest ones jump up and down, waving with their whole bodies in answer. My family. I can't tear my eyes away. They look small, already distant.

The door swings shut, creaking hard enough to send a chill over me. It sounds so final, that kind of closing.

The bus shimmies and shakes and finally lurches forward. For a second, I get a little sad about it. Not the leaving—just the way it seems like the world is always changing, right underneath my feet.

Lansing, 1937

We used to be so happy. Even after Papa died, when things got hard, nothing was so bad because we were together. But then things got harder, and the government social workers started coming by our house. Started pulling us apart, because there was never enough money. For food. For clothes. For the day-to-day necessities.

By the time I was twelve, things got so bad, we'd be nervous every day when we came home. Often as not, there'd be a black car out front. The welfare man calling.

As Philbert and I crossed the porch, we could see Mom through the window, sitting with him in the living room. As if he were a guest, not an intruder. This time, there was a woman, too, someone I hadn't seen before. They often sent someone new. As if they wanted us to know there was a whole chain of people with power over us. And they were all watching.

Philbert opened the door. We stepped inside, and the three adults turned to look at us.

Wilfred wasn't there. He was still at work and wouldn't be home until well after we'd gone to bed. As the oldest, he had to take a job, to help keep food on the table. Hilda had the rest of our siblings herded into a corner, as far from the adults as possible.

Mom sat all tightened up, her body stiff from holding back her fury. Those people always made her angry and tense.

"Hi, Mom," we murmured.

"Boys," she said. "You remember Mr. Franklin. And this is Miss Castle, from Social Services."

"Where have you been?" Mr. Franklin said. "School's been out for hours."

Philbert opened his mouth, but no sound came out. We'd been down at Doone's Market, swiping fruit from the barrels out front.

"We were setting traps, down by the creek," I answered. It wasn't even a total lie. We'd walked down there earlier and set some. Maybe we'd even have a rabbit or a musk-rat to sell in the morning. We couldn't eat these things ourselves—Mom's West Indian culture viewed them as unclean—but we could turn a buck off of them.

Mr. Franklin looked at our empty hands. "And you didn't catch anything?"

"We were *setting* the traps, I said. Not checking them."
I crossed my arms over my chest. *He thinks I'm stupid. He thinks he's better than us.*

The government man stood up. He pulled me aside, away from my brothers and sisters, away from Mom, to the corner by the window. He always tried this and often on me. Maybe because I was the loud one, the tall one, the one who seemed like the leader, even though I was only twelve. Philbert and Hilda were older.

"What are you doing, sir?" I asked. He had his hand on my arm. I hated him touching me, but I knew better than to pull away.

"I just wanted to get your thoughts," he said, releasing me. "Your mother doesn't seem well."

"She's fine, sir." I looked at her, sitting erect on the edge of the living-room sofa, her bottom lip tight. She would be fine as soon as these people went away.

But they played this game sometimes, telling us that they'd take us away from Mom if we didn't act right. If things weren't perfect. If we ever admitted that we were hungry.

"Malcolm," Mr. Franklin said, like he knew me. He spoke quietly, beside my face. "If you have any concerns, you can share them with me."

He stood close. Too close. Breathing his nasty breath on me. I could smell his lunch. Maybe a sandwich. One with thick slices of bread and actual meat. I willed my stomach not to growl. I was grateful for the fruit I'd swiped earlier.

Stealing might be wrong, but if it helped our family stay together . . . I wasn't so hungry that he needed to know about it. Mom could take care of us just fine.

I stood by the window, watching the lingering cloud of dust dredged up by the car tires as the government people drove off.

"OK," Mom said. She brushed off the knees of her skirt as she stood. "Back to work." My siblings un-bunched from the corner of the room and came toward her. Mom pulled a volume of poetry from our bookshelf and began to read the verses out loud. There was a determined quality to her voice, like she wasn't going to let those people break us, and before long, her words pushed to every corner of the house, sweeping the intruders' stench right out of our home. Finally she closed the book and set it aside.

"Keep studying," Mom said. "I expect stories from everyone over dinner."

My siblings knelt around the coffee table, studying Mom's encyclopedias and history books. I leaned against the window frame. Inside the house, it might have felt like old times, but outside I could see everything that was wrong. The churned-up dust settled back against the road, some of it mingling with the large dirt rectangle that had once housed Mom's vegetable garden. Next to it, the chicken coop stood empty, as it had for years. Papa would have torn it down by now. Then again, if Papa were still here, it wouldn't have been empty at all.

"You, too, Malcolm," Mom chided me gently. I came away from the window to join my brothers and sisters in studying. My hands found a favorite volume of philosophy. I flipped to a familiar chapter, but I found it hard to focus on reading. Mr. Franklin's words had shaken me more than usual this time. Wasn't so easy to put him out of sight, out of mind.

Mom didn't seem worried. She went about her business, sitting at the table writing an article for her periodical, a furrow of fierce concentration on her face. She sighed occasionally as she wrote, and rubbed her fingers along the side of her face. She softly whispered, reading her drafted words aloud from time to time, or slipped into a light, cheerful hum as she worked.

I closed my eyes and let the sound of her voice wash over me, but the heartbeat of worry in my chest wouldn't subside. How could Mom keep on doing her Garvey work? Couldn't she see this is why they were after us?

The house was otherwise quiet, apart from the simmer of boiling greens on the stove. Dandelion stew, which we ate at our most desperate. With the Great Depression on, food was often scarce. No matter how hard Mom and Wilfred were willing to work, jobs were scarce, too.

Hilda tended the pot of greens from time to time, as if there were anything she could do to make it better. I wanted to tell her, *It's steamed weeds—just let it be.* But some things become worse when spoken aloud.

The sound of simmering and the scratch of Mom's pen and the light scrape of book pages turning took over. Reginald and Wesley headed out to see if they could find something to add to our supper, and when they came thumping in a short while later, their fresh noise nudged us all out of our quiet reflections.

Hilda turned away from the stove. "Did you get anything?" The bakery sometimes sold us day-old bread at a discount, but it was hit-or-miss based on what was available.

Today was a day with bread. Wesley was carrying a sack about half the size of his slight seven-year-old body.

A full sack of bread was a feast as far as we were concerned. Dandelion greens had some nutritional value, Mom promised us, but their broth wasn't exactly filling. On Sundays we would go down to the Seventh-Day Adventist church, which Mom had joined after Papa died. There was always a big old spread of food after the service, which meant that one meal was guaranteed. But it was only Wednesday; half a week still to go.

Any time we could make do without the government handouts was a good day. It made us feel like the Great Depression hadn't gotten the best of us. Times were hard for everyone. Didn't matter, though—it was still an awful feeling not to be able to get by on our own, as we had when Papa was alive.

Back then we'd never heard of welfare. Papa took care

of everything. He built our house with his own hands, and Mom's vegetable garden fed us year-round. We kept chickens for eggs, and our table was always full of good food. The wood walls didn't creak; they echoed with music and laughter and powerful stories.

Now Mom worked even harder. So did Wilfred. All of us did our part, but with the Depression on, working hard simply wasn't enough.

"Dinner," Hilda said.

Mom sat still, pen poised in hand, eyes fixed on her papers. She seemed to be staring straight through the page, thoughtful. Unmoving as we gathered around the table.

"Mom, let's eat." I laid my hand on her shoulder. My touch brought her out of whatever thoughts were swirling in her mind.

"What is it, baby?" Mom said, glancing at me. I guessed that she was so caught up in her writing, she hadn't heard me the first time.

"Dinner's ready. Looks like it's going to be a good one," I added, trying to stay positive and proud, like I knew Mom would want me to.

Mom looked at me, her gaze liquid-soft. "I know, baby. We're OK." She wrapped an arm around me, and her strength seeped through me and beyond. The government people wanted us to believe there was something wrong with her. Because she was strong. Because she stood up for what she believed. Times were hard, but she was still Mom, and she refused to let anyone reduce her.

We took our seats around the table. Hilda ladled dandelion greens into our bowls. Yvonne chopped the bread into chunks and slices, then distributed them among us. We prayed over the meal. It was supposed to be a moment to thank God for the nourishment before us, but through my cracked eyelids, the meager offering didn't look like much to be thankful for. "Lord, may our dinner be filling to our minds, bodies, and souls," Hilda said, which sounded to me less like a blessing and more like wishful thinking.

The amount of food on the table could be eaten in under five minutes. But we ate slowly, as if the longer we stretched each bite, the more it would become.

The greens were stringy and chewy, but I tried to remind myself to be grateful. Yvonne and Wesley must have spent more than an hour picking them from what was left in our garden.

The bread was crusty, halfway stale. We dipped it in the dandelion broth to soften it. The only sounds were of our occasional chewing. No one talked about anything. We just sat there together. The lack and the hunger floated around us like a cloud, withholding everything—all hope, all satisfaction, every single drop of cleansing rain. There seemed to be no help for the way we were stuck.

We chewed the bland greens dutifully. My mind streamed, full of thoughts; I could feel the government people circling like carrion birds. We were still alive, and yet they circled. Lying in wait.

"What did he say to you?" Philbert wanted to know.

It was almost like he could tell what I was thinking. But I didn't see why he had to bring it up now, here at the table with everyone.

"Same old," I murmured. "You know."

"No. He always talks to you," Philbert added. A little miffed about it, I guess. Him being older and all. He stabbed at the dandelion greens with his fork.

Hilda shot me a look across the table. Why me, I didn't know. I didn't start it. I widened my eyes back at her.

I got the message. Had already had it in mind. Mr. Franklin's visits put everyone out of sorts enough, without rehashing things. Philbert knew better, too.

"All right," Mom said in a tone of voice that stopped us from fussing at one another. "Tell me about your studies." She glanced around the table. "Did you learn anything new?"

Mom was always teaching us new things, telling us stories that we repeated to one another until we knew them by heart. We could recite passages from Shakespeare and legends about African kingdoms going back thousands of years. We could share facts about the transatlantic slave trade, the largest forced migration of a people in the history of humankind, and about the great military strategist Queen Nzingah, who defended the nation of Angola against Portuguese invaders in a powerful effort to destroy the slave trade entirely. And more recent events, like abolitionist efforts and the many revolts against slavery in the United States.

"I have one," Yvonne piped up. "How about Frederick Douglass and his *North Star* newspaper that helped free the slaves—I mean, the enslaved Africans?" She briefly told how Douglass's words had helped change the nation.

Over the meager meal, we took turns repeating the lessons Mom had taught us over the years at this very table. "There's so much beauty and strength in our history," she'd say as she'd recite the works of black people who had come before us. "You must be able to read thoughtfully, speak clearly, and understand everything," she'd tell us, and point to a new page in the dictionary.

Philbert and I talked of Papa's friend Marcus Garvey and their movement to unite black people in demanding their equal rights. We all chanted one of Garvey's famous phrases together: *Up, up, you mighty race. You can accomplish what you will.*

Mom sat listening, a slight smile on her face. Her expression grew distant at times, the same thinking expression she had worn earlier while she was working. And when we came around to discussing Papa's work, a fresh shadow crossed her face. I wondered, somewhere deep in me, what Papa would do if he were here. If I concentrated hard enough, I could almost hear his voice: *Malcolm, my son, you can be and do anything you put your mind to.*

So why couldn't I figure out how to help our family?

I sipped the gray-green water gathered in my bowl. Dandelion broth? Not exactly. A surge of desperation growled low in my stomach. There had to be something we could do to get everyone's mind off the meager supper. The stories offered some distraction, but not enough.

I caught Philbert's eye across the table. Then I tapped my remaining heel of bread against the side of my bowl. When I let go of it, as if on cue, Philbert reached over and snatched it. Jamming it between his teeth, he tore a huge bite.

"Hey!" I grabbed at his face. "That's mine."

In retaliation, I snatched his piece of bread, which was identical to mine—the opposite heel. I bit into it.

Philbert squealed in mock outrage. "That's mine."

"It's mine now," I mumble-shouted, my mouth jammed with crust.

We gnawed the heels, staring at each other like bull-dogs. Reginald's laugh snapped through the air like a starting pistol. Philbert and I dove dramatically across the table at each other. My fingers at his lips tried to retrieve the remains of my supper. He scratched my face in return. I squealed in response.

We both chewed frantically, trying to down as much bread as we could before the other wrenched any out of our mouths: teeth versus fingers on tough old bread that didn't want to give in to either. My brothers and sisters laughed, choosing sides and chanting our names.

"Philbert! Philbert!"

"Chew, chew, Malcolm!"

"Boys!" Mom's tone turned sharp. "What's this? Stop it, now." She laid her hands flat on the table and leaned into them. "Sit down," she ordered us. "And finish your suppers." Then she fell quiet again.

We turned our heads away from each other, toward her. Philbert, no doubt, thinking the same as me: *That's it?* Mom, when things were right, would scold us raw for fighting over food. Scold us for not being grateful. For not being civil. For not doing everything we could for the family. That's the reaction we were expecting. Hoping for, even. To see the spark in her eyes. To feel like things were normal for a minute.

But this time, Mom just shook her head, as though she were too tired to deal with us. "Please, boys," she added.

"Yes, Mom," we mumbled. I drew my hands back, coming away with the last morsel of my bread. Victorious, at least technically. Philbert chomped through the rest of his own meal, freshly silent. Sullen.

My plate was nearly empty. My hands. My heart.

Mr. Franklin wanted us to believe that Mom was crazy. Crazy for being too proud to take more welfare handouts. Crazy to let us go hungry during the Depression when what they're giving free is pork, which we don't eat. Crazy for standing on her principles: no buying on credit, no giving up her children, no eating of unclean meat.

Across the table, Mom dipped her spoon delicately into her bowl of foraged greens, as though she were eating a gourmet meal. But her forehead was wrinkled. She still looked distracted. Frustrated. Thoughtful.

Mom wasn't crazy. Our family was broken. Her strength

25

was in keeping us all moving forward and in holding the pieces of our sorrow together, but we were living with shards of it. You never knew when one was going to prick you or how sharp it would be.

Sooner than later, the greens and my final nub of bread were gone. My stomach rumbled on. The ache of it filled my body from toes to ears.

Despite the way I'd misled the welfare man, Philbert and I did a pretty good business trapping and selling meat. We'd catch frogs, rabbits, muskrats—basically whatever creatures happened along our stretch of the creek. We could sell it all to white folks, who apparently would eat just about anything. Maybe that was the secret to always having food on the table: no standards. Mom definitely had standards, and we all kept to them. For instance, I was hungry enough to eat a pig, a rabbit—heck, I'd have eaten a muskrat when things got really bad—but Mom still refused to serve it in the house.

With the money we got selling the meat one afternoon, a few weeks after the government man's visit, we bought some potatoes and some eggs. I figured Hilda could boil them up nice and they would make a decent dinner. The store guy looked at us a little funny when I laid the money out on the counter. Lately, he was used to us coming around for the welfare parcels. I could see them stacked in the corner, small brown boxes stamped NOT FOR SALE, waiting for other families to come along.

26

Papa would be proud. Tonight we were paying customers. Didn't even have to put a cent on credit, which Papa used to forbid. Buying on credit was a system created with no way to ever catch up, he'd say.

We stepped outside, me swinging the sack of food. I had it clenched up in my fist real good, though. No way would I drop our dinner.

"They've got a nice melon patch over at the Bolls'," I said.

Philbert nodded. We were always in sync, Philbert and me. Without another word, we changed course. We circled around so that we could come up from the woods side rather than the road side. Mrs. Boll was bound to be inside, cooking up the fresh muskrat we'd sold her, so we might have a clean shot at swiping a couple of melons and not being noticed.

I'd already made up my mind that we weren't going to crack them open and eat them on the spot. We'd bring them home and let Hilda cut them up for supper. Since we had the bag of what we'd bought, a little extra wouldn't raise her suspicions. Tonight, the Littles were going to eat like old times.

Behind the Bolls' property, we crept out of the woods. Tiptoed straight into the melon patch, all viny, with melons ripe for the picking. The melons had grown large and oval. We knocked on their tough green flesh to be sure they hadn't gone soft, then we scooped up one each and hightailed it back toward the woods.

Hot damn. I had a melon under one arm and a sack of eggs and potatoes in the other hand. It was gonna be one fine supper. I wanted to stick it in the face of the welfare man. We were fine. We were gonna be just fine.

"You boys, stop right there!" a woman's voice rang out behind us.

Of course we didn't stop. We kept on running, even though I recognized the voice. Mrs. Stockton, one of our neighbors and a friend of Mom's.

"Malcolm and Philbert Little!" she called as we were scrambling. There was no purpose in running after that point. The jig was up. If we ran, she'd just be on our porch waiting when we got home.

Mrs. Stockton was a beefy, no-nonsense woman in a plain blue skirt and blouse. Her thick shoes shushed her through the grass toward us at a surprising clip. When she reached us, there was a high red in her cheeks from the exertion. Or the anger. Hard to say.

She circled the Bolls' melon patch as if checking to be sure we hadn't done any damage. We stood dutifully with our heads bowed, while she muttered woefully about "these niggers and their antics."

Mrs. Stockton loomed over us finally. "Come with me." She grabbed each of us by an ear and marched us straight down the road into town. Soon enough, we realized that she was taking us toward the dress shop where Mom worked, sewing clothes in the warehouse.

At the rear entrance, Mrs. Stockton let go of my ear long

enough to pound her fist on the door. After a moment, a blond woman, hair knotted atop her head, answered. She wore a thicker, darker smock than the one Mom would come home wearing. She must have been the shop owner or at least the head seamstress.

"Yes?" she said. Her gaze flicked up and down, appraising Mrs. Stockton.

"These niggers were down by the creek causing trouble," she reported.

"How is that my problem?" the head seamstress asked, appraising us, too.

"Their mother works here," Mrs. Stockton said. "She needs to know what they're up to."

The head seamstress glanced at us, brow wrinkled. "No. I don't employ any Negroes."

Mrs. Stockton shook her head. "I'm just sure . . ."

The door to the workroom opened wider. A stream of women dressed in the paler blue smocks began to exit. Mom emerged, along with the others finishing the day shift. "Ah, there she is," said Mrs. Stockton. "Louise!"

Mom's steps faltered. Her brow furrowed. She swallowed hard.

The head seamstress balked, looking from Mom to us. "These are your children?"

Mom drew herself up straight. "They are." The gaze that pointed to us promised a significant whipping to come. My backside smarted in anticipation.

The head seamstress paced around Mom, peering more

closely at her features—her fine bones, creamy skin, and straight dark hair. "You're a Negro!"

"Yes, I am." Mom didn't blink.

Philbert and I dropped our heads in shame. Mom didn't flinch, didn't shy away from the discomfort of it. Stood firm as the woman poked her skin and squeezed the ends of her hair while the other seamstresses looked on. Mom had never looked prouder to me.

Finally the head seamstress stepped back. "I don't know how you fooled me," she said. "But I don't employ niggers. Take your lot and go."

Mom nodded curtly. She stepped toward Mrs. Stockton, who had released our ears and now stood with her hands over her mouth.

"Louise, I'm so sorry," Mrs. Stockton whispered.

Mom ignored her. She spun Philbert and me each around by a shoulder.

"Home," she ordered us. "Now."

"They thought you were white?" Philbert said to Mom on the long walk home. He should have known better than to speak. Mom smacked him on the back of the head. We both knew there was a good paddling awaiting us at home.

How could anyone mistake Mom for white? Mom was a proud black woman, the proudest I knew. She hated us having to take welfare food, hated accepting anything we needed but did not earn. We had a picture of Marcus Garvey on the living-room wall, talking about going back to Africa, talking about the power of blackness and the strength of the Negro heart. I couldn't imagine looking at Mom and not seeing that.

"They all think I'm white," she said after a moment. "That's how I keep a job."

Trudging down the road that day, I didn't give what Mom said all that much thought. I was more worried about what punishment she'd lay down when we got home. I guess that's why I didn't notice until later how, in the space of that instant, everything Mom and Papa ever told me became a little less true.

Chapter Two

On the Bus, 1940

The fact of the matter was you had to be white to keep a decent job in Lansing during the Depression. Mom was just doing what she had to. It stung like a betrayal, but I know better now. Mom talked a good game about the power of blackness, but she knew that the white world held even more power. You just needed to find a way to break in.

Out the bus window, the air is somewhere between black and brown and gray. Rural Michigan looks like a landscape on ink-stained canvas. There's day and there's night, and somewhere, I guess, there's a line between them. Just like black and white. A moment when it stops being day and starts being night or vice versa. That's what we're driving on right now. That line. I look out the bus window and it's night, and it's night, and it's night, and then suddenly it's not. The sun hasn't come up, but you get the feeling that it's out there, somewhere, lingering, like a promise. And nothing changes, except everything. And the bus just rolls and rolls into the lightening sky.

Lansing, 1938

With Mom out of a job, the pressure came on the rest of us to bring in money and food. She would get a job again—she would—but there might be a bit of a wait. Jobs came and went for Mom, always. Now that I understood why, it smarted.

I thought that was just life. I didn't know it was a Negro thing.

Down at the market, I was thinking about how to acquire some things that we needed. A sack of flour, maybe, or some cheese rounds at least. I paced the outskirts of the parking lot, planning it.

The squawking distracted me.

I was familiar with the sound of chickens. We used to raise them on our farm when Papa was alive. They made me think of dinner, which made my stomach speak, which threw off my thinking.

I followed the squawking.

In the parking lot, I found a farmer's pickup truck, chock-full of farm-related wares. Bushels of corn, bundles of raw wool, and a pile of three-foot crates that proved to be the source of the squawking.

Six chickens in each crate.

Loud, plump, red-and-white hens, ripe for the plucking—just like the ones we used to have.

It was too tempting, that big crate of chickens. We could eat some and keep some for the eggs, as long as we could hold out without eating those, too.

I sidled up to the truck. The closest crate was right on the edge, beneath a bundle of rope.

First things first. I moved the bundle. Easy enough.

No one appeared to be around. The farmer was still in the market. No one else was in sight.

I slid my hands up, right into place inside the looped rope handles at either end of the crate. Easy enough.

I glanced around. Then in one smooth arc, lifted the crate. And started walking away. Easy.

Picked it up to a jog. Had to get out of sight.

Not as easy. I had to keep my elbows bent to raise the frame above my jutting knees. The chickens strutted and squawked, changing the weight distribution of the crate. It rocked in my grip and began to feel heavy.

"Hey!" I heard shouted behind me. "Stop! You thieving nigger. You stop right there!"

I didn't stop.

I'm fast, but I was running with the chicken crate. Holding it in front of me was breaking my stride.

Before long, thick hands landed on my shoulders. The farmer panted heavy in my ear. "Them's my chickens," he said. "Goddamned nigger."

I dropped the chicken crate and tried to wriggle free, but he had me good and tight by the arms, and there was no way to get loose. I kicked and thrashed and stomped, but his boots were thick—no match for my shoes' soft soles—and his muscles were like rocks after decades of hard labor against the earth. I could do no damage.

So I stood limply in his grip until the sirens came, and the policemen in their little black caps chained my wrists together and shoved me in the back of their car.

Wilfred came down to the police station to collect me.

"Malcolm, you gotta stop this," he said. "What's wrong with the rabbits and the traps?"

Trapping was no kind of guaranteed supper. Stealing, on the other hand . . . "We don't always catch anything, you know." That's what I said out loud, but in the meantime I was thinking about how to get better at swiping things from the store. This whole back-of-the-truck concept was new to me, but it seemed like a good direction to go. I didn't care much about the man whose chickens I'd taken. He had a whole truck full of chickens and things. I didn't even figure he'd miss them.

On the whole walk home, Wilfred went on and on about how we were in this together. And something about reflecting on the family.

"What would Papa think, to see you getting hauled in?" Wilfred said. "You can't, *you can't* get on the wrong side of the law like this. You know what happens. . . ."

I tuned him out all the way at that point. Papa wasn't there. He wasn't there and I was hungry, and I didn't want to wait for welfare package day, or walk along the creek and hope to find a rabbit in the trap we couldn't even eat ourselves, or go down to the Seventh-Day Adventist meeting so Mom could pray for our daily bread.

I did what I had to. Didn't see anything wrong with it. Not a thing.

"I understand you're out of work," the government man said first off.

Mom stood with her body in the doorway, as if to block his entry. He pushed past her, of course, in a way that made me feel ashamed of her for even trying. It made everything worse, the way she fought it.

"I'll get work again," she protested. "I always do."

It was true, so far. No job lasted forever, but before the seamstress work, Mom was cleaning in a white family's home and, before that, another family's. In the meantime, we'd take the welfare packages, with their bundles of meat and cans of things.

"The larger issue is that there are simply too many mouths to feed," the man said. "And too many children to discipline."

"My children are very well behaved," Mom answered. Her gaze cut to Philbert and me, about which this was absolutely untrue. Like a warning. "They are excellent students as well." Mom folded her hands. She did not offer him a seat or a beverage, which was rude. But then again, politeness is about making a guest feel welcome, which the government man certainly was not.

He sat down anyway. Right in the middle of the sofa, with his legs spread wide. He had a thick folder of papers, which he opened like a suitcase. He riffled through and extracted a group of clipped pages.

"Malcolm Little," he said. "Yes, here he is. Malcolm, come over here."

I separated myself from the others and edged around to stand beside Mom.

"It's time to make a change," the man said.

"A change?" Mom's voice rose. Her arm went around me, over my shoulder, clutching me to her. I don't know if she felt herself do it. It was like a reflex. But she grabbed me tight. "What sort of change?"

"It's like I've told you. If you can't control all these children, we'll be forced to find another arrangement," the slim man said, pushing up his glasses.

Mom sputtered an indecipherable protest.

"In fact," the man went on, "we've already made arrangements for Malcolm here to stay with another family."

My heart exploded in my chest.

"No," Mom declared. "These are my children, and this is our home. Malcolm is staying with us."

"That's no longer your decision."

"You can't take him," Mom said. "You can't."

The man slapped his portfolio closed. The soft smack screamed finality. "The foster home is only half a mile away. He won't be far."

Tears rolled down Mom's face. She was no match for him.

"They have the means to take him in, and clearly his behavior indicates that he's beyond your control," he said. "Malcolm obviously needs a father figure and a firm hand."

My chest filled with scalding heat. I shook loose from Mom's arms. The firm hand against me had always been Mom's. But for these white men to say anything against Papa or our loss of him . . . "No," I said. "I'm not going."

"I'm not asking," the government man said. "Your recent trip down to the police station?" he added. "This move is an alternative to some kind of detention."

The chickens. It all came back to the chickens. I wanted to laugh. Out of the hundreds of things I'd successfully stolen, I was being punished for the only time I'd ever failed.

"Detention?" I repeated, uneasy.

"He won't do it again. Anything like that. Ever," Mom insisted.

I glanced at her. Sure I would. Put those chickens in front of me again, they'd be mine. I'd just take a minute to learn how best to run with a crate.

But the government man shook his head anyway, as if he knew what I was thinking. For a quick second, when he met my eyes, I knew what he was thinking, too. Malcolm, the troublemaker. Malcolm, the one who won't toe the line. Looking in his eyes—a thing I maybe never did before—it speared me.

The government men who were always coming around, they were always talking to me. Up on the side, just me. *Malcolm, this. Malcolm, that. Malcolm, you need to . . . Malcolm, why don't you . . . ? Malcolm. Malcolm. Malcolm.*

Maybe it had been me causing this trouble all along. All my antics. I was the problem, the one who couldn't do right, no matter what.

If I would just go, maybe it would all stop. Maybe they would leave Mom and my family alone.

"Pack your things, Malcolm," the man said.

So I did.

Chapter Three

On the Bus, 1940

The bus grows warm, with all the light through the windows. I shrug out of my jacket.

"Yeah, I reckon it's getting a mite warm." There's another Negro on the bus now, an old coal miner on his way back to Philadelphia. He unbuttons his sweater, as if agreeing with me about the temperature. "But you ain't felt heat until you're mining in a six-by-six shaft with twelve other men."

"Well, at least you're out of the sun down there," I say.

He laughs. "I reckon. So you're a silver-lining kind of lad, huh?"

I wouldn't say that. Nothing I've ever touched is lined with anything but lead.

He reaches across the aisle with an open hand. "Name's Earl Willis."

I flinch. Hope the old guy doesn't notice. It's strange, hearing Papa's first name on people who aren't him. There was a kid in my class at Mason Junior High called Earl. Every time he got called on, I got goose bumps.

Across the bus aisle, Earl Willis's hand hangs there, waiting. I stretch to meet it. His hand is warm and work-roughened. Big. I have long fingers, but his grip makes me feel small and tucked in. Maybe there are lots of old guys in the world called Earl. Maybe there's only one that's missing.

I tug away quick. "Malcolm Little."

"Where you headed, Malcolm Little?"

"Boston. My sister lives there." I've decided to call Ella my sister instead of my half-sister. We all share blood, my siblings and I. I'm not sure it matters how much. It ties us together, although it doesn't make us the same.

"The call of the big city," says the old miner, shaking his head. "You young 'uns can have it. All that hustle and bustle's too much for me. I like a small-town way of life."

I just look out the window. I don't really want to be talking to him, actually, but it does sort of pass the time. He sits across the aisle from me in his own spread of two seats mirroring mine. Except he sits in the aisle seat. I sit by the window, keeping watch so I won't miss anything.

"Ain't nothin' to see," he says. "Just more and more o' the same."

So far, he's not exactly wrong about the scenery staying the same, but I look anyway. Everything's new to me. Every cornfield under its wide-open sky seems fresh and broad and exciting. The world unrolling like a carpet in front of my feet.

I pull out the map my siblings gave me and turn it right side up. It's the eastern United States. I see Michigan right away, shaped like a mitten, near the top. Under it, Indiana and Ohio. To the east, Pennsylvania, New York, and Massachusetts. All the states we're going to pass through on this ride.

"Do you know where we are?" I ask the old miner.

"Not far outside Toledo, Ohio."

Outside the window, there's still nothing but corn. "How can you tell?" With my finger I trace an imaginary path until I find the dot marked TOLEDO.

He smiles. "I've ridden this route once or twice. You're pretty sharp," he says. "Where you from, little man?"

"Nowhere." It's what comes to mind. It's what comes out of my mouth.

The old miner laughs. "Everyone's from somewhere."

I shake my head.

He frowns. "To understand a man, you have to know where he comes from."

"Nowhere," I answer. "I'm starting over." *Words have*

power, Papa used to say. *Speak what you want to be true.*

"Where'd you get on the bus, then?" he tries.

"Where I used to live."

He hoots with laughter. "You're a wily one. You must be trouble."

"That's what they tell me."

I can hear the voices. *Troublemaker. No account. Just a nigger.*

I couldn't ever be more than that in Lansing. Can't ever be more anyplace, it turns out, as long as I wear this brown skin. I used to think things were different, because Papa used to tell me stories about all the great things I could be and could do, and how mighty this brown skin was. But now I understand. Now I know they were just stories. Just ideas in his head.

Lansing, 1930

A long time ago, when Papa was alive, I believed that I was special. I was so small, four and five years old, riding on the long seat of the old black touring car, with Papa at the wheel. These were the greatest days, when it was just him and me, going to one of his important meetings. It would be afternoon or evening, when the sun was dipping low. He would drive around the outskirts of Lansing, because

Negroes weren't allowed inside the city limits after dark. He would park alongside somebody's house, look down at me, and say, "Keep quiet, remember?"

He might have been talking about my behavior in the meeting. Or he might have meant, *Don't tell anyone that we were here.*

Then we would go inside, and there would be a living room full of black people waiting. Quietly. They would speak together with Papa about the tragic lynchings of young black men and women, and other challenges afflicting the black community. Papa would quote the great leader Marcus Garvey, saying: "Up, up, you mighty race, you can accomplish what you will!"

But the meetings were still kept quiet.

There were always secrets to keep, it seemed. And so many rules for how to be a black person; you could not say how you felt or what you thought, and you had to keep your head down low when a white person passed you on the road. You had to use a low, dirty water fountain, right next to the high, clean one for the whites. You had to ride in the back of the bus or the streetcar, and you couldn't sit down unless no whites were on board.

Papa was different, though. He went ahead and said the forbidden things and did them. Black people looked up to him because of it. He preached and he promised better days. A whole new world for all of us. He talked about the beauty and wealth of Africa. About how, before we were enslaved, we governed ourselves and ruled our own land.

After the meeting, it would be very late at night. Papa would say, "Time to go home and go to sleep," and I would let him scoop me up, because it was nice to ride so tall and be protected by my papa.

We rode home on the long bench seat in the big black car, and by the time we got to the house, sure enough, I felt sleepy. Papa picked me up and held me against his shoulder, and in the circle of those strong arms, nothing could touch me. He whispered, "Pay attention, Malcolm. One day you will preach and teach like I do."

"Really?"

"Of course," he said. "You'll go to school and learn and grow, and then when the time is right, you're going to be a great leader. Even greater than I could hope to be."

"OK," I said, even though he was being silly. No one was greater than Papa. I snuggled against him, warm and sleepy, halfway dreaming of all the things I could become. A preacher. A lawyer. A businessman. With Papa there to show me the way, anything was possible.

On the Bus, 1940

I didn't think Papa could ever be wrong, but he was wrong about me. Of all the things he promised, none have come true.

I'll always be there.

You're meant for great things.

You have nothing and no one to fear, for God is with you.

I hate the feeling that Papa lied to me. I don't want to think of it like that, but it creeps in under my skin anyway. He lied. He told me these things about myself and about the world like they were true. But they were only his hopes. Wishes for some dark and distant future only he could see. I know Papa was trying to build such a world, a world where we could be treated as men. But he died long before it got done.

Up, up, you mighty race!

The thing he forgot to mention is, in order to come up, you have to be coming up from somewhere. And that place is pretty far down.

Case in point: we're in a small town somewhere in Ohio. Bus parks right on Main Street, in front of a storefront station that's in line with all the shops and businesses. I get up to stretch my legs and use the bathroom, and the old miner says, "Don't wander from the station, you hear?"

"I know." I hear the nervousness in his breath. *Don't get uppity. Don't get out of line. Act like a good Negro, and everything's going to be fine.*

I've told him one too many stories, I guess. About how I got expelled from school for putting a thumbtack on my teacher's chair—he had it coming—and how I almost went to reform school because of it. And how good I was at figuring out exactly how much food I could steal from Doone's Market without anyone noticing. And how Philbert and I, and some of the white boys from school, would pull pranks on the townsfolk back in Lansing. Tip their outhouses. Swipe melons from their gardens. That kind of thing.

So he's nervous about me making trouble at the bus stop. It makes me want to laugh. Just as truthfully, I could've told him I was class president. On the football team. Straight-A student. But what was interesting about any of that?

"I'm serious," the old miner says. "They might have known you around your hometown, but you can't go around acting up in these parts."

It makes me want to break a window or something. Just to show him. What I do is up to me now.

Coming back, I see we have a new bus driver. He's a skinny man in the same green jacket and cap the first one wore. He thumps up the stairs and plays with the mirrors, then walks up the aisle, surveying all the passengers.

When he gets to me, he stops, looks me up and down, and says, "You all by yourself?"

I nod, open my mouth to speak. The glint in his eye and the curl of his lip scare me a little. He leans in toward me.

"Ain't anyone ever tell you the road is a dangerous place for a lone little nigger?"

"He's with me," says the old miner, coming up from behind the driver. He slides into the seat row in front of me, because the driver is blocking the aisle. There's a fierce expression in his eyes, tucked behind a thick layer of contrition. I only see it because I'm sitting. His head is bowed respectfully, as every "good" Negro knows instinctively to do.

I think: *This is the one thing Papa couldn't do.* Papa only knew how to stand up, how to never bow down. Mom, too. So the white world sliced and diced them.

"This is your boy?"

"Yeah," says the old miner. "He's my—"

I hold my breath, hoping. *Don't say "son."*

"Nephew."

I glance out the window, relieved.

Other passengers start reboarding the bus. The driver checks our tickets and starts to return to the front. He turns back as the old miner eases into his regular seat across the aisle.

"Hey, now," the driver says. "If you're traveling together, you sit together, niggers."

Never mind that the bus is nearly half empty. Almost everyone has a seat to themselves.

"Yes, sir," says the old miner. He gathers his things and moves across the aisle to join me in my seat. I squish myself against the window. He's not a huge man, but big enough to stop me from sprawling the way I have been. Our knees and elbows bump.

"Sorry, son," he whispers.

The word "son" burns like a little fire sizzling my skin. "You didn't have to do that," I tell him. "I can take care of myself."

"Maybe," he says. "If the world was fair. As it is, we got

to look out for each other." He looks at me slant, not smiling, but clearly tempted to. "If you came from somewhere, you might know that."

Here is what I know: Papa was wrong, about all of it. Day after day, there's more and more proof. The values he taught me were only things he wanted to be true.

Lansing, 1939

I believed in Papa's stories a lot longer than I should have. He'd insisted I was exceptionally smart, and I always got perfect grades in school easily. He said I was going to be a leader, and people tended to look to me like I was in charge without me even trying—my siblings, the welfare people, my classmates. Not just black people—white people, too.

When I got expelled from school in Lansing, I got removed from regular foster care and sent to live with the Swerlins, who ran a pre-detention foster facility twelve miles away in Mason. Mrs. Swerlin enrolled me in the all-white Mason Junior High. I still got straight As. They elected me class president my very first year there. Destined for greatness? Sure. It was easy to believe everything Papa ever told me.

The English teacher, Mr. Ostrowski, was definitely my favorite person at Mason Junior High. Some of the things he talked about even reminded me of Papa in some ways, as much as any white man could. From time to time, Mr. Ostrowski would clap me on the shoulder and say I had potential. I liked to pretend it was someone else saying it. Someone who loved me. I missed Papa's deep, strong voice, and being away from home, away from my siblings, it was extra nice to hear something so familiar and uplifting.

Mr. Ostrowski was always asking us—the whole class, I mean—what our dreams were and what we wanted to be. The way Papa had always done, telling me the sky was the limit.

So it was no real surprise when Mr. Ostrowski motioned me up to his desk after class one day, saying, "Malcolm, have you given any thought to your future?"

"My future?" I echoed. I mean, I was used to hearing him talk about stuff like this in general, but not really one-on-one.

"Yes," he said. "Let's have a little talk about that."

While the other kids cleared out of the room, laughing and joking and starting their after-school games, I gathered up my stack of books and came to stand by Mr. Ostrowski's desk.

"You're working now, aren't you?" he said.

"Yes. I've started a job over at a restaurant in Lansing." Mrs. Swerlin had recommended me for it, knowing I wanted some spending money.

"Well, that's just fine, for now, isn't it?" he said.

"I suppose." I didn't especially like doing the work, but

I sure didn't mind the little bit of pay I was getting. A handful of cash that was just my own. That was the key to the good life, as far as I could see.

"I wanted to talk to you because I want to be sure you're thinking about what you want to do for work in the future."

"Sure." I nodded eagerly.

"Have you given it any thought?" he said. "You have a lot going for you."

"Well, yes, sir," I answered. "I suppose I've been thinking I'd like to be a lawyer." I certainly didn't want to wash dishes in a sweaty kitchen for the rest of my life. I won all of the debates at school, and I wanted to help people like Papa had; being a lawyer seemed like a good fit.

Mr. Ostrowski's reddish cheeks puffed outward as he smiled. "Now, Malcolm," he said, "you know that's not likely to happen."

I blinked at him. *Not likely?* I had heard him say it plenty of times—that there was more out in the world than just being a farmer, like most of the other kids' parents. He talked about a whole life to be lived beyond Mason, or even Lansing, about striking out on our own, making a go of it, especially to those of us at the top of the class.

"You ought to be more realistic," he went on. "A lawyer? That's no kind of realistic goal for a nigger."

My stomach began to clench. "But, I—"

"What can you really be?" Mr. Ostrowski mused. "A carpenter? You're good with your hands, I think. That's respectable work, carpentry."

"Sir, I'm at the top of the class," I managed. "I really think . . ." My voice trailed off. Beneath my protest, I could feel the dream slipping away. Right through my fingertips, like air.

I tried to hold on to Papa's belief in me and to the things Mom had always said about making him proud.

"This is the real world, boy," Mr. Ostrowski said. "Be as good as you want in the classroom, but out those doors, you're just a nigger."

Just a nigger.

Those words haunt me. I can't get out from under them.

I've been a Negro my whole life. Light-skinned, sandy-haired, and olive-eyed, yet a Negro nonetheless.

Up until that moment, I'd never, ever heard it as a bad word. It had been tossed my way a thousand times. People on the street: *Nigger.* Boys in school: *Hey, nigger.* Playing around after class: *Come on, nigger.* I rolled with it. Always felt it was all in fun. We were friends, all of us.

Now I saw it all new. What it really meant to be called a nigger.

It was like hurting in retrospect, each repetition of it a pinprick. A thousand tiny stabs, felt all at once. *I'm a nigger.*

But that wasn't the word that hurt most, it turned out. The one that sliced me.

Just.

Just a nigger.

I'd always been colored, but now I saw the walls that came along with it. Thick and white and holding me in place.

I thought about Mom, passing as white at all those jobs, burying her blackness beneath the way she looked. Trying to get us the things we needed. Things we couldn't rightly have.

I thought about Papa.

Just a nigger. You try to be more than that, you get cut down.

I thought about the white boys I used to play with, the ones who would go along with any game or prank I came up with. *Great idea, nigger.* They used to follow me anywhere, looking up at me like I was smart and wise. A leader. And I thought I was. All this time I thought they were seeing me. Now I knew they were seeing just a *nigger*.

I started to feel restless, an itching under my skin that I didn't know how to scratch. One that couldn't be scratched, maybe.

Chapter Four

On the Bus, 1940

When the sky turns black again, the air through the window cracks turns to slices of cold. I huddle deeper in my seat. My coat is too thin to make a good blanket. Even though it's summer, night is night and the air is cool.

I'm far too hyped up to sleep. The old miner snores softly beside me; I don't even have his constant chatter to distract me from the weightless feeling. Like we're hurtling into infinity. Like the night will never end and the black sky will conquer us all. But I love that black sky. The mystery of it. I can't help but wonder about the pitch-dark secrets it holds.

If I could turn off my mind, my heart, it would be perfect. But I just keep thinking about how far from home I'm getting. A little farther. A little farther. It still doesn't scare me, but I guess I'm waiting for the moment that Lansing is so far in the rearview that it gets smaller. But it's all still here with me, stowing away.

Papa's in my mind. Memories from a long time ago. And shadows of the things I don't know. Maybe Ella remembers him, can tell me the stories that never got told back home, about how Papa was young once. He'd ridden on a bus before, I know that much. But there's plenty I don't know.

We're all family, Ella says, on account of the Little blood that we share. I try to think of it that way. Not like two families, but like one big family, just spread out. But it isn't exactly the same. Ella seems familiar to me and close, but not like my whole brothers and sisters. That'll change, I hope, once I'm staying with her.

At the bus station saying good-bye, it felt not quite real yet. Hugging everyone. The whole history of our lives in those hugs. Days and days and nights and nights together. I know every hair on their heads. I can tell the difference between my brothers' breathing in their sleep. We don't even have to speak. Every single glance and tiny movement is a language of its own.

There have been good-byes before. When the welfare man sent me to the first foster home, and again when I ended up with the Swerlins in Mason. We've been split apart in all directions, time and time again. But they were always see-you-tomorrow good-byes, not see-you-I-don't-know-when. We've always been a walk or a shout away from one another. This is different. This is huge.

It's huger now. Now that I'm alone on the road and the world outside seems so much bigger than it ever has before.

Lansing, 1939

I would swing by our house pretty often, to see about Philbert and Hilda and Yvonne and everyone. Mom always seemed glad enough to see me, but I started to think that my dropping by only reminded her of how things were coming apart.

I came around one time, and everything was going to shit. I saw the familiar black car out front, as well as another car and a small sort of truck with a closed-in back. Different from usual.

My heart thumped faster as I bounded into the house, into a living room crowded with people. My siblings stood in a loose half circle around the room, facing the four intruding adults: three large, unfamiliar men, plus a woman I'd seen before, from the welfare office. Mom sat on the couch, with Yvonne clinging to her arm. "You cannot separate me from my children," Mom declared. "This is wrong!"

The woman looked away from Mom and spoke to Wilfred instead.

"She's not in her right mind," the welfare woman said. "She needs psychiatric care."

She handed Wilfred a pile of papers with small print. Important, scary-looking papers. Wilfred glanced at them. "A mental institution?"

The woman nodded. "The state mental hospital. In Kalamazoo."

"For God's sake," Mom said. Her eyes lit with anger. "Can't you leave me and my family alone?" She wasn't crazy—we all knew that. Something else was going on. *They'll try anything to destroy us,* Mom had said once. I hadn't believed her. I mean, they couldn't . . .

"Please don't take our mother from us!" Hilda cried. Kalamazoo was an hour and a half away. Too far to visit regularly.

"She's not crazy," Wilfred said.

"Leave her alone," I blurted out. But the men ignored us.

"Get the girl," one of them said. "Move her out of the way."

Hilda reached for Yvonne and drew her back, away from Mom. "Mama!" Yvonne cried. But Hilda was larger and stronger. She pulled Yvonne close, despite her growing cries. To fight would only make things worse.

"Take my babies to the kitchen," Mom ordered Hilda. The men were moving in on her.

"Let's go," they told her, reaching for her arms to help her up. At the first hint of contact, Mom began to fight. They gripped her instantly and hard.

"No. No!" she cried. "Wilfred—" She stretched an arm out toward my brother. He started toward her automatically, but the men pulled her back. "Take care of your siblings," Mom called. "We have friends who will help you. Remember that!" She looked at the rest of us. "Be strong. Make me proud. Make your papa proud!"

The government men dragged Mom out of the house. They held her by the elbows and ankles and shoulders and thighs, their harsh, meaty hands digging into her softness. She flailed against their touch, but they overpowered her with ease, the way those white men always knew how to do.

Still, Mom did not go quietly. Her hair came loose from the neat bun at her neck and flew in long frizzes down to her waist. The determined, proud expression we all knew so well surfaced from beneath the sorrow. I thought, *No way can they take her. Not Mom. Not really.*

Yvonne cried on. Her retching, choking, uncontrollable cry was the sound that rose above all the rest: the scuffle of boots on earth, Mom's angry protests, and the slamming of paddy-wagon doors, with its cursed finality.

A cloud of dust rose as they drove Mom away from us. The usual cloud that turned the air brown and silty, but this time it failed to dissipate.

Right there and then, this happening shot to the top of the pile of moments that defined our family, in darkness and in light. I put my arms around my sisters. We fell into a familiar sad huddle, which took me back seven years, to the night Papa never came home. I was so small then, comforted by the others, who were bigger and older than me. Now Hilda laid her head on my shoulder. Her tears dripped into the space between my collar and my neck, directly onto my skin. Soft. Warm. Wet. I stared straight ahead, my own eyes dry as desert bones.

We held hands in a small tight circle. We had already lost Papa. Forever. Losing Mom this way was worse than forever, almost, how she was just out of reach now. To know she was out there and not be able to touch her.

Hilda sobbed. Philbert turned away to hide his trauma. I wanted to tell them it would be all right, but it didn't feel all right. Didn't feel like it ever would be, not for a minute, ever again. Wilfred's face was like a statue in the rain. I don't think I had seen him cry but once in my life: at Papa's funeral. It tore my guts to see my siblings so shattered.

"Come on, then," the government man said. "You can't all stay in the house alone."

"We're not alone," I said. "We have each other."

The government man's face twitched. If he had laughed outright, I would have leaped across the room and punched him. Couldn't have helped it. "It's the law," he said. "A bunch of kids can't live alone. We got places for all of you."

Hilda's head snapped up. "Places?" She emphasized the *s*.

"Yeah."

"No. We will stay together," Philbert said.

This time the government man did laugh. "Ain't no one that's going to take in all of Earl Little's stray niggers."

I would have leaped then, but Hilda was holding my arm.

"I'm twenty," Wilfred protested. "I can take care of them." He'd been doing it all this time anyway.

"You can stay," said the man. He nodded at Hilda. "And you. For the rest, we have homes."

Wilfred led the government man to the side of the room. There was nowhere to talk without us hearing, but he appeared more like the man of the house for trying. He argued. He pleaded. He offered himself, time and time again, as our caretaker. And then he stopped. He stopped because the game was over and we all were outplayed. He returned to us.

"You have to go," Wilfred said. "For now, you have to go." He urged us to our feet.

The government people waited by the door while my siblings each packed a small bag of clothes and things. I didn't have anything to pack myself, of course. I had already moved. I tried to help Reginald gather his things, but he shooed my hands away, glaring at me through the tears.

60

Philbert, too, held his back to me, and I wondered how many more ways this day would find to cut me. My brothers turned to one another to stem the sadness, but not to me. Because I was already gone for them. And so I began to hate myself for leaving. What had seemed like not a big deal at the time now seemed like the first wave in a terrible ocean tide. The waves just kept on coming, larger and harsher and saltier than ever before.

My limbs grew heavy, and after a time I found myself sitting on the porch, the corners of the boards digging into the backs of my thighs. The light mellowed as the afternoon deepened around me. My breath frosted into thick, sad clouds. The trees arced shadows over the snow. I no longer lived here, but everything around me was home. Snowdrifts covered the stretches of grass that I had walked every day of my life, the mounds of garden earth that I had turned with my bare hands. Beneath the blanket of white, the land now seemed empty, its history erased. What would this place become now? Without Mom, without the others, could I ever again think of it as home?

One by one, my siblings came out onto the porch. Philbert. Reginald. Wesley. Yvonne. Robert. From inside drifted the echo of Hilda's weeping. She had been our second mother for so long—would she now become the one to grieve us?

The government people bundled my brothers and sister into their cars. I could hear them talking about where everyone was going—Philbert and Reginald to one home,

61

and Yvonne, Wesley, and Robert to another. I suppose it was a relief to hear that no one would be sent away alone, the way I had been. They couldn't have managed it, to be torn away from the family. Not like me.

Neither Wilfred nor Hilda came out to the porch, so I sat there, long after the thick billowing exhaust fumes faded into the white landscape. I sat until my fingers were numb where they curled against the familiar planks of wood that my father had laid with his bare hands all those years ago. I sat until the sky went dark and my stomach growled, low and insistent, and I realized that I didn't have to sit here any longer. I could go get supper with my foster family.

I pushed off the porch and crunched across the ground. In the cold air, I caught a whiff of the promise of fresh snow; soon it would obscure my footsteps leading away. I couldn't feel my fingers or my toes or my face. I just wanted to get warm. I picked up my feet, faster and faster, until I was dashing full speed across the frozen earth. Thinking: *I'm alone now.*

Trying not to think.

Thinking: *I'm alone still.*

Trying not to think.

Thinking: *Put it behind me and go. Go. Go.*

I ran to my foster home, where, indeed, the walls broke the chill wind. Ate my fill of hot biscuits and chicken stew. Stood by the hearth until I could feel my fingers, if not my heart.

Chapter Five

On the Bus, 1940

The farther east we go, the brighter it gets. As the sun rises, casting fresh, full light through the windshield, I sigh with the simple relief that comes along with daytime. My mind relaxes and my eyes have enough to take in to distract me from my melancholy thoughts. The landscape is textured now, rolling hills covered more often by trees than farm fields.

We pass through small rural towns nestled in the Pennsylvania mountains. The old miner reports the names of many of the towns and their approximate sizes, which he knows off the top of his head and apparently finds very interesting. The numbers don't mean all that much to me.

I find the trees especially striking, the way the rising sunlight glints off the leaves, highlighting various shades of green in different places. In the middle of admiring these colors, I spot something that makes me look again.

"What's that?" I say aloud. I squint into the distance at what appears to be a long something hanging from a branch of a tree up on one of the hills.

The old miner follows my gaze. "Oh," he says. Then softly, "Oh, rest his soul."

The bus winds along the road, bringing us closer to what I had seen. Eventually I can make out what looks like dangling legs. Arms. The rounded top of a head. Black hair. Brown skin.

"Is that . . . a person?" I ask. It's hard to say the words.

"Surely was," the old miner says in a leaden voice. "Until they strung him up."

The branch bows with the weight of the . . . body. Heavy with the cruelty of such an act. Yet at the same time, the thing that once was a person seems narrow and strangely weightless, swaying slightly in the breeze. Weightless because it's lifeless, I suppose, but all dressed up in now-ragged clothes. Did it hurt? I wonder. Was he a papa? Was he someone's son?

The bus rounds a curve that brings us closer still. "Avert

your eyes, son," the old miner says. "No cause to be looking at that."

He reaches out with a callused hand and covers my eyes.

It doesn't matter. I've already seen.

"Why?" I say.

"There's never a why," he answers. "They'll give one, but it ain't . . ." His voice trails off. "'Round these parts, they can lynch a Negro like that." He snaps his fingers in front of my face. Lowers his hand. The sight is behind us now. Yet in my mind, it's still along for the ride.

"Maybe he owed a debt," he says. "Maybe he looked wrong at a white woman. No way to know."

Lynch. A too-familiar word. It floats back to me from long ago. Things I overheard at Papa's funeral, when I was much too small to understand:

There might not have been a rope, but it was a lynching all the same.

They done lynched Earl. Didn't even have the courage to do it outright.

"I'm sorry you had to see that," the old miner tells me. "Shame of a thing for a kid like you to carry. We were having a nice ride, I thought."

No way for him to know: I'm carrying it already.

I know without knowing: the man in that tree was a proud black man. Uppity, some might say. Out of his place, some might say. Too smart for his own good. I can hear the words, see those pink lips moving, spitting the words that promised his death. His back never bent underneath it, and they hated that most. I know plenty.

"It's OK," I tell him. "It's just how it is. I know that."

"There's gonna be a better time," the old miner says.

"How do you know?" I ask. "Isn't this how it's always been?"

"It's been all kinds of ways. It's been worse." He looks at me. "Son, you don't know your history."

I do know it. It's etched on my bones. Too deep to dig up. Better to bury it. "You don't know me."

"Hmm."

I could tell him all the things I know. Mom used to sit us around the table, teaching history. Way-back history, about queens and princes ruling Africa, and close-up history about black people breaking the chains of slavery. She made it sound like black people are great and powerful: we can rule again; we can overcome. We could rule when we were on our own, maybe, but not in this white world. In this white world, they enslaved us. In this white world, they lynch us. White families take their children out onto the hillsides, sit on blankets with lunches, and watch. Black men, women, and sometimes even children strung up from trees. Never cut down. No dignity.

I look away from the window, straight forward at the dingy gray back of the seat in front of me. The old miner's staring at me. Or past me, I can't tell.

"What's the point of looking backward?" I tell him. "I'm going to Boston."

Lansing, 1931

I was six years old. Too young to understand much of anything. Not like I understand it any better now.

The policeman came long after supper, after we were all in bed on our way to sleep. We heard his heavy footsteps on the wooden slats of the porch. We knew enough to be afraid, but not enough to know why. Mom did. She started screaming before the knock even came at the door.

"Earl, Earl!" she yelled. But Papa wasn't home. He'd left hours ago, headed downtown to pick up money people owed him for some chickens he had sold.

"Earl, Earl!" Mom yelled again. If any of us had been asleep, we weren't anymore.

Then came the knock. Heavy with dread, it seemed to shake the whole foundation.

Mom was crying. The policeman came in. We could hear the voices from the other room, but not what they were saying. My brothers and I sat up in bed and listened. Wilfred slipped out from between the sheets and went to the door. He cracked it open so we could hear better.

"It was a terrible accident," the policeman was saying to Mom. "Your husband's been badly injured."

Philbert scooted close to me and slid one arm around my shoulders and the other around Reginald's. That's when I knew something was really terribly wrong. Last time Philbert had an arm around me, it was to wrestle me to the ground. My stomach knotted with fear.

Wilfred opened the door all the way and went out into the main room of the house. He was eleven years old, but he stood straight and tall and talked to the policeman, just like Papa would have wanted. Hilda came out of the girls' room and took baby Yvonne from Mom's arms.

"Go on, Mother," Hilda said. "We'll be all right."

Philbert kept on holding us, and together the three of us tumbled out of bed. We tiptoed to the doorway.

"It doesn't look good," the policeman said. "You'll want to be with him."

"Of course. I'm coming." Through her tears, Mom blew us a kiss, picked up her purse, and followed the policeman to the door.

"I'm coming with you, Mom," said Wilfred.

We had never seen this police officer, a white man, before. And here Mom was about to go with him and get into his car, a thing that she would usually never do. I didn't like it. A lot of the police around Lansing didn't like Mom or Papa very much. *Uppity troublemakers,* some white people called them. Papa always said it was because he and Mom were smart, and they had big ideas about what black people like us could be and could do.

The police car rumbled off down the lane, away from our farm, and toward the rest of town. We all looked to Philbert, wondering what to do. He was looking out the window, standing perfectly still. I heard him murmur under his breath, and it sounded like he said, "They're trying to kill him."

I started to cry. Philbert turned and looked at me. "Shh, Malcolm," he said. "It's all right."

But we both knew it wasn't.

Hilda nudged me. "Go get Wesley," she said. I went into Mom and Papa's room and scooped up Wesley out of the crib. Just two years old, he'd managed to sleep through the commotion. When I picked him up, he stirred, then slumped against me. I brought him into the living room where the rest of us were.

The four of us sat around the table, Hilda, Philbert, Reginald, and me, plus baby Yvonne in Hilda's lap and Wesley asleep on a pillow on the floor. It felt important, to be all together. We waited.

"Papa doesn't have accidents," Philbert said sometime in the night, out of nowhere.

"Hush," Hilda said. "We don't know what happened."

"Yeah, we do," Philbert said bitterly.

"What happened?" I asked, confused.

He sighed. "We don't know," he said, even though that's not what he had said a minute ago.

By morning, when Mom and Wilfred returned, we did know. The policemen brought them back to the house, two of them carrying Mom inside. She couldn't stand up. She couldn't stop crying.

"A streetcar accident," one policeman told us. "He fell on the tracks and was run over."

Wilfred saw the policemen to the door with his back straight. Proud, like the man of the house, which, of course, he was now. Then he joined the rest of us in our small, sad clump, where we stood, very, very frightened.

Then the women started to come, friends of Mom's. They swarmed into the bedroom and brought food with them and took her in their arms and tried to stop her crying. The men who followed them came with whispered stories about what might have really happened to Papa. Sinister words on their lips, like "murder." "The Black Legion was out to get him," they said. "The Klan. Some white folks thought Earl was stepping out of place."

I knew what it meant. Papa didn't have an accident. He died for being a proud black man. He died because someone killed him. Someone who was going to get away with it.

I knew this, but I didn't know what to do about it. My thoughts were with Papa.

Papa, who sat and told us stories by the firelight in the evenings.

Papa, who would take the strap to our backs if we failed to finish our chores.

Papa, who instructed us to always hold our heads up, who promised us we were worthy, who assured us we were descended from kings—and from architects and farmers and healers and visionaries—no matter what all the hateful people in the world had to say about us.

Papa, who always took care of us, and who always knew what to do to put things right.

Papa was never coming home.

On the Bus, 1940

The old miner gets off at his stop somewhere in Pennsylvania. He shakes my hand and says, "Fare thee well," which strikes me as the kind of thing people say in books.

"Bye," I tell him. I don't know what else to say. *Thanks? I'll be seeing you?* Except, of course, I won't.

I watch as he disappears into the bus station to wait for his connection. He settles a tight little cap on his head. From the back he could be almost anyone. Not quite a stranger, not quite a friend.

This is how it is, I suppose, now. People drift in and drift out. Foster families and welfare men, and so-called friends and schoolmates. Family. Some you remember and some you forget, whether you want to or not, in either direction. It's a far cry from my first world, full of my brothers and sisters and Mom and Papa. When everyone I loved was always there with their arms around one another, laughing and building our home.

The bus pulls out, and I'm alone again.

My family is far behind me now. I don't know what's ahead.

Chapter Six

Ella meets me at the bus station. She might be my half-sister, but she looks wholly happy to see me. She folds me in her arms straightaway and says, "Welcome."

My feet and my behind still vibrate from the engine's constant rhythm. It's a relief to be on solid ground again.

"I'm glad you made it. How was the bus ride?"

"Good, I guess." Not that I have anything to compare it to. "I'm glad it's done." I tell her about the old guy I talked to. I don't tell her what we saw.

Ella keeps her arm around me, walking us along the sidewalk toward her car. She's strong and tall and warm. I'm tired from the long road, and it almost seems like I can lean on her and rest. But the cacophony of the city around me is too exciting. I'm folded into more than Ella's embrace; I'm a part of Boston now.

The city is alive. More than alive—it's hopping, thriving, breathing. Never have I seen so many people at one time. It's a Sunday afternoon, and folks are dressed up in their churchgoing fineness. Women in neat knee-length dresses with delicate hats or large sculpted curls in their hair. Men in dapper suits of all colors and neatly brimmed hats. Children scampering everywhere, enjoying the summer sunshine. We drive past a park, nestled right among the tall buildings, and I can hear laughter as the youngsters run and jump and play.

Up until now, I thought Lansing was a big city. But here, there are stores for every kind of thing you can imagine. Dress shops and tailors. Haberdashers and cleaners. Groceries and fruit stands and butcher shops and bakeries. Shoe stores with windows chock-full of the latest fashions, with people clustered on the sidewalks peering in to see what's new. We pass tobacco shops and jewelry dealers and movie theaters with grand marquees ten feet high. Nightclubs and bars and restaurants, too, with glittering metal signs, or ones made out of lightbulbs so that they'll glow in the dark. Department stores with a whole city block of windows, full of appliances and clothing and knickknacks and things whose purpose I can't even guess.

I try to read every sign, every message scrawled in paint across a picture window, but there's too much to see. Impossible in one sweep to take it all in. Through the open car windows waft the scents of food cooking. Each delightful whiff lingers for a second, and then it's gone. Spicy tomatoey something. Fresh bread. Smoke from passersby's cigarettes. Steam from the laundry vents. The fur of a wet dog I can't even see. Something sweet and strong that makes my mouth water, like a swirl of cinnamon and sugar.

Everywhere there are signs for city buses and subway trains, going every which way. There are streetcar tracks here, too. It's weird, but I didn't expect there to be. I won't ride those. I wish they weren't even here, in my new life. I look away from them quickly, toward the things that are new and exciting.

Ella's neighborhood is called Sugar Hill. It seems like a nice area. The people walking on the sidewalks are dressed well, and the sounds of the traffic and the commotion make everything seem alive and important.

Ella's home is an impressive three-story house with a porch out front and a driveway for her car. The second floor has one of those three-sided windows sticking out. She leads me inside. The house smells good, like home cooking, with hints of Ella's perfume. There's a basement, too, so it's four floors altogether. A big place.

Ella shows me my bedroom, a small rectangular room upstairs. "Why don't you settle in while I get some dinner ready?"

"Thanks."

She leans forward and kisses my cheek. It's little things

like that, all warm and familiar, that make me know I'm doing the right thing. This is where I'm supposed to be now. I've only met Ella one time before, but she really does feel like family.

Ella leaves me alone to unpack. In a room of my own, I can put my things anywhere I want.

Lansing, 1939

At first, when I learned Ella would visit us in Lansing, I didn't know quite what to make of the news. Hilda told me that she'd written to Ella about Mom being taken away from us and committed to the center in Kalamazoo. I guess, being slightly older and having some measure of means, Ella wanted to help us.

Our half-siblings from Papa's first marriage had always been something of a mystery to me, so I was curious to learn more about Ella, and Hilda brought her out to Mason to meet me. Ella took a special interest in me right away—Hilda must have mentioned some of my troubles in particular, since she was always concerned about me being separated from the family. Stealing chickens and swiping melons—the kinds of things we did to get by—had made me seem like a problem to the child-welfare people. My bigger pranks had been all in fun: moving outhouses to trick farmers and things like that. But I may have gone a little far when I put a thumbtack on my teacher's seat during class. I had been expelled and was living at the Swerlins' group home, where the welfare people sent the most troublesome boys. It was one step away from a real juvenile detention center. My sisters — Hilda and now Ella — felt like they needed to do something to get me back in line.

Ella looked every bit like a well-to-do city woman. Her black hair was coiled in waves around her head, beneath a pert, proper cream-colored hat. She wore leather gloves and a fur coat that looked warm. She was a tall woman with a strong presence. She seemed enormous to me, like Papa, so full of blackness.

She held her arms out to me, and I let myself be folded into her all-encompassing warmth. I hadn't been hugged warm in such a long time. I pulled away early, because it made me feel a little too good, and I didn't want to get accustomed to that kind of thing.

Hilda headed back to work, but Ella wanted to spend some time with me. "Let's go see about your mother," she said.

Ella took me into the car, and we rode the seventy miles to Kalamazoo. I peppered her with questions about Boston, the city I had only seen pictures of in magazines and newspapers. I couldn't imagine much of anything outside of the Lansing area. Kalamazoo was certainly the farthest I'd been that I could remember, anyway. Our family had moved from Nebraska to Wisconsin to Michigan when I was a baby, but it was beyond my memory. This was the only world I knew.

"What's the best thing about the city?" I asked her.

"Oh," Ella said, gazing patiently at me. "Well, I suppose we have access to a great many things." She glanced out the window, at the stores and houses flashing by. "And we live among friends."

All of it sounded wonderful to me. Hard to imagine, but wonderful.

"You could come visit," she said. "Maybe over the summer?"

"Really?" I asked.

"It's quite a long ride," she said. "But we would be very happy to have you."

I tried to picture it, me going all the way to Boston. Hours and hours on the train or bus just to get there. And what would I find?

Going into the state hospital was easier having an adult with me. Last time we had visited, just us kids together, they had given us a hard time about getting in to see Mom. Ella, in her big black way, took charge and walked me in without a bit of fanfare.

She put her arm around my shoulders and eased me forward. It helped. I didn't like how much it helped, so I shrugged away from her and went toward Mom on my own.

It was strange to see her. Strange because I spent my days now putting away thoughts of her. It was easy enough to lose myself in all the school things. Football. Class-presidential things. All the distractions that came along with being popular and adored.

She was draped in a white-and-green gown made of thin fabric, its loose folds billowing around her. Her pearls were gone. There were flat green slippers on her feet, and she tapped one toe against the tile floor. She sat in a tall-backed chair with high arms. It made her look small.

I walked toward her because I had to, but I didn't want to. Even though we'd come all this way, I just wanted to turn. To look away.

Ella came up beside me, then fell a little behind again as we got close.

Mom stood up. Put her hands on my face. "Honey."

I felt relieved that she knew me, because I barely knew her. It had been a few months since I'd seen her, the longest time ever between visits. She was gaunt, with these haunted, saggy cheeks, but her shoulders were still broad. She put her arms around me, and I tried to find the warmth in her hug that had surprised me in Ella's earlier. But this hug felt vacant of comfort. I held her tight anyway. "Hi, Mom."

"Mrs. Little?" Ella stepped up behind me. "Ella Collins."

Mom's attention flicked to her. She stepped forward and embraced Ella, seemed to draw strength from her large dark presence, but then pulled away, smiled, and brought her attention back to me and me alone. She talked to me softly, pulled me to sit beside her. Ignoring Ella, who stood aside and watched.

In a sudden rush, I felt myself blurting out, "I have all As." I knew it would make her proud. "I'm class president."

Mom clapped her hands lightly. She praised my efforts. We chatted about everything—everything except all the trouble I was in—and for a while I found a way to close out the white hospital walls and the acidy smell and the squeak of wheels and the occasional troubled shriek that pierced our bubble. She was Mom again, and I was me, and the ugliness faded for a moment.

A brief moment.

It didn't last long enough. Never long enough.

Ella came closer. "Mrs. Little, I'd like to talk for a minute, if you don't mind."

I ducked my head, because I'd known this talk was coming. I knew it was going to be about me. Someone had to break the news that I was in big trouble, and that I'd broken every expectation that had ever been held for me. The joy over my achievements at school would fade for Mom once she learned I was one strike away from juvenile detention.

"Ella Collins," Mom echoed, addressing her directly for the first time. "Ella Collins."

"Yes," Ella said. "I'm—"

"I know who you are," Mom snapped. She waved her fingers in the air, dismissing Ella. "You're one of *them*."

Mom clamped her fingers on my shoulders. I closed my eyes. Would have turned away, but there was nothing to turn to. She had a grip on me, so strong that it hurt. I could feel her pulse through the tips of her fingers—or maybe it was just my own heart pounding, fast and fierce, as though it wanted to bust out of my chest. I opened my eyes, and the pounding ache drummed deeper. Mom's fierce grip on me felt strong enough to last forever, but I knew the system hated us and would keep on tearing us apart. Behind these walls, she seemed caught, and helpless in a way I'd never imagined she could be.

Still gazing at Ella, Mom whispered something, so softly I barely heard.

"What did you say?" I asked.

Mom's attention flicked back to me, her eyes thickened by the clouds of pain and grief she usually kept above us, out of sight. I would have closed my eyes against it if I could have, but there was no escaping it. The air grew thick with sorrow.

"He left them," Mom said. "I should have known he'd leave us, too."

"She didn't mean it," Ella said as we walked away. "You know she didn't mean to say that."

But he did leave, I thought.

"I don't think badly of him," she told me in a distant, floating voice. "He was always a father to me." I watched her wipe a tear from her cheek. "Even when he wasn't near. Can you understand that?"

I couldn't. I couldn't, because what I remembered of him was small, dark flashes. His smile. The proud look in his eye. A few of his words and the rumble of his car beneath me, the way he made me feel safe, but not much more than that. In all this long time that had passed, what I knew of him had only gotten smaller.

"Can you understand that?" she whispered.

There was so little that I understood. Least of all this.

Why I was here. Why Papa was not. Why I felt like I was leaving Mom, too. Why when Ella put her arm around me for a second time, I let her.

"We're family. And we have to stick together," she said. "That's how we get through it."

"Through what?" I asked her, but not because I wasn't in it. Only because I didn't know what was on the other side.

"Oh, Malcolm." Ella hugged me, with both arms this time. "You miss him, like I do. Don't you?"

I let her hold on to me, but I didn't say anything. We didn't talk about this. About the hole in us, or how it got there.

"It helps me to remember Papa's work." Ella talked on, maybe because I wouldn't. "He believed in something. It's never wrong to fight for what you believe in. What you want."

All we have is want, I thought. *All we do is fight. And he did leave.*

It was dark already, in the car on the way back to the Swerlins'. It had been a long day, and my eyes were drooping. I caught my neck jerking forward a couple of times.

Ella patted her shoulder. "You can rest your head, if you like," she said.

I could lean on Ella, it seemed. Everything around me had holes in it, and she was something solid. It wouldn't hurt me to rest awhile. I moved closer to her. She wrapped a thick arm around me, and next thing I knew she was tapping me awake.

Out the window, the Swerlins' place. Time to step out in the cold and back to my room.

"You stay out of trouble," Ella insisted. "You hear?"

"Yes, ma'am."

She hugged me—so like Mom's hugs used to be: safe, firm, and loving.

"You come visit me," she told me. "You'll like Boston. There'll be a place for you there. I can promise you that."

But Boston seemed big and far. Like a dream. A place to visit in my sleep, like the memory of Mom's arms.

"I don't know," I said, edging away. "I don't know."

"Well, think about it," she said, pushing open my door. The chill of the night caught me. I hurried the few paces to the Swerlins' front door. I stood on the porch and watched as Ella's car chugged off down the lane. As she disappeared, I felt a sinking return to everything normal. Everything cold.

* * *

82

I woke the next morning feeling no warmer. That very day I started setting aside money for the bus fare to Boston. Visiting Ella over summer vacation seemed like it would be the best idea ever.

Then, barely a month of saving later, Mr. Ostrowski saw fit to enlighten me about the truth of my great potential. The world turned upside down. What was the point in going back to school after that? I didn't need a high-school diploma to be a nigger.

I had to second-guess everything. The classmates who had elected me president—did they really think I was the best in the class, or was I just a novelty object they wanted to play with? *He's just a nigger, but, hey, we've never seen a nigger who can do what Malcolm can do.* My stomach ached every day and every night, thinking about it.

And Papa—all the good warm memories I was holding slowly faded. Moment by moment, I realized how deep into me all his stories had burrowed. His promises. His lies. Pulling them out hurt more than anything, like yanking myself up by the roots.

No, I couldn't stay in Lansing. Not after the way things had changed for me. I counted my money first thing when I woke every morning and last thing before I went to bed. The good news was now I only needed to earn half the money I'd been working toward. No round-trip ticket for me. The minute I had enough money saved to go one-way, I'd be out of there.

Boston, 1940

To celebrate my first night in Boston, Ella prepares a large dinner of baked chicken. Bowls full of side dishes adorn the table: okra, sweet potatoes, corn on the cob, greens, homemade bread. The food is plentiful and tasty. After the meager meals I managed on the bus ride, I delight in eating my fill.

"I don't want you to look for a job just yet," Ella says over dinner.

I raise my head in surprise. "You don't want me to work?"

"Well, I want you to go to school," she says pointedly. I can see Papa in her face, the way her cheeks drop sternly as she levels a familiar gaze at me.

Education is vital, son. Knowledge gives you power.

I look away. If knowledge is so important, how come Papa didn't tell me the truth?

"Naw." School used to be fun, back when I thought something would come of it. But now I figure I'm better off just getting on with my life. "I'll get a job. Help pay my way."

"Eventually," she answers. "But first I want you to take some time to experience the city."

I step out onto the front porch, looking left, looking right. Which way to go first?

I want to go everywhere. Walking around Sugar Hill, I do my best to keep hold of the street names, but it's easier just to remember the landmarks and the turns. I keep the route real smooth in my head. But I don't want to know just this neighborhood. I want to go everywhere. Yesterday I might have said I've had enough of buses for a while, but it's a brand-new day, and riding the city bus seems more exciting. I buy a handful of tokens and jump on board.

In downtown Boston, the buildings are tall and stately. A hundred years old or more. With plaques drilled into them, from the days of the American Revolution, the one promising freedom and the right to pursue happiness. No one mentioned that the pursuit would be so long.

Back near Ella's house, I get off the bus and just walk. Sugar Hill itself is something of a mixed neighborhood. Black folks and white folks, walking together. Together as in among one another. And together as in holding hands. I see some couples made up of one black, one white. It's amazing to me. In Lansing things were very separate. Here people of different races pass on the sidewalk without seeming to even notice each other.

Down the Hill, though, I discover the most exciting things I've seen in Boston so far. Walking down from Sugar Hill into the next neighborhood is like getting to the depths of something. The heart. It's a beating pulse of a place, full of music and laughter and energy. Most buildings aren't so shiny, clean, and new. They're solid and worn and real. Some blocks are run-down; others are really nice. Every door looks weathered but approachable. Places you can get into, things you can actually touch.

People lounge around on their front porches, laughing and talking. Some might think they're no good, but to me they seem like the sort of people you want to spend an afternoon with, just shooting the breeze. A lot of the young fellows, not too much older than me, wear the most amazing billowing suits. They walk with a sort of swagger, swinging their arms and looking left to right with their hats pulled low.

They use long lines of words I've never heard before. Everything is "cool," and the guys look "hip," which is how they score "chicks" and take them out dancing. Afterward they might go back to someone's "pad" and "pull some tones" off a record or the radio. You dig?

Roxbury, the neighborhood is called. It's not the mixed place that the Hill is. Nearly all of the faces you see down here are Negro. And it isn't a buttoned-up polite sort of place like the Hill, either. It's tough and energetic and makes my senses come alive. Jazz strains leak from behind the doors of the hippest clubs. Any given block might steam with the scent of chicken and rice or sausage and fries or a simmering vat of chowder. The people move fast, and they're all so different, covering every imaginable size, shape, and shade, with skin light as mine to darker than even Papa was. And style. I've never seen such swinging threads. Shop doors are propped wide so it's easy to see in. The sort of place where everything's all out in the open.

It's not so hard—being black—when I'm surrounded by so many others, and everyone seems to be getting along just fine, from the rich-looking dark men in pressed suits to the vagrants in the alleys. Mothers lugging babies and groups of pretty girls in short, smooth dresses with purses to match. Schoolboys with satchels and newsboys on bikes. Milkmen and mail carriers and shopkeepers and barmaids. All Negro.

No such thing as "just a nigger" in Roxbury. I love it.

Chapter Seven

Boston, 1940

Ella frowns with concern over my repeated explorations into Roxbury. "You should stay on the Hill," she tells me. She reminds me about a place nearby, called Townsend's, a drugstore and soda fountain, where I can get friendly with teenagers my age.

"You should go there," Ella insists. "It's where everyone your age spends time."

To please her, I go on over to Townsend's Drug Store. Loud, snazzy pop music plays on the radio. I recognize a few tunes I like by Erskine Hawkins. Other songs remind me of the music my classmates at Mason used to play, but a lot of it feels too high and light to me now, after hearing the deep soulful tunes that guys play on the streets down in Roxbury.

Ella's right: the place is full of people my own age. Boys and girls in dark and light hues, dressed in skirts and slacks, looking like they've just come out of school. Some carry books or satchels or have stacks of textbooks on the table beside them. They look and sound like Mason students. I guess I know these people, and I could fit in if I wanted to, but I find myself looking out the window.

They order French fries and milk shakes, banana splits and grilled burgers and sandwiches. The air's full of laughter and the general hum of people chatting over one another, trying to get a word in edgewise.

With the dollar Ella gave me, I order a raspberry soda and fries. I perch on a red swivel stool at the counter, turning from time to time to see what's going on around the room. The waiter stands inside the U-shaped counter, going from side to side taking orders, gliding to the register to ring people up. The fry guys manning the grill in the back move swiftly, every other second shouting, "Order up." A waitress in a black-and-red-striped dress with a red smock takes the table orders. The place is hopping.

I keep to myself for the little while it takes for my food to come. I know it's important to Ella that I try things out here, but there's no one I especially want to talk to in this place. Even though everyone appears to be with friends, it seems like at the same time everyone's putting on airs.

Some of the tables are all white, and some are all black, but plenty are mixed. I've been in groups like that, with my so-called friends from Mason. I know that you can be black and get all up with white folks, feeling like you're fitting in, trying to ignore the fact that when you step outside, you're still a Negro. Still low. It makes me a little sick. Or maybe it's just the sweetness of the soda—which I suck down quickly. Delicious. Munch my way through those fries pretty quickly, too. Then I make my way down the Hill.

Down to where people stay real. Down to where the guys on the corner laugh low and shout dirty jokes to one another, cracking up and slapping skin as they try to top each other. Down to where music drifts out the doors of bars, and people are looser and altogether more free.

Down the Hill is where I belong. The sights, the smells, the rhythm of the folks, the feeling in the air. I circle the blocks again and again, trying to take it all in. Yeah. Roxbury's where the action is. And I'm here to stay.

Back in Lansing, I would have been talking to everyone I passed. Everyone says hello. Here you can just move. Still, there's no reason not to make Roxbury my own. This place is gonna be home. The blood in my veins was meant to keep pulse with the rhythm of these streets. My heart beats faster, and my eyes move quickly from one face to the next.

There's a cluster of young guys gathered around the hood of a car, down in front of the barbershop. They're often there. I've passed them a couple of times now. They laugh and hoot and bump against each other while they're bent over whatever they're doing. Eight, maybe ten guys. Looks like they're playing cards.

Circling to the rear of the car, I lean in and peer over the hood. Just to see. Down the long slope of the windshield, I see a heavyset guy pull three cards out of his breast pocket.

"Who's up for a little Find the Lady?" he says. He's wearing a fedora with the brim pulled low. He lays out the three cards faceup. Two jacks, one queen. "Money down. Place your bets."

"All right," says the guy to his right. He moves a toothpick between his teeth. "Fat Frankie's swapping. Who's up and who's in?"

"Me," says a tall, thin cat about my size. He throws a dollar on the hood.

Fat Frankie flips the three cards over and starts shuffling them over one another. He picks up the far right card with his right hand, the center card with his left. Drops the right card in the center, grabs the left card with the same hand. Drops the center card in the left slot and so on in a kind of rhythmic pattern that gets faster and faster until he finally stops. "Where's the lady?" he says to the cat who bet. It seems that the game is about keeping track of the queen. But the guy loses his dollar.

Another guy goes. He loses. Fat Frankie's shuffling gets faster and faster.

Another guy goes. Another dollar down. But I've been right about where the queen is every time.

I can do better than these clowns. I reach into my pocket for a dollar. A hand lands on my wrist. "No, my man. Don't fall for that stick."

"What?"

The hand and the voice belong to a short, dark cat with a long black briefcase. "It's a hustle."

"A what?"

"A game you can't win."

I grin. "Maybe *you* can't. I've been right every time."

He smiles back. Shrugs. "Minute you lay your money down, it's gone. I guarantee you."

"What's it to you?"

Now he sort of frowns, sticking his lips out. "Eh. Just a bit of friendly advice."

Fat Frankie's been watching. He groans. "In or out, kid?" He starts the shuffle. "Where's the queen? Find the lady and double your money."

"In." I slap my dollar onto the windshield. It slides down to the wipers.

"This kid's green as a thistle," the new guy says. "Have some shame."

"Shorty, lay off," Frankie says. "He's here to play. Maybe he's got what it takes. You got what it takes, kid?"

"Oh, yeah," I answer, refusing to tear my eyes from the cards. *I've got her, I've got her, I've got her . . .* Fat Frankie suddenly stops sorting. The three cards stand like little sentinels, waiting.

I point to the one on the left. Frankie flips the card and the crowd cheers, "Ohhhh!" I'm looking at the smug, tiny face of the queen.

"See?" I gloat to the guy they call Shorty.

Shorty moves his briefcase to the other hand. Despite the case, he doesn't really look like a businessman. He's wearing tan slacks and a shirt halfway unbuttoned so you can see his underclothes. His flat newsboy hat tapers in the front, and underneath it his hair is straight and combed back toward his collar, like a white man's. Plenty of cats in Roxbury have that look. I don't know how they do it.

"Beginner's luck," Shorty mumbles. "Y'all take care now." And he ambles off.

Fat Frankie peels a dollar off his impressive cash roll and tucks it in under the windshield wiper alongside mine. "Double down?" he asks me.

"I'm in." I match my winnings with two more dollars down. I'm betting four.

"That's my man. Give him some room!" The crowd shifts, putting me at the center of it. My toes are against the tire now; I'm leaning my palms on the side of the hood, watching close. The metal is sun-warm, and the guys around me jostle and hoot. My heart skips forward, elated by the rush. Frankie's hands move fleetly, but I've got a good eye.

I can't afford to double after that—I've only got four more dollars. So I throw two in. I'm betting ten. Next round, my winnings are up to twenty. Not a bad return on a five-dollar bet. I throw in my last two dollars. "Here we go again," Fat Frankie says. My skin is sweat slick. His hands move faster and faster. Forty-four dollars will be the most I've ever held in my hand at once. But then again, I'm on a roll. Maybe I'll let it ride, without adding anything. Eighty-eight? Unimaginable.

The cards fly. My gaze darts along with them. "Where's the lady?" Frankie says. "Show her to me. Keep your eye on the skirt, man. Where's the lady?" He stops. The cards wait. With confidence, I point to the center.

Fat Frankie's slow grin. Right away I know. My heart sinks. I swallow. He flips the center card. Sure enough, it's one of the two jacks. He scoops my twenty-two dollars off the windshield and adds it to his roll.

In my room that night, I write a letter to Philbert, telling him all about my failed wager with Fat Frankie. We used to go down to the creek or up into someone's barn and play cards or flip coins and bet on them. Cards, we could win, but matching nickels, Richie always had some kind of crazy luck. You each flip a nickel, and it comes up heads or tails. If it matches what you called, you win. If you both match, or both don't, it's a draw, but if one matches and the other doesn't, the winner gets to keep all the money in the pot.

I scrawl the whole story for Philbert. How I recognized the wily grin on Fat Frankie's face, at the moment when he knew he'd hustled me but good. I warn Philbert not to match nickels with Richie Dixon anymore. Richie used to smile just like Fat Frankie when he won. We only *thought* it was luck.

Lansing, 1938

Walking home from school, I pretended to be Joe Louis, the Brown Bomber, the greatest boxer who ever lived and the only black boxer headed to the heavyweight championship. I tried out my uppercut, right hook, and blocking with the left. Philbert had given me some moves to practice.

Philbert was a really good boxer. He trained and took on real matches and everything. My own skills left something to be desired, but I was working on it. I thought about Joe Louis and the sound of the crowd on the radio, the thump of gloves and the grunts and the cheers. I pretended it was all around me right now. I went up on my toes. *Boom. Swish. Pow. Pow.*

"Look at this," said Richie Dixon, coming up from the side, along with some of our other friends. I hadn't seen them coming. I dropped my fists, embarrassed to be caught swinging into midair.

"Hi, Richie," I said.

"Hey, nigger. You think you're some kinda Joe Louis?"

"Maybe," I retorted. "I could be." This was not entirely true, but that was the whole point of practicing.

"Oh, yeah?" Richie started rolling up his sleeves. "Let's see what you've got, nigger."

"You're on." We danced around each other for a moment, all in good fun.

"Let's go," he said.

"Right here?" I asked. "On the road?" I wasn't about to walk away from the challenge, but it didn't feel right to go it alone. If I was going to beat Richie's behind once and for all, I wanted witnesses.

Richie looked like he was thinking. "OK," he said. "Let's do it official. How about up by the Coleman barn? Meet you there tomorrow, daybreak. Then you're going down."

It sounded sufficiently dramatic to me. We shook hands to settle the deal. A day meant all the time in the world to gather an audience. It wasn't just a challenge; it was a showdown. I ran ahead, to meet up with Philbert. If Richie was going to bring some people, I had better, too.

The Coleman property had been abandoned for a number of years. For as long as we could remember, at least. Behind the barn was nothing but a patch of dying grass. We had heard that by night it used to be a moonshine spot, where the booze runners would make secret deliveries to paying customers. But now it was just a place kids would meet and kick a ball around or set up a makeshift diamond for stick-ball or whatnot.

Richie Dixon was on one side of the group. I was on the other. I thought about Joe Louis and how he ruled in the ring. Today I could be Joe Louis. Today I could fight. Today it would be easy.

I thought about my victory lap, knee-high jogging with my gloves in the air. Not that I was wearing gloves; it was just a backyard fistfight, but still. I could imagine it.

"Come on, Malcolm. You can beat him," Philbert urged. Just because I always lost to Philbert didn't mean I didn't have skills. He was just really good.

I hopped up into the makeshift ring, which was a circle of our friends and classmates.

"Go, Malcolm," some shouted.

"Go, Richie," others proclaimed.

I thought I had a fair share of the cheering section, and I was feeling pretty good about it until Richie stepped forward, fists raised. His knuckles flew at me.

I saw stars. "Malcolm? Can you hear me?"

Philbert's face loomed over mine. "How many fingers am I holding up?" he said.

I honestly could not have told him. His hands and face were swimming. "Uhhh . . ."

"The fight's over, buddy." Philbert reached for my hand and helped me sit. "He knocked you out in one punch!"

Not possible, I thought. "That's just the first round, then, isn't it?" I said.

Philbert's worried face gave way to a laughing face. "Not when you stay down as long as you did," he chortled.

"Why? How long was I out?" I noticed that the other boys were already some distance away. Were they leaving?

"About a minute," Philbert answered. "Boy, you are never going to live that one down!"

"Noooo," I groaned.

"Richie Dixon, boxing master?" Philbert shook his head. "I should never have let you go up against him."

"Let's get a rematch," I said. "How about that?"

"That seems like a good idea," Philbert said, dripping sarcasm. "How bad did he ring your bell?"

I rubbed my neck, and we started walking. I tried to work out what had happened. It should have been a fair fight, me and Richie. But Richie Dixon always seemed to have the upper hand.

Boston, 1940

Richie Dixon's greasy pink grinning face floats in front of me, keeping me awake. Damn him. He was hustling us all along. How can you cheat at nickels? I wonder. Nobody could really be as lucky as Richie seemed to be. How did we not see it?

I pound my fist on the mattress. And the knockout. It should've been a fair fight between me and Richie. I should've at least got a punch in. Maybe he cheated at box-ing, too. Did he throw his punch too early?

Hey, niggers, Richie'd say.

Hey, we'd answer. Like it was no big deal. Just what they called us. A nickname.

I thought Richie was our friend. I even thought I had one up on him, actually. I could boss him around, get him to do things the way I wanted, like tip outhouses for a Halloween prank.

We got caught tipping outhouses once. Some old farmer dragged me and Philbert out of his yard by the elbows, so screaming mad we thought he was going to kill us dead. Meanwhile Richie and Ben, who were just as guilty as we were, scampered off into the woods lickety-split—as if they hadn't even been there.

I never noticed at the time, but whenever there was trouble of any kind, Richie and his friends got off scot-free.

It makes me want to pound him, for real this time. Him and everyone like him, the lucky sons of guns who slide through life like they're greased.

Chapter Eight

Boston, 1940

Through the window, the pool hall appears dim but inviting. Low strains of music drift out through the cracks in the door. Shorty, the guy I met over bets with Fat Frankie, is in there corralling balls atop each table with a wooden triangle. Shorty seems nice enough; he tried to help me and all. He might be someone I'd like to know. I could use a friend who plays everything straight up and real. I go on in.

Inside, the pool hall is brighter than I expected. A dozen or so tables are spread around the room, their smooth green-felt surfaces looking pristine. Most of the tables have a triangle of colorful balls all laid out and waiting, plus one white ball at the opposite end. Lamps hang from the ceiling over each table, casting cones of light. The uneven wood floor creaks and rocks with every step. A hundred pool sticks of different lengths stand at attention in their cradles on the walls.

Shorty sees me coming but keeps on racking balls. I go on in, get pretty close. Trying to figure out exactly what to say. Not sure what I want from him, except maybe a few words of advice.

"Wouldn't have pegged you for a billiards man," he says.

I run a hand over the edge of a table. The green-felt surface is firm but smooth under my fingers. "I dabble."

Shorty grins. "Right. Well, go on, then." He spreads his hand wide over the table, as if inviting me to just dive in.

I hesitate. My gaze flits from the sticks to the balls to the can of white powder on the side of the table.

Shorty's amusement deepens. "You even know how to play?"

"Back in Lansing, I never even set foot in a pool hall," I admit, surprising myself a little. I've been pretending to everyone as much as I can, about what I've seen, where I've been, what I know. But Shorty brings out something honest in me.

"My man," Shorty exclaims. "You're from Lansing? I'm from Lansing."

"Really?" We slap hands. I'm thinking, *This is great— what crazy luck to meet someone who's been where I've been.*

101

"What do you know." Shorty glances around, as if looking for someone to tell the good news. "My homeboy!"

So we chat easily for a couple minutes, about people and places from back home. Shorty throws out names, and I know some, but we don't have friends in common. He's almost ten years older than me, so we didn't exactly run in the same circles. I go along with it, because any talk with Shorty is good talk, but I don't really want to think back on Lansing anymore. What I really want is to know about Roxbury.

Shorty is dark black, like Papa. Not really as dark but close. He's thick and muscled, but doesn't have much height. Hence "Shorty," I suppose. I've got inches on him, even though he's in his twenties. He's not treating me like a kid, though. He talks to me like we're the same. Just two guys from Lansing, getting to know each other.

"How'd you get to work here?" I finally ask, twisting the conversation. "Seems like an OK setup."

Shorty nods knowingly. "You're new in town. You need a slave?"

"What?"

"A slave. A job, homeboy. You working someplace?"

"Naw. But I'm looking," I lie. Ella's plan aside, I can't have it around that I'm the kind of guy who isn't earning his keep.

"We'll find you something," Shorty says. "Yeah, my boys'll keep their ears out."

"Thanks," I tell him.

"Sure thing, Red."

"Red?"

"Look at you," Shorty says. "I never seen a Negro with red hair, high yellow or otherwise."

"It's not so red," I say. "Only in the right kind of light."

Shorty grins. "Yeah, we got the best kind of light down here in the pool hall."

I shuffle my feet, feeling self-conscious. Nothing to say, except I want to fit in, not stand out.

"We also got to do something about that fuzz," he says. "Get you a clean conk, like so." Shorty smooths his hand over his own slicked-back hair. "You'll see, Red. I'm gonna hook you up."

I know enough to know that everyone needs a street name. Red. It has a ring to it. Real definitive. Real simple. Sleek.

When I get back up on the Hill later that afternoon, Ella's on the phone. "Yes, actually, here he is now," she says. She holds out the phone to me, wearing a pinched expression that says she doesn't quite approve. "Someone called Shorty, for you?"

"Hey, Red. I found you a slave," he says straightaway.

"Really?" I tuck the phone closer. Turn away from Ella's hands-on-hips, narrow-eyed scrutiny.

"Freddie, the shoe shine down at the Roseland, hit the numbers. He's quitting tonight. Job'll be yours if you want it."

"That's fast work," I tell him. Meanwhile, my pulse starts thumping, about to beat out of my skin. Work at the Roseland Ballroom? Where all the bands would come to play?

"I said I'd take care of you," Shorty says. "You in?"

Did he even need to ask? "What time do I need to be there?"

"About seven. Ask for Freddie."

"I'll be there. Hey, thanks, man."

"No problem, homeboy."

We hang up.

"New friend?" Ella says.

"I got a slave."

"You *what?*" Ella catches me in a sharp gaze.

"I got a slave, down at the Roseland. Shining shoes."

"What are you talking about, Malcolm?"

I feel swelled up for a second, knowing something that she doesn't. "A slave. You know, a job."

Ella wipes her hands on her apron. Her weighty stare unyielding. I squirm.

"Well, I told you, you don't have to work yet, but if you're ready . . ."

"My friend Shorty hooked me up," I say. "It's a good slave, he says, in the ballroom, with all the people and the music. Gotta jump on it."

Ella shakes her head. "I don't want you up in this house talking about 'slaves,'" she says. "You don't know slavery, so don't act like you do."

What am I supposed to say? I have to learn to talk like the guys down the Hill. The "cats" down the Hill, that is. I have to be hip.

"Will you be paid for this work?" Ella asks.

"Sure. And probably tips on top of it."

"Well, all right, then," Ella says.

"You must be Red," Freddie says. It's weird to shake a guy's hand while you're standing in the middle of the bathroom.

"Yeah. Red. That's me." I'm owning it, fast.

Freddie chuckles, a kind of high-pitched whine beneath it. "Shorty wasn't kidding. You're green as grass."

What can I say to that?

"How long you been in the city?" Freddie asks.

"Three months," I tell him. A lie.

Freddie scoffs. "Full of it," he says. "No wonder you're getting on with Shorty."

I don't understand.

"You've been here a month if it's been a day," he says. Catches me spot-on. I fight off the urge to say, *How'd you know?* To ask would be to give up the lie.

"Step into my office," Freddie says, sweeping his hand toward the shoe-shine corner. It's a big bathroom, with stalls and a long row of sinks. Along the wall Freddie leads me to, there's a raised wooden chair with footrests where the guy will sit while you shine. Various bottles line the counter, beside stacks of towels and bowls of mint candy.

"So this is how it goes," Freddie says. "They wash their

hands, you hand them a towel. Usually you get a nickel. Not everyone's gonna tip, but that's just life." He touches the ceramic bowl strewn with coins.

Freddie demonstrates the shining process on his own shoe. "You take the brush, like so." The stiff bristles scrape the shoe along the sides and over the top. *Buff, buff.*

"Then the polish." The bottle makes a puckering sound as he squeezes a dark dollop onto the toe.

"And brush it in." *Buff, buff.* His hands move fleetly. I try to imitate it, turning my wrists in the air.

"Then the rag." *Swipe, swipe.* Freddie whisks away the excess, finishing with a snap of the rag, loud like a firecracker.

He slaps the brush into my palm. Drapes the rag over my wrist. "Your turn. Do the other one." He jumps into the chair and offers me his other foot.

Buff, buff. Pucker. Buff, buff. Swipe, swipe. I pull the rag up to finish with a flourish, but it only hangs limply from my fingers.

"Not bad," Freddie says. "But you gotta get much faster. They're in here just between dances, you know?"

"How'd you do that snap?" I ask, yanking the rag taut. It makes no sound at all.

"It takes practice," he says. He takes back the rag and shows me the basic move. "But you get better tips off it."

I snap the rag till my palms sting.

"Getting there," Freddie says. "It's all in the wrist." He shows me again.

"One more thing," he adds. "You go down to the drug-store, and you pick up a couple packs of rubbers."

"Rubbers?"

"Yeah, you know," he says, making a humping motion with his fists beside his hips. "They're a quarter each down the store, but you can sell 'em in here for a dollar. Sometimes you get a tip besides. For going the extra mile, right?"

I nod. "I can do that."

"Some nights you might go through a pack of 'em, easy."

"Wow." I'm already thinking about all those dollars.

"Yeah." Freddie looks me up and down. "I think you'll do just fine once you get the hang of it."

There's something in his expression that makes me ask, "So that's it?"

"Yeah, that's the basic gig," Freddie says, eyes darting around the room as if checking to see what he might have forgotten to show me. But he still has this look. I've been around the block enough times to know when someone's hedging.

"What are you leaving out?"

"You'll figure out the rest," he says. "There's more to the job in terms of giving people what they want. But you gotta work up to it."

"Up to what?"

Freddie sighs. "Look, you're new," he says. "All you gotta have for now is rubbers."

"OK." I'm starting to feel uneasy. "For now?"

"Later on, you might be wanting to offer some more extras." Freddie leans in conspiratorially. "Cats'll be asking for hooch from time to time. Or reefer. Or . . . well, you'll get to see how it goes." He claps me on the shoulder. "Up to you what you want to go in for."

"OK."

Freddie leans back and gives me a strong finger point. "But don't move up from rubbers until you're one hundred percent sure you can pick out who's a cop."

"OK."

Freddie laughs. "You're like a broken record, man. I'll be right back," he says. He points again. "Towels only. Don't shine anyone's shoes till I get back."

"OK."

Freddie glides out with a grin. I spin a slow circle on the tile, taking it all in. It might be just a men's room, but it's the fanciest men's room I've ever set foot in. The shoe-shine chair gleams in the low light, the faucets and fixtures all clean and polished. Freddie reigns in this room—I can see that. People coming to him, asking for things, money changing hands. Freddie is king—and that mantle is about to be mine.

Once the dance is in full swing, the music becomes a constant distraction. It seeps up the stairs from the ballroom, in loud and soft bursts as the men's room door opens and closes with traffic. Freddie lets me do a shine, but all the while he watches over my shoulder.

"It must be hopping down there," I say.

"You've never seen one of the dances?" Freddie says, giving me that look again, the one that makes me feel green as a dollar bill.

I shake my head. I hate to admit all the things I don't know, but Freddie's been sharp enough to see through my bluffs so far.

"It's slow right now," Freddie says. "You can go look. But don't go down." It's a white crowd tonight. No Negroes allowed.

Eagerly, I rush out of the men's room, onto the landing over the stairs that lead down to the ballroom. I can't believe my eyes.

The room positively swirls with dancers. White men in the crispest, slickest suits—black and navy and tweed, some with loosened ties and coats unbuttoned or cast aside over chairs. White women of all sizes and shapes, in bright puffy gowns that spin gracefully as they step and twirl and rock their hips.

The music strikes me as familiar, and I realize it's the Glenn Miller band, playing live! We'd listened to their records back in Lansing. I hold back the urge to laugh out loud. If the kids at Mason Junior High could see me now, they wouldn't believe the magic that was right in front of me. They couldn't even imagine how their little Negro mascot was quickly surpassing them all. I lean on the railing.

I couldn't go to the dances at Mason, either, but leading up to it everyone would be dancing in the hallways and

to get ready. I tap my feet in a semblance of
pening below.

    ot to think about how bad I want to go down
    walk among the dancers. Just to feel what it's like
    se to the music and swinging. But it's whites-only
on th. dance floor. Negroes are allowed to serve, and that's
as far as we can go.

    Freddie calls me. "Red. You got a shine."

    I dart back into the men's room. More than anything,
I want to be down there in the throng. Someday, maybe.
Freddie tells me they often hold Negro dance nights, and
he promises they'll be even better, more exciting and viva-
cious than anything I've ever seen. Ooh, I'm looking forward to those nights.

Ella doesn't hear me come in for the night. I climb the
stairs, stepping long over the two that tend to creak.

    In my room, I sink onto the bed and close my eyes. The
swirl of syncopated rhythms sticks with me. I feel myself
swaying on the mattress. I don't want to sleep. It's hard to
come down off the feeling of being in that room. The walk
back up the Hill couldn't shake it.

    I lie in bed, thinking I'll fall asleep, but I don't. The
house's creaks and settling groans swell around me. Start
to make me feel small.

    I reach into the desk for my stack of notepaper. Who
do I feel like writing to? I'm dying to tell all those kids from
school what I've seen and done tonight, but I won't write to

them. Ever. One clean sheet under my wrist and a pen in my fingers, I pour it all out to Philbert instead: the music, the dancing, the snap of my rag. I'm getting the hang of it, and fast, I tell him. It feels good to report it. Like it's proof or something. I'm moving on. Moving up.

There's so much to tell, but only so much I can actually say. How do I describe the heat and the swirl and the lights and the sounds? How can I possibly bottle that on a flat page? I sign off and fold the letter.

When I finally stretch out again and slide my bare feet between the sheets, I huddle against myself, trying to get warm. I don't need to tuck so small. I have all the space I can imagine. A bed all to myself. Nobody there to kick my feet, to hog the covers. To whisper with. Compared to the coziness of sharing with my brothers, my bed for one seems large and lonely.

Chapter Nine

Boston, 1941

In addition to setting me up with the shoe-shine gig, Shorty schools me on everything to do with the street life. No matter what crazy thing he starts talking about, I just nod like I understand. Most everything is pretty clear once you got the hang of it.

Like the numbers. On the surface it's easy enough. You pick any three numbers, like 346 or 937, and then you place your bet. If you place your bet on Tuesday, then on Wednesday you get up and look at the paper and flip to the finance page. You see where the stock exchange closed on Tuesday night. If the last three digits of the total value of stock sales match your numbers, you get to collect winnings.

It's a good system. Easy, because the stock exchange guarantees there'll be a new random number every day. And it always posts in a place where any old body can look it up and know for sure if they hit.

There's a thousand possibilities, no one of them any more likely than the other. You can play a quarter a day or a dollar, or more; any amount you choose. You can play straight, so that your number has to come up exact, or you can split your bet six ways to cover the mixes. For a split, if you bet 347, you'd also win with 743, 437, 473, 374, or 734.

Some people play the same numbers every day, like a religion. Their birthday, maybe, or some other lucky digits they arrive at somehow. Others build a whole superstition around it, looking for numbers all over the place. Like if the grocery bill lands at $9.25, they might run around the corner and place the change on 925. As if there's divine writing on the checkout slip or something.

The payout is six hundred to one, so when you bet a dollar and hit, you'll come away with six hundred dollars. Most people are more likely to bet a penny for a six-dollar payout, or if you split the bet, a penny will bring you a dollar for any combination hit.

However you come about the numbers, and however often, everybody plays. Hustlers and hookers and schoolkids and grandmas, working stiffs and even upper-crusters who are in it for the rush.

Shorty tells me all about it. He tells me everything, and he introduces me to just about everybody. He greets the other guys by slapping hands. It isn't really a handshake. They come in from the sides, arms outstretched, and then meet in the middle in a kind of slap. Just the quickest of grips, maybe, then a slide away.

"In this world, everything's a hustle," Shorty tells me. "If it doesn't look like a hustle, you got to look at it from another angle."

We stroll through the neighborhood, checking out the knots of people hustling one way or another. Fat Frankie, it turns out, is known for hustling at Three-Card Monte. The seven bucks he took off me still smarts, even though we're friendly now.

"I shoulda listened to you that day," I tell Shorty as we're passing Fat Frankie's spot.

Shorty does a kind of halfway smile. "Yeah."

Frankie's hunched over the car hood out front of the barbershop, as usual. "Find the lady. Where's the lady? Who wants to ask her out? Step right up." As Shorty and I scoot past, Frankie and Shorty exchange a glance. Shorty tips his chin up, and in response Frankie shakes his head. It was so subtle, I barely even caught the exchange. But it sticks in my mind. Something just happened. We keep on walking.

It dawns on me. "You were in on it, weren't you? With Frankie that day."

Shorty grins wide. "Don't take it personal, Red. I was just doing a favor for a friend."

"Everything's a hustle, eh?"

"You know it."

"What was the point? I was already going to play. You tried to stop me."

"It made you want it more, didn't it?"

I thought back. "Yeah, I guess. But I would've bet anyway."

"Let me show you something." Shorty stops walking. "Reach into your pocket," he says. "Like you're about to bet."

He's a half step behind me now, so I turn to face him.

"No," he says. "I came up behind you, remember?"

I turn back. Put my hand in my pocket. "Hey, man," Shorty says, laying a hand on my arm. The same arm that's reaching for my thin stack of folded bills. I automatically look at him when he speaks to me. "I really want to show you this thing I can do that's pretty neat," he says. Then he lets go of my arm.

"So show me," I say.

Shorty smiles. "You have twelve dollars in your pocket right now."

"How do you know that?" I reach the rest of the way in and pull my money out.

"I just counted it."

"How?"

"With my hand. While I was distracting you."

Puzzle pieces fall into place. "Then you somehow told Frankie how much I had on me."

"Yeah. That way, he knows exactly when to pull the plug before you walk away with any winnings."

I feel like the biggest dupe. But at the same time, it's pretty dang funny. "I want to learn that," I tell him. "The money part and the cards, too. How does he switch out the cards?" It looks so cool when Fat Frankie shuffles faster and faster. And guarantees your win or loss, depending on how he wants it to be.

Shorty keeps walking again. "It's just sleight of hand," he says. "A trick."

"But how could you count my money with a briefcase in your other hand?" I ask.

"Briefcase? Oh, that's my sax case. I set it down for a second."

I shake my head, because I don't remember seeing him do that. "Cool. You play sax?"

"I'm a musician," he says. "I mean, I'm trying to be. That's what I want, to perform in a jazz band. It's why I came here."

"Wow." That seems like the coolest thing I've ever heard. It's so easy, just listening, to get lost in the jazz tunes and rhythms that fill my head in Roxbury. How amazing, to be a part of making that.

"What do you want to do, homeboy?" he says. "Why'd you come here?"

The question makes me uncomfortable. "To figure it out, I guess."

Shorty seems OK with that answer, which is a relief. All that matters to me right now is getting to the bottom of the Three-Card Monte hustle.

"Instead of counting my money, you coulda just picked my pocket, you know," I tell him.

Shorty's grin becomes epic. "Well, that would be a crime."

Soon as I have some money saved, I go into the haberdasher and buy myself a fedora like Fat Frankie's. I stroll through Roxbury all afternoon, tipping my new hat to every lady I pass. Slapping skin with every Negro I know.

"Yo, Red."

"Red, my man."

"Red! How's my homeboy?"

I'm making friends. Feeling good. My new name makes me feel lighter on my feet. With a new name, anything is possible.

I can learn to hustle, learn some sleight of hand of my own. In Roxbury, there's always a way to get what you need. A way to start over.

Roxbury's a clean slate, my fingertips the purest chalk. Ready to write a new destiny.

*　*　*

The one thing still missing from my fresh ensemble is a zoot suit. I try to tell Shorty I need more time to earn into it, but he's all, "Let's go take a look."

He takes me down to this shop he knows, the same place where he buys his own zoots. "What color do you like, homeboy?"

I run my hand over the row of hangers. Pick out a suit in a rich royal blue.

"That's nice," Shorty says. The salesman nods. He draws back a curtain and lets me go behind.

I slip out of my shoes and pants, into the zoot. The fabric plumes around my legs, but down at the ankles I have to tug to get the tight cuffs over my long feet. The jacket hangs long and smooth. The broad shoulders make me look wider and tougher. Just like one of the cats off the block.

I duck out from behind the curtain, holding back my smile. Acting cool.

"Looking good, homeboy."

"Yeah, I think so," I say. "I can't wait until I can have it."

"Don't look now, Red, but I think that day's today."

I shake my head. "I can't afford it."

Shorty laughs loudly. "Afford it? What are you talking about, Red? You never heard of credit?"

"Shorty's gonna vouch for you," the salesman says. "It's yours if you want it. Five dollars down."

I finger the lush fabric, thinking.

I remember Papa talking about credit. *Don't ever owe anybody a cent. You pay your debts up front.* We learned it the hard way after he was gone. What it meant to be in debt. What it meant to owe. It meant what you had wasn't really yours, no matter how you worked for it. It meant there was always a hand in your business, someone else's hand, some white man who could make it rain dollars, and then came through sweeping up more than what he dropped. *Owe* rhymes with *low*, we learned, for a reason.

"Yo, Red," Shorty says. He whistles. Waves a hand in front of my eyes. *"Pssh."* He makes a sound like radio static. "Come in, homeboy. *Pssh.*"

It jolts me. "What?"

"Where'd you go, man?" Shorty nudges me. "You want the suit or what?"

Yeah, I want it. I rise out of the thick cloud of the past. Only way I can afford the zoot: credit. My fingers smooth one crisp, tailored sleeve. In the mirror, I barely recognize myself. I can't go back. Can't even imagine putting on that country coat again. Not after seeing myself new.

I grab up my fedora and flip it onto my head. Can't get over it. Is that really me? I shimmy my shoulders a bit. Give a little shift, smooth my collar. Run my thumb down the side of my nose, the way I've seen the cats on the block doing. Looking fly.

"Whoa-ho," Shorty says.

"Yeah." I grin. Settle a little deeper into those broad shoulders. "Yeah." I toss down a couple steps of something approximating the Charleston. Raise my eyebrows at Shorty in the mirror.

Everyone uses credit. It's the city game. I'm here to play. "I'll take it."

Ella shakes her head when she sees the outfit. "I should have known it would happen," she says. "No real way around it."

I strut through the living room, modeling it for her anyway. She disapproves, but I don't really care. It's clearer now, how different we are. She's really a Hill woman, through and through, while I am a creature of the street. No way can she understand what it feels like to go down there, to be folded in.

Most people who live on the Hill take a strange pride in it, I've noticed. Being above. I don't want that. Ella can have it. Down the Hill, everyone lives for the now and everything is raw. No going wrong down the Hill. No manners to mind and no one pointing fingers.

In the mirror, I practice. Try to perfect that swaggering kind of walk. Arm swinging out front just so. A little lilt to the hips, a little bend and sway. Like a dance-floor move. Just rolling out down the sidewalk, all six foot four inches of me, turning heads and looking fly.

At closing time, there's plenty of business to be had up in my office. Guys are coming at me, left, right, center.

"Can I get a rubber, Red?"

"Any reefer, man?"

"I need a girl tonight."

I dole out the packets and the joints and the folded slips of paper. I ride high on being the guy who can get it for them. The guy they can't live without, for those fifteen minutes at the end of the show. The guy who's going to make or break their night. Everything's a hustle, and I got my own hustle now.

"Thanks, Red."

"You're the best, man."

"Catch you later."

The swirl and the excitement quickly fade until it's me alone in the men's room. It starts to seem again like toilets and stalls and fixtures, nothing special.

I click the lights up full and sweep the floor clean, like I'm supposed to. The maids will come in the morning to scrub down everything with soap, but I do my part anyway. Grab the dirty towels. Gather my tips, carefully folding the bills. One unusual tip tonight—a mostly full bottle of whiskey given in exchange for a handful of rubbers, from a guy who was as close to falling-down drunk as I'd ever seen.

The Roseland itself is no longer a thing of magic once the dancing's done. The lights go up, and what seemed glitzy and alive moments ago now seems like a shell of itself.

Bottles and bottles, a ton of bottles, strewn among the tables and even on the empty dance floor itself. A few shawls and jackets and bags, forgotten amid the swirl of liquor and the lull of the tunes. I take a turn around the floor, just to see if there's anything worth picking up.

I think how amazing it would be if I wasn't behind the scenes, but just one of the throng out on the floor. Right in the swing of things. The thick of it.

At the doorway, Shorty's waiting for me. Passing the time with Clyde, the big guy who watches the door. We slap good night, and he steps back into the coatroom.

I'm holding the whiskey by the neck. "Where'd you score that?" Shorty says. "That's a nice bottle."

I tip up my shoulder. "Some cat left it for me."

"That's a good tip." Shorty chuckles. "We're gonna get some use out of that." He reaches for the bottle and takes a long swallow. Wipes his mouth on the back of his hand. Takes another. "You don't mind, do you, Red?"

"Course not," I say. I've never even tried any kind of liquor. Never been around it until I came to Roxbury.

When Shorty hands the bottle back, I just hold it for a minute. He goes, "Well, you have to take some, too."

I sip. It burns on the way down. *Liquid fire,* I've heard some of the cats say. That makes sense now. The flames spread over every inch of my throat. *"Whoo,"* I say, shaking it off. I push the bottle back at him.

"Naw," Shorty says. "You barely got a swallow."

I drink a little more, a little faster. Just try to choke it down. I like how it makes me feel after a minute—a little fuzzy. I no longer mind the burn so much.

"Yeah." Shorty takes the bottle, takes another swig. "It's gonna be a good night."

We head out into the street, huddling in our

jackets against the chill night air. It's only a matter of time before we're passing the bottle back and forth as we walk. It's nothing wild, I realize. Just a little liquid in my mouth. A little fire in my gut that burns so nicely.

"Where are we going?" I ask.

"Anywhere we want," Shorty answers.

We wander. We sip. Minute by minute. I'm bounding with it. Where are we going? Anywhere we want. I realize the power and the potential of that. Absolutely anywhere.

The house party's jumping, warm and alive. Shorty himself isn't really into the dancing. We stand on the side of the room, near the spread of liquor bottles on the kitchen counter.

"You ought to get out there," he tells me.

"Nah. I'd just like to watch for now." The minute I get onto the dance floor, my secret'll be out. I don't know how to dance a lick.

Back in Lansing, all the white folks knew all the steps to all the dances somehow, but I never learned them, and so I never got out on the floor. Too easy to make a misstep when you don't know what you're doing. Anyway, black boys weren't supposed to dance with white girls.

I danced around the house often enough. With my sisters, all silly, laughing and twirling them around. We'd put on a record, and Mom would sing, and Wilfred or Philbert would drum while the rest of us galloped and swung. But it doesn't count. A thousand turns around the dance floor in my memory—our living-room rug—are not so helpful right now. This room is not so warm or safe, and everyone is looking to judge.

I lean against the wall by Shorty and just sip away. I manage to try a whole array of beverages laid out. Whiskey. Wine. Clear liquor. Not dancing is pretty fun anyway, watching the girls dance. The way they step, rocking forward and back. Twisting their hips and swirling their skirts, in all the different colors they're wearing. Mesmerizing.

There's one girl I watch closer than the others. Not on purpose, but my eye keeps straying her way. After a little while, I realize she's looking back at me.

"Come here, cutie," she says. "Why aren't you moving?" She pulls my arms, giving me no choice but to follow. Over my shoulder, Shorty's laughing. I'm turning to him to get me out of this, but he just leans against the wall and grins something fierce.

"She'll school you in the Lindy, for sure," he calls with a chuckle that makes me wonder if this was part of his plan all along.

"Relax," she tells me. "Just move."

Good thing I've been standing near the bar all this while. No way I could stand the pressure without a little drink in me. My shoulders work back and forth, following the movement of her arms.

"What's your name?" I ask, but she just shakes her head like she can't hear.

Soon enough, my legs start to loosen. It helps that

everyone's dancing close; no one can really see me. We become one with the crowd.

I discover there's a kind of release on the floor. Arms and legs flailing. Following the music, getting filled by the rhythm. I'm dancing OK, it seems. Almost like it comes sort of natural to me. The girl smiles. Still has her hand in mine. I'm feeling good.

I stumble back toward the wall. Shorty gives a little smile, looking me up and down. "Not too bad, homeboy."

He's puffing on a reefer. He lights a second one, pushing it against the lit end of his until they both glow red-hot. He tips it toward me, and I don't even hesitate. Take it between my fingers like it has always been there. The thin cloud of smoke clogs me. Fills me. Spreads me like butter against the wall.

"There you go," Shorty says, sounding satisfied. "You're getting the hang of everything now."

Yeah. Yeah. I'm floating. Between the liquor and the reefer and the music and the girl . . . Yeah.

I've never had a better time. It's like I can't feel my body. My brain is quiet. My heart aloft.

Nothing tugging. Weighing. Haunting. I don't even have to try not to think about how things were back in . . . the place I'm from. I can't even get there in my mind. Not that I want to.

"Hey," Shorty says. "You want to call it a night? Head home?"

The very idea is like a blur to me. "I'm not going back," I answer. "Everything is here." In this room, I feel like I'm getting close to the answer to something. It's not safe and warm, but fresh and exciting. Not closed in, but wide open.

"The night is young," I say, slugging Shorty's arm. "And so are we."

"What are you doing tomorrow afternoon?" Shorty says out of nowhere.

I shrug. "Why?"

"That hair's looking long enough now," he says. "You ready to lay on your first conk?"

Shorty hands me a list of ingredients. About the strangest combination of items I could have imagined. Soap. Eggs. Vaseline. Potatoes. Lye. The only thing on the list that makes any sense is a comb—but I have to get two: one with wide teeth and one with narrow teeth.

Shorty waits for me at his cousin's house, where he lives. I bring over my bags of conk supplies. We get to work straightaway.

"It's gonna hurt," Shorty warns. "The first time's the worst. It'll never hurt this bad again. Just think on that."

"Sure." Nervousness sets in a bit. I want the conk. Have to have it. I've been growing my hair out for weeks now, getting it long enough to straighten.

Shorty sets me up at the kitchen table. He dumps out a couple of potatoes. Hands me a knife. "Peel, homeboy."

I scrape the skin off the potatoes.

Shorty's in high spirits. "Gotta earn that conk," he says. "Slice 'em thin, now."

The potato slices go into a big Mason jar. Shorty pours the lye over them, cracks two raw eggs into the mix, and stirs it all up with a wooden paddle. The smell rockets to potent immediately.

"Whew." I fan my nose. "Get a load of that."

"You ain't smelled nothing yet," Shorty warns. "And it's nothing compared to the feel. Touch the jar."

The sides of the glass are piping hot. After the merest contact, I flinch away.

"That's what'll be on your head in a minute," Shorty says.

As if he needs to remind me. I pat my bushy kinks. Time to say so long. It'll be good riddance as far as I'm concerned, but the heat in that jar has me worried about getting from point A to point B. I glance at Shorty's smooth head, figuring that if this homemade gel straightener is what he uses, it's bound to work for me, too. "Congolene," Shorty calls the goop. "Conk" for short.

"You ready, homeboy?" Shorty uncaps the Vaseline. I sit in the chair and let him rub it into my head by the scooped-out handful. He works it into my kinks and smooths it all over my neck, forehead, and ears. I might as well be a greased rabbit.

"Now's when it gets hot," Shorty reminds me, reaching for the steaming jar. "Keep it in as long as you can stand it. Makes a better conk."

He pours the congolene on top of me. It's warm. He grabs the wide comb and rakes it through my thicket of hair. This really isn't so ba—*oh!*

Oh, sweet mercy!

It burns!

It burns like the sun fell out of the sky. Like a hot coal in your fist. Like a whipping with a lash of flames. Hotter than the flames that once licked around my bed before Papa pulled me out of our burning house.

"*Aaaah!*" I shriek. I let loose a string of curses— probably every one I've ever heard, plus a couple I make up right here on the spot.

"Get it off! Get it off!" I yell, stamping my foot.

"Hang on, homeboy," Shorty yells back. "Just a minute. Just another minute."

The stench of the congolene absolutely fills me. Everything I breathe, everything I taste. And above all that, the pain. I hold fast to the sides of Shorty's cousin's kitchen table, crazily contemplating whether the fire of a conk could lead a man to splinter wood with his fingernails.

Shorty scrapes and tugs with the comb. My scalp screams for mercy. There's nothing in the world for me except the burning. A pain as deep as some sorrows I've known.

My eyes stream. My nose runs like a faucet. But how can I care, under the stinging? I leap up and race for the sink. Shorty follows, cranks on the water, and hoses down my head.

The cool water eases the burning, but only somewhat. My eyes drift closed. It's all I can do just to breathe.

"Lie back," Shorty orders. He scrubs the bar of soap against me. Rinses me off with a hose like a showerhead attached to the sink. Wash. Spray. Wash. Spray. Wash. Spray. On and on, until the fire on my scalp dies down to embers.

Back in Lansing, when I was small, Mom would wash my hair like this, pouring bucket after bucket over me while I squirmed. Not as rough, maybe. But similar.

Hold still, love, I hear her scold me lightly.

"Hold still. I gotta get it all," Shorty says, hands washing every inch of my skull. "If I miss a spot, it'll keep on burning. Scald you something fierce."

"Keep rinsing." I tap the tears out of my eyes with shaking fists.

"OK, Red. Let's take a look." Shorty whips the rubber apron off my neck and blots my hair and neck dry. "You feel any spots still burning?"

"No." Everything stings, but it isn't the active sort of flames. "It's just sore now."

"That's normal," Shorty says. "It'll fade." He dips into the Vaseline again, massaging it all over my hair. "It took real nice," he says. "OK, get up."

We look at me in the mirror. It worked! No more tangled, kinky bush. Each strand of my hair is razor straight. Straight as any white man's hair I've ever seen. Straighter. It lies flat back, gelled smooth with Vaseline. "Whoa," I keep saying. "Whoa." I touch my new crown tenderly.

"That's a nice conk." Shorty wipes his hands clean of all the mess. "You're a new man, homeboy."

A brand-new man, I agree, running my fingers through the straight reddish-brown locks. In the afternoon light, my hair looks almost golden. I barely recognize myself. It's shocking. It's beautiful. I love it.

My scalp still buzzes a bit. But I can handle the pain if that's what it takes to erase the old me. All his stinging sorrows, washed down the sink like congolene. Nothing left to scald the new me. Rinsed clean.

Ella lights into me the minute she sees my conk. "What have you done to yourself, Malcolm? You have taken out every beautiful curl that the Lord gave you! Why are you putting these chemicals in your hair? I don't like these characters you are hanging around with."

I smooth my palms over the sides of my head, like I've seen other cats doing. "What's the big deal? It looks fly." I admire myself in the mirror over the table in the entry hall. In the reflection I can see her pacing and flaring.

"Why do you persist . . . ?" Her voice trails off, and she throws up her hands. "I have to get supper on. Wash your hands and come set the table."

I go on into the bathroom to scrub up. Ella might not approve of much of what I'm doing, but that isn't going to stop me from doing it. She's not my mother. And she's not my father, either, even though she takes after him. I don't have to do her bidding. I'm my own man now.

You are my son.

I look around, like he's actually there, speaking to me.

The Almighty God has granted you a great destiny. Do not lose faith, son.

I run the water louder. Ella doesn't get a say. Papa either.

Seeing myself in the mirror over the sink just makes me all the more sure. I'm a whole new me.

Ella starts bringing dishes to the table while I set our places. Fried chicken, okra, greens, and corn bread. A regular southern feast. We eat this kind of food a lot. Ella says she likes to eat food that reminds her of growing up. I'm glad enough about that for her, but I'm even gladder because this kind of food doesn't remind me of anything.

I chow down on a chicken leg. I've gotten used to eating my fill now; no longer any need to force away the memories of hunger churning deep.

Ella's still muttering about my conk. "What would Papa think about this?" she drones on. "Not in school. Out in the streets at all hours . . ." I tune out her voice. Imagine Lindy music playing in my ears.

"You better be careful," I hear. "All this new, new, new. You're gonna wake up one day and not recognize yourself."

I smile to myself. Isn't that the point?

Ella can say what she wants. Starting fresh feels good. Nothing's going to bring me down.

Chapter Ten

Boston, 1941

Every night after work, it seems, Shorty knows of some house party or other we can swing by. The result: I sleep half the day and I'm up all night. It's practically daybreak by the time I stumble in. The foyer smells like brewing coffee. Ella's downstairs in the kitchen already, getting ready to cook up some breakfast.

Good timing. I can grab a plate of whatever she's fixing, then catch some shut-eye.

I call out hello but don't wait for an answer. I go up into my bedroom, dump out my bag of tricks.

I've got a reefer high going, and everything is soft. It was a good night; between tips and sales, I have about twenty bucks in ones and change denting my mattress.

I riffle through my pouch of extras, cataloging what needs replacing. Rubbers. Reefer. A laugh escapes me. Always low on reefer. Nobody can get enough reefer. Me included.

A knock at the door.

"Yeah?"

Ella pokes her head in. "Are you going to want some breakfast?"

"Sure."

Frowning, she pushes the door wider and steps inside. "Malcolm."

"Yeah?"

Ella takes the pouch out of my hand.

"It's not mine," I blurt out. "It's just for work. Extras, you know?"

"Extras." She studies me. "This is what you do?"

"Mostly shoe shines," I say. "But you have to have extras."

"Malcolm, no. This is not acceptable." Ella paces my room, hand on her forehead. "This is over the line. I'm responsible for you," she says. "I took you in. To protect you. Not to have you . . ." Her voice trails off.

"I want you to get a different kind of job," she says. "I don't want you going down to that club anymore."

"But—"

"No." She all but shakes her fist at me. Then her eyes widen. "Townsend's Drug Store."

"What about it?"

"They're looking to hire a new soda-fountain clerk. You worked in a restaurant before, didn't you?"

"Yeah." Back in Lansing. All the more reason I'd rather be doing something new.

"Then it's settled. I'll talk to the owner. He's a friend of mine."

How well I know. I can't mention anything about this town without Ella name-dropping someone she knows. It's one of the things I hate about the way you have to be to live on the Hill.

Ella presses on. "I'm sure they'll be thrilled to have you."

"No, but . . ." My reefer high makes me feel like I'm protesting from under water. "I really don't want—"

"Well, you can't keep doing this." With my reefer pouch, Ella points at the other incriminating items strewn over my bedspread. "I won't permit it."

She has that look on her face, the insistent one that I hate, that makes her look exactly like Papa. I yank the pouch back from her, sweep all the things toward one corner of the bed, and lie down with my back to her.

"Malcolm, did you hear me?" Ella demands. I close my eyes, but I can still see that face, hovering, disapproving, trying to push me in a direction I refuse to go.

"Malcolm Little!" The voice is loud in my ear. The hand on my shoulder, trying to nudge me to turn and face it. I can't win if I let myself face it. Instead I try to shut my mind and hope it goes away.

"So help me, Malcolm, if I have to go down to that club myself . . ."

"No, don't," I blurt out. I spin upright and face the voice. It's a surprise, somehow, that it's Ella I'm looking at. I blink. My mind is reefer-blurred. My heart is under attack.

This is not who you are, my son.

"I can be anything I want to be, right?" I repeat the refrain, nearly shouting it. "Isn't that what you're always saying?" Looking her straight in the eye, I want to grin. It's only Ella I see now. Maybe I *can* win.

Ella flinches and purses her lips. "You can *achieve* anything," she amends softly. It sucks the air out of me.

I duck my head. Ella still believes in Papa's stories. Papa's "someday, maybe" dreams. Papa's lies.

That's the fire in her eyes, and it's a thing I used to have, too. I can take it away with three little words: *Just a nigger.* I should say them. Eventually, she has to know the truth so she can go about living in a way that's real. But I can't bring myself to be the one to tell her.

"Malcolm?" Ella says.

"All right," I tell her. "I'll go see them tomorrow."

When I tell Shorty the news, he doesn't seem surprised. "You were going to outgrow that deal eventually," he says. "Once you got the hang of everything."

135

"Ella's got me a job on the Hill. Soda clerk at Townsend's."

Shorty hoots. "Damn, homeboy! You're moving up in the world."

"I'm not thrilled about working up the Hill," I admit.

He looks at me kind of funny. "A slave's a slave," he says. "Anyway, tips are probably good up the Hill."

Maybe so. Still, I'm not looking forward to it. The only thing I'm happy about is the schedule. At Townsend's I'll have a normal working day and get off for the night at eight. Now, unlike ever before, I'll have my nights free. I can come to the Roseland just to dance.

Shorty's way of thinking about my Townsend's deal gets me cheered up about it. It isn't just a new job. It's a change of station. Moving up in the world. Instead of doing what's right for people's feet, I'll be working for their mouths and for their bellies.

This is a time to celebrate. A brand-new slave for a whole new kind of man. So I go back to the suit shop. This time I don't need Shorty to back me up. They know me at that store now. I've been paying my weekly bill on the blue zoot suit, real steady. When I walk in, they look me up in their book. Tell me I have an A for my credit.

"You only missed one week. That's nothing," the guy says. "You're good for it."

He lets me look at any suit I want. Of course, I want

something nicer than the first time. On account of how I'm moving up in the world.

The high-end zoots look slick. Sharp as a tack and hip as a hip bone. Made of fabric that barely has any feel to it at all, it's so nice.

I pick out a zoot in sharkskin gray. So fine.

I pour myself into that sharkskin suit. Tug on the tight cuffs. Smooth myself into the blooming sleeves.

Looking good.

I spin before the mirror. Strike my pose. Feet apart. Toes out, heels in. Knees in, elbows out. Head down, hat low, fingers on the brim.

I peek at myself. All right, now. All right.

It's an expensive zoot, more so than the last one. That means my weekly payment will go up. Harder to make it.

But the zoot feels so fine on me. The line it cuts is nice. I've never looked so hip in all my days.

Where's the question? The sharkskin zoot suit is coming home with me. I can handle the payments. I've missed one already, and it was no big deal. You just make it up later. Papa was wrong about this, too. Credit is just about the best thing imaginable.

I pluck off the tags and wear that sharkskin zoot down to the Roseland for the Negro dance. All those nights working the shoe-shine rag hadn't prepared me for how it would feel to be down in the throes of it all. The heat radiating off the dancers. The scents of whiskey and perfume and sweat. The blinding shine of the stage lights if you catch one in the eye. My shoes skid nicely across the waxed floor, and all those nights in dark apartments, leading girls and learning the steps, have paid off. I'm confident. I'm in the Roseland, on the floor, and ready to take the place by storm.

I dance with every woman I can get my arms around. Beautiful Negro girls: short and tall, slender and big-boned, smooth skin, sun-kissed mahogany, ebony, or creamy caramel. I swirl them, lift them, flip them side to side off my hips while their legs fly through the air. The minute one girl gets tired or takes a breath, I spin away, pick up the hands of another. I'm so tall and so slick. They love me. I love them, too.

I sweat through dance after dance.

I go upstairs to my old office to take a little break myself. There's the new guy, crouched in my old spot, scrambling with his rag.

"Where you from?" I ask him.

"Kansas." He hands a towel to a guy, who takes it but doesn't even tip a nickel. Some people. *Them's the breaks, kid.* I'd managed, and so would he.

"How you like Roxbury so far?" I say to the kid. He's my age, probably. Thereabouts. He seems younger, though, on account of being so green.

The new kid grins real wide. Real country. Couple months from now, he'll be smirking. Slick as owl shit.

Probably in a zoot. Not as fine as this one, though. I smooth my lapels.

"I'm getting the hang of it," he says.

"Good for you."

I flip him a quarter, slide into the chair, and get my shoes shined. Sip from the flask in my jacket pocket. I stare down at the crown of his nappy head. Damn. I've come so far.

Chapter Eleven

Boston, 1941

Next day I start at Townsend's. When I come down the stairs wearing the white server's coat, Ella could not be more pleased. She fusses over me for what feels like an hour. "Oh, you're going to meet all kinds of lovely people," she says. "Girls your own age. Nice girls. This is a good opportunity, Malcolm." She smiles, for the thousandth time. "You'll see."

What I mostly see are things that drive me mad: the same kinds of people I saw when I first visited. The kind who put on a certain face to go out, a prim and proper mask. They chatter, all flushed and breathless, climbing a ladder that's going nowhere. Everything's a hustle, like Shorty always says, but these folks are hustling after something they can't get. Down the Hill, we hustle after what's real. Being happy. Getting rich. The important stuff.

Ella has these high hopes about all the people I'll meet here, so I go home and tell her all kinds of stories about everything. She eats it up with a sugar-coated spoon. Meanwhile all I really do all day is pour soda over ice cream. Root-beer floats. Coca-Cola floats. Ice-cream cones. Ice-cream sundaes. Smile real nice and big. Plop cherries on top with a flourish.

But there's always something good about even the crappiest job. The thing I get to looking forward to day after day is the quiet girl with the book. Banana split is her standing order. Glass of water with ice. She comes and sits in the corner of the bar on one of the tall red stools with her nose in one thick book or another. Never looks up except to place her order and to pay.

My attention strays to her constantly while I work. Her glowing brown skin. The delicate dark hairs that frame the sides of her face. Her full lips teasing the ice-cream spoon. I wonder what it would feel like to touch the smooth back of her hand, to lace our long slender fingers together. I stare, hoping I can catch her glancing up with those sparkling eyes.

Just about every day she comes in. It gets to where I'll start slicing the bananas from the moment I see her through the window. But girls like her don't really talk to the soda jerk, except, I guess, to order.

"Banana split, please," she says. It's the sweet, sincere "please" that gets me. It's surprising how often people forget to say it. All these people, so uppity and polite, can't manage to get that little word out, or at least can't make me believe they really mean it.

"Coming right up," I say. She has a nice smile, which she tends to offer me for the small price of an extra cherry or two. No skin off my nose. I give her a real smile in return, not the big corny fake one I've been practicing.

All along, I know I'm eventually going to talk to her. She seems different from the others, less affected. Down-to-earth or something. Real. So I'm going to talk to her for sure someday. Just not today. Maybe tomorrow.

Tomorrow comes and goes a couple of dozen times before I get around to opening my mouth.

"What are you reading?" I ask her.

She looks around for a second before glancing up. "Me?"

"Sure," I say. "You're the one with the book."

She flips the book upright and shows me the cover. I reach over and place her glass canoe of ice cream in the space between her elbows. "Thank you," she whispers.

"*Their Eyes Were Watching God,*" I read off the jacket. "Is it any good?"

She nods, more enthusiastic. "Oh, yes. I can't put it down. I love her writing. Have you read her?"

I glance at the spine. Zora Neale Hurston. "No." Last time I picked up a book was . . . I don't even know. Some school thing or other. Back in Lansing.

"Is it for school?" I ask.

"No," she says. "Just for fun. School reading is too boring. Don't you think?"

"I'm done with school," I say. "Now I'm just a guy who makes a mean banana split." I really want to know her name, so I add, "I'm Red."

She frowns. "Then who's 'Malcolm'?"

"Oh, right," I say, glancing at the name tag pinned on my chest. "I'm him, too."

"Nice to meet you, Malcolm. I'm Laura." She swirls her spoon, studying me. "You don't look old enough to be done with school."

Laura. I roll the name around, tasting it.

"I'm going to college," she adds. "Aren't you?"

"No way."

A different song comes on the radio, from the speaker at the edge of the room. The kind of beat that sets your toes to tapping. Laura starts drumming the fingers of her free hand.

"You like that song?" I ask.

"Yes," she says. "I like anything with a nice rhythm." She moves her shoulders a bit. Kinda flirty. Kinda sexy. I start to think maybe there's more to her than a big stack of books.

"You ever do the Lindy?" I ask her.

"Oh, I love to dance," she says, closing her eyes. Her shoulders move.

I close in on that remark. Hawklike. "Really? You been to the Roseland?"

Her eyes pop open. "The Roseland Ballroom? Oh, I've never been there before! I'd give anything to go," she wails. "My grandmother would die."

"I go from time to time," I tell her. "Let me know if you would ever want to. . . ."

"Oh," she exclaims. "Oh, I wish I could."

She's a good girl. Too good, I suppose, for the likes of me. She's a college girl, or will be soon enough. But I'll be going to the Roseland, next Negro dance. It'd sure be nice to have a pretty girl on my arm walking in the door.

I meet Laura outside of Townsend's Drug Store. I wear my new gray zoot, hat and everything. I stand on the sidewalk, trying to look hip.

She comes rushing up to me, breathless. "Sorry I'm late, Malcolm," she says. "It was harder than I thought to get out of the house."

"You sneaked?" I ask. Her grandmother doesn't approve of much of anything, it seems. Dancing. Dating.

"Not really," she says. "I told her I was coming to the soda fountain. She just kept talking. I couldn't tell her I had to be here at a certain time." She tucks her hand into the crook of my arm.

The party at the Roseland is already pushing out beyond the bounds of the club. The sidewalk is full of people working their way in.

"I hope we can get in," Laura frets.

"We'll get in," I say. One of the few things around town I know without a doubt is how to get into the Roseland.

We push toward the door. I put my hand on Laura's waist, real casual. My fingers nestle into the curve of her body, drawing her to me and guiding her through the crowd at the same time. She glances around nervously at the people shouldering against us, but when she looks back and up at me, her gaze becomes trusting and soft. I've wondered how it would be to hold her and dance with her, when I've never even so much as touched her hand before, at the fountain. I know now it's going to be fine. We fit.

When we're close enough, I nod to the doorman and he motions us in. The crowd parts, and I nudge Laura to lead us through the gap. As we pass the doorman, I slap his skin with my free hand. He says something under his breath to me, and I don't totally catch it, but I sure get the gist. *Nice catch,* he's saying, about Laura.

We're inside, and I check her coat. She seems impressed by how many people I know. I'm slapping skin left and right. Her eyes go wide as we approach the dance floor. I keep my hand on her waist and ease her forward.

The music soars; it aches; it glows. Sour notes turn sweet, and the rhythms of the night thrum deeper and deeper until every beat of the song becomes a part of me. Beside me, Laura closes her eyes and sways. I know she's feeling it same as me. If the song is me, and the song is her, then she is me and vice versa.

I fold her hand in mine, some kind of magic. Soft brown skin, fingers interlaced. The tips of her nails graze the back of my hand. We rock in the rhythm.

Dancing with Laura is unbelievably smooth. She glides as easy as a hand on the surface of water. No weight to her.

"Where'd you learn?" I ask her.

She half shrugs. Spins. "Around."

As good an answer as any, I suppose. Where does anyone learn? I'm just trying to make conversation. Don't really need to. She's smiling like the sun. I'm feeling smooth enough. Seems OK for now to just get lost in the music, to feel the flow and the jive and ride along with it.

We're walking around the Hill one day when Laura says, "I don't see why you aren't in school. You know you're smart."

"Nah," I say.

She tugs my arm. Insistent. "You're so smart. Don't you know it?"

Smart enough to be top of the class. Smart enough to rise to the top at any school. Smart enough to get by without it, too. "I'm OK," I tell her. "No point in any of that."

I can't go back. I'm only moving forward.

Laura loves school. Can't imagine the road I'm walking. "I'm so looking forward to college," she gushes. "Haven't you ever wanted that or wondered what it would be like?"

I try to ignore the little flutter in my heart. "I wanted to be a lawyer once, maybe."

"Oh," she exclaims. "You still can be. That's perfect for you. You could go back to school. I know you can catch up on everything, and fast. We can go to college together."

Feels like a long time since I've thought about school. Grades and classes and problems and reports. It would be like stepping back into a box I was lucky enough to break out of.

"No way," I say. "That was just me thinking crazy one day. I don't even know why I just said that." Now Laura's getting stars in her eyes about this future, the two of us lugging books across a lawn from building to building. I've walked around the campuses nearby, seen all the buttoned-up students with their books and their satchels and their studious expressions. I rarely saw a dark face.

"Not that many people like us actually go to college," I tell her.

"Of course they do," she insists. "There are lots of Negro colleges."

I've been all over Boston, and I've never seen one. "Around here?"

"Well, no," she admits.

"Then, where?"

Laura sighs. "Atlanta. I would love to go to Spelman," she says. "But Grandma thinks it's too far from home."

"So . . ."

"So I'll probably go to Howard, in D.C. Or else maybe Cheyney School for Teachers, in Philadelphia."

"Sounds like you have it all planned." I could see it. Laura and all her books, striding across the quad with her curls bouncing.

"You should come too," she says. That I can't see. When I picture the future, I see myself tomorrow, hanging with the guys down at the pool hall. Shorty, wailing on his sax, working hard to save for his dream. Blowing off steam, throwing rhymes in the alley. Smoking reefer to feel good. Never thinking too hard, just taking the days as they come. Me, I'd rather be out in that world than stuck in those closed-up ivy halls that weren't meant to fit me.

"It's not for me."

She frowns. "Why not?"

We swing our hands between us. The words weighing on my mind are *Can't. Just. Nigger.*

"You can be anything you want to be, Malcolm," Laura says.

She's one of the only people who don't call me Red. I never really noticed that before. "Around town, they call me Red, you know."

"I like your name," she says. "Don't you?"

Nothing really to say to that. My name is my name, and the guys call me what they call me. Never occurred to me not to like it. It's how I came to feel like one of them.

"Your hair's not really red," Laura says, squinting up

at me. "It's light brown, like sand. A little golden." She puts her hand up and touches the patch of hair in front of my ear.

I grimace. "Sand" would be no kind of street name. "Just let it be." I lift her fingers away. Since I'm holding both her hands, I use them to swing her close to me. I do a little Lindy move, right there on the sidewalk, and spin her. She lands against me, all smiles.

Always a sure way to change the conversation.

"How'd you get so beautiful?" I whisper.

"Who, me?" She tips her cheek up, playing coy.

"Um-hmmm." I peck the side of her face. My arms lock around her delicate waist. She's tiny and lightweight, and touching her like this wakes my whole body. I'm aware of every single breath.

She kisses me, all sweet in my arms. It's getting harder, I realize, to hold her. All the talk takes it real, takes it deep. Down into things that I've put away. Things that can't ever be.

When I get home, I poke around my bedroom closet first thing. I think it's in here somewhere. My suitcase is empty except for a couple of tufts of lint and a small crawling beetle that scurries off at the first hint of light, but hanging in the far corner, pushed all the way to the end of the closet, is my old green suit. To think that when I came here, it was my best outfit. Now it looks so incredibly country. I stick my hands in the pockets, find the bus ticket stub in one, and in the other, sure enough, the folded-up map my brothers and sisters gave me.

I take the map over to the bed but, on a whim, return to the closet and pull that old green jacket off the hanger. Sure enough, I can't even get both arms into it. My shoulders are broader now. I'm taller, too. I stick one arm into the sleeve, and the cuff lands well above my wrist. It makes me happy, thinking about how much I'm changing. I push the old suit back to its dusty corner. Won't be needing it anymore.

The map, though, still interests me. I unfold it and look. There's Michigan, right where I left it. I put my finger on Boston, as if to say, *Here I am.*

Laura's grandma is right. Atlanta is far. So far I can't even span it with a spread of my pinkie to thumb. I can get as far as D.C., though. Howard. I don't need to stretch at all to reach Pennsylvania.

I don't like the thought of Laura at Spelman in Atlanta. That's Deep South. Ella's family came up from the Deep South, and she makes it sound like that, like it comes with capital letters. Ominous.

Howard, in D.C., might not be so bad, but I still don't like it. All the laws that are made to hold down black people—where does Laura think they're made? A Negro college in D.C. sounds like bait in the lion's mouth, if you ask me.

Cheyney, in Philadelphia. Heck, no. That's Pennsylvania, a large, scary state covered by mountains. I've seen firsthand what happens to uppity Negroes in Pennsylvania. Hard to get more uppity than trying to go to college.

The map folds easily along its worn creases. It's been tucked away so long, I almost forgot about it.

I pull out my notepaper to write a letter to my sister Hilda. Hilda especially will want to know I'm not entirely clueless when it comes to matters of romance. *I've been out with a girl called Laura,* I scrawl. *She dances well and she eats banana splits. You'd like her.* My fingers hover over the page, uncertain where to go next. I want to ask Hilda: *What can I tell a girl like Laura that might convince her to stay?* But there's no point in asking. I already know.

A girl like Laura won't believe me if I tell her about being just a nigger. With the stars in her eyes and the Hill under her feet, she'll never stop fooling herself into wanting the whole world. I don't have time for such dreams anymore.

Duke Ellington's band is onstage when we get to the Roseland. The music comes from every which way. Laura and I make our way onto the dance floor. Soon we're sweating and smiling as we swing.

Then Duke calls out for a showcase. Most of the couples groan and clear the floor. The showcase means that the best of the best dancers go all out for a while, in a little competition.

Laura tugs my arm. I'm busy steering us to the

sidelines, thinking about securing a good place to watch.

"Let's dance it," she says.

"The showcase?" I ask. "Uhh . . ." I don't want to say it—she won't want to hear it—but we both know we aren't at that level. We're pretty good and all, but the dancers in the showcase would be the very hottest of the hot.

"Yeah," she insists. "What do we have to lose?"

Not a thing I can think of. I shrug. "If you're up to it."

Laura smiles. We head back to the dance floor. The Duke strikes up the band, and skirts start swirling.

Laura fairly floats. She's really into it, stepping and twisting, throwing herself into every move I lead. The crowd begins to cheer for us. Maybe it's clear that we're out of our element, but no one's making fun.

The showcase goes on and on. The music seems never-ending. Laura's arms begin to soften, showing her tiredness. We're dripping sweat, our hair out of place, but still smiling.

"Enough?" I mouth to her. She offers the slightest of nods. I spin her silly, one final time, then catch her and dip her to uproarious applause. Around us, the other showcase couples keep spinning, but I lead Laura off to the side of the dance floor. Breathless but proud.

The crowd surges around us, still cheering. They chant our names. Hands clap my shoulders; everyone jostles me. Laura's separated from me now, folded into a press of onlookers wanting suddenly to get close.

"All right, Red."

"Great job!"

The kinds of things I'm hearing lift me up. Everything blurs for a while, and then right into the center of it walks a woman. Silky blond hair styled in two symmetrical curls above her shoulders. Skin like cream. Lashes black as a curtain beneath slow-blinking, black-lined lids. Bloodred lips that part, smiling at me. Stunning.

It's normal to see a few white folks mixed in with the crowd at the Negro dance. White skin will get you into the Roseland any night. But I've never seen anyone who looks anywhere close to this good. She comes toward me, so close that I'm about to move out of her way. Until she leans right into me. "Nice moves." Then whispers, "You caught my eye."

"I was fishing for it," I whisper back. Which would have been true, if I had ever seen her.

"Push me around the dance floor, why don't ya?" she says. She snakes herself against me, surely knowing there is no way I can refuse.

I put my hand on her waist and steer her toward the floor. Thinking I've never had my hands on a white girl, even back in Lansing. It went the other way around sometimes; they always wanted to know what it would be like to touch a black man's skin, or what my hair felt like. I would bend, and they would put out their small pale fingers and bounce them off my kinky curls. Then they would giggle every time—over how it felt? I used to wonder. Or over the rush of breaking the rules?

This woman isn't giggling. Her eyes are serious and so are her hands. If she were to run them through my hair, it wouldn't be like it was back then. I've got a conk now. This Negro is good enough for her.

The crowd parts to let us through.

I squeeze her hands and start leading her. She's no Laura when it comes to the dance moves, but she has this whole other thing going on. Sexy and throaty and rich. Her dress is one of the finest in the room. I can tell that for sure, now that I'm touching it. My hands on her waist steer her in circles.

"Are you as good as you seem?" she purrs.

"Baby, I'm better," I promise. I spin her, lift her, and dip her, showing off my skills.

"I've got a car," she says. "You wanna take off?" She kisses me, somewhere between my cheek and lips. Promising me a drink of milk, sweet as cream, smooth as honey.

"Sure," I say. "But I've got a thing to do first. Meet you back here in an hour?"

I wind back through the crowd, searching for Laura. "I need to get you home," I tell her. "Before your grandmother sends out a search party."

Her gaze is locked on the dance floor. I can tell she just

wants to keep going all night, but she nods reluctantly. "Yeah."

The whole walk up the Hill, Laura chats on and on about the showcase. "Malcolm, I don't know what's come over me," she says. "I just had to be out there. You know, I just wanted to feel like one of those girls." She twirls in the street.

I wonder for a second if she's been sipping at my flask. Probably not. She's the sort of girl who gets high easily, off the music, off a moment. Maybe I was like that when I first came down the Hill. All wide-eyed and trying to take it all in. Everything was exciting.

Laura twirls and laughs, the stars in her eyes. "And Duke Ellington," she gleefully chirps. "Playing for us. Live. Did you see how he nodded to us when we stepped off the floor?"

"Sure," I answer. Thinking, meanwhile, that a nod ain't nothing. I used to shine that cat's shoes. He put nickels in my hand. The fingers that make that magic, I've felt them in my palm.

It takes a bit more to impress me now. And I was impressed tonight. I didn't catch her name yet, so in my mind she's Miss Cream. I can still feel her arms. Hope to heaven that she's still waiting for me. That some other cat hasn't caught her eye. Out of sight, out of mind. Not for me. But for her?

Laura grasps my hand and comes kissing at me. It takes

me by surprise. All these weeks together, it's been hard to get more than a how-do-you-do.

I scoop her close and try to push it a little. Tonight we've danced among the stars—maybe her cherry ice is melting.

She lets me kiss her for a while, then she ducks her face away. "I have to get home."

I know. And I have to get back to the Roseland. "Of course." I put my arm around her shoulders, real polite. No reason to make a fuss with her. I'm gonna get mine tonight.

Laura tucks against me while I'm thinking how to tell her about the white girl that I met. Most girls you wouldn't even have to tell. Surely she saw me dancing up on Miss Cream. Everyone saw. I went out of my way to make sure of it. I've never had so many eyes on me. Never had a bunch of hip cats all drooling and wishing they were me. I was hot stuff on the dance floor for a minute there.

I want that feeling back. Coming down the Hill is a rush, for sure, but it's not enough anymore. Maybe for Laura, but not for me. I've come too far.

And she isn't the girl who can go far enough for what I need.

"There's so much out there for us, don't you think?" Laura's saying.

"Out where?" There's plenty for me right here, and plenty for her anywhere she wants, but it isn't the same plenty and what does she mean by "us"?

"I'm so happy I met you," she gushes. "I'm so glad we're

together now. I always wanted a boyfriend." She's giggling, all flustered.

Boyfriend? The word echoes in my ears.

"I just wanted us to have a fun time," I say. "It's not that serious."

In fact, it has been fun. She dances like a dream. She's pretty enough to turn heads. It's been a lot of fun, right up until this point, but we're heading in different directions. Right now all I want is to go back in and dance with other girls. One in particular.

My arm around her grows heavy. "This is what we should do," she starts. "Tomorrow, let's go . . ." She keeps talking, but I stop listening.

Yeah, it's getting too deep, and she's holding me back. Holding me down when all I want is to fly high and free.

Laura leans against me. "You know?" she says.

I have so much in my heart for her. Too much, really. No space for it, in the end. And Miss Cream, moving against me like a scoop of molten vanilla. That's where I should be.

Time to move past holding hands, two straws over a raspberry soda.

"Look, baby," I tell her. "This isn't working out."

When I lean away, she falters, stumbling backward, like I've pulled the very earth out from under her. She stands a little apart from me, just breathing and staring. Eyes wide.

"Come on. I'll walk you home."

"No," she says. She holds up a slim gloved hand. "I'm fine." But I walk her anyway, and I wait until the front door is closed.

I'm half expecting Miss Cream to be gone. I scope the dance floor. Searching. Searching.

I let out the breath I've been holding. There she is.

Sure enough, she's dancing with some other guy. A conked black guy. As tall as me. Maybe taller. Definitely thicker, body and mind.

She stands out like wine on a tablecloth. Well, the opposite of that. I look around, thinking for the first time clearly how strange it is for a white woman to be at a Negro-night dance. Why did someone like her come here? For the thrill of doing something daring—something the world wouldn't approve of? I can relate to that.

She has her arms coiled around that Negro's neck, and a jealous fire flares in me.

I move right up to the sideline of the dance floor and stand where I'm sure she'll see me. Our eyes catch within a matter of seconds. But she doesn't move toward me or even unwrap her arms from his neck.

Shit.

What am I going to do? I can't lose her to some black-as-midnight fellow who just happened along at the right moment. I can't blow this shot.

She doesn't make a move toward me. And I don't know what kind of move to make on her.

So I just stand and wait. A long, long minute or two, while the song rages on and Miss Cream sways on, entwined with the man I'm planning to throw my fists at in a minute. The only thing holding me back is the memory of my last fistfight, which didn't end so well. Not exactly the impression I want to make. But Miss Cream is rightfully mine, I figure. She came to me first. Danced with me first. And promised me a ride. Promised me the rest of the night.

She's worth the fight.

The song winds down with a shivering vibrato on the cymbals.

I ball my fists by my sides. She unwraps herself from the man. Kisses him on the cheek. The blood in my veins is steaming hot. But I can't make my feet move. He's bigger than I thought, now that I'm closer. Now that Miss Cream's gaze is no longer distracting me from a full view of him.

Her mouth moves near his ear. "Thanks."

I grip the back of a chair. She winds her way through to me as the band pipes up with a fresh jiving number.

"You're a patient man," she says.

I raise one shoulder. No good reply comes to mind. So I don't say anything. I've seen men whip a victory out of silence. When Papa was most angry, he'd just stand there, looking at us, and we'd fall into line. We knew that the next thing after the silence would be the strap, so the silence had some kind of power in it.

It cuts both ways, though. In the silence, in trying to re-create Papa's strong silence, it could become all too easy to hear his voice again. I push the thought away, concentrating on the pulse of the music and the stirring blond beauty before me.

"I like that kind of confidence in a man," Miss Cream purrs, curling against me.

"I like you," I answer. "And I've got all night."

"You wanna get out of here?" she says.

Boy, do I. We head for the coat check. She hands me her ticket, and I retrieve a stylish fur stole.

"It's mink," she remarks, offhand. The mink hugs her neck and shoulders as I usher her out into the night.

Every move I make, cats are staring. Surely thinking, *Who's he to land that hot piece of contraband?*

"What's your name?" I ask her on the sidewalk.

"Sophia," she says. Her car is parked right outside. A white convertible. Top raised.

I hold open the driver's door for her. "They call me Red."

"I know all about you," she answers. Her voice drops to a low, sexy pitch. I still can't believe she's talking to me. Guys around the doorway are watching us leave. Every minute spent in Sophia's company, my stock ticks up a couple notches.

She slides into the seat. I run around and hop in the front beside her. It's easy enough to slide across the bench seat to get close.

"Wait until we park," she says.

As far as I'm concerned, we are parked. But she puts the

car into gear and pulls out. She drives us to a wooded area outside the city; it's a spot she must know well, because despite the dark, the car glides into a space with ease.

The radio hums soft, sexy jazz. Sophia cuts the car engine off. Turns to me, all creamy warm. "You were saying?"

I slide across the bench seat and remind her.

Chapter Twelve

I'd thought my sharkskin zoot and my swagger made me big stuff around Roxbury. Turns out, that was nothing compared to having a white woman on my arm—and it sure doesn't hurt that she's among the most stunning women any of us have ever seen.

I squire Sophia everywhere I can. Night after night, down around town. I take her dancing everywhere. Mostly I keep my hands on her, make it known to the world that she's with me.

But it's just as fun to watch her twirl and flirt. Negroes in the club swarm her like bees on honeycomb. If I step aside for a second, they come surging forward, tripping over themselves to ask her to dance. And she dances. But after a minute, I come back. All I have to do is stand next to her. She lets go of whoever, snakes her arms around my neck, and suddenly I'm king. The waters part around us, and we stand there, just the two of us, looking in each other's eyes and knowing. Just knowing.

Sophia is the best thing that's ever happened to me. I guess this is what all the songs mean when they talk about love. I want to swim in her, swallow her, breathe her. I've decided it's time I take her to the fanciest restaurant I can afford in Roxbury. She has money, and so she often pays for the things we do, but I've saved my tips so I can treat her to something nice for a change.

Sophia's the perfect kind of woman. Fancy but not prissy. She never minds sliding to the underbelly of things, even though she deserves much better. Usually I take her to my favorite restaurant, a little hole in the wall that's open all night. They serve everything fried, and they know us by name, and we lick grease off our fingers in the wee hours of the morning and relish the free life we're living.

But here tonight, in the candlelight of a nice place with white tablecloths and heavy china, she looks like a goddess across the table from me.

"Do you like this place?" I ask her, just to make sure.

She nods. "Yes, I've been here before. It's safe for us to

eat here." She leans closer to whisper: "But I can't wait to hold you."

I hold back a smile. *Safe?* Says the woman who comes to the Roseland on Negro night. "We'll be dancing in no time," I promise. "Until the sun comes up. I'll never let you go."

And she smiles at me, and I wish I could pour myself into her. Our hands entwine alongside the bread plate, and I'm weirdly grateful all of a sudden that my mother made a point of teaching us why they sometimes give you two different forks and how to behave in a nice restaurant, even though we learned it around the circle of our own dining table. I never actually thought it would be useful, knowing what a bread knife is and where to put it. But here I sit, hand in hand with Sophia. For a second, I feel kind of hopeful that maybe there really will be better days.

I call Sophia up at her house. "What time are you coming by tonight?" She always picks me up in her convertible.

"Not tonight, Red," she whispers, like there's someone to overhear. "Another night, maybe."

She hangs up. In the silence, I hear the echo of it. *Maybe. Maybe.*

Maybe? I thought what we had going was getting to be a sure thing. We're fun together. We're downright hot together. All those steamy nights in the club, not to mention the equally steamy aftermath, stretched out on the seat of her convertible.

I hang up the phone. Resist the urge to dial her back, to ask, *What other night? When will I see you?* The idea of walking back onto a dance floor alone makes me cringe. I'm somebody now. She makes me somebody. I'm not about to go back to how it was.

Days pass without seeing her. I'm desperate to know where she's gone, if it was all just a fluke. I'm going to have to find a way to show her I'm worth her while.

Shorty says jewelry is the quickest way to get and keep a girl. He takes me to a hole-in-the-wall shop he knows. The guy behind the counter knows Shorty, of course. They slap hands.

"This is my homeboy, Red," Shorty says, by way of introduction. "He needs to impress a lady."

"Sure," the guy says. "We'll take care of you. What sort of item are you looking for?"

"Umm . . ." The amount of jewelry in the glass counter is staggering. Through the top, I can see several large pieces laid out in half circles. Necklaces, I suppose. Scattered in between, some smaller items. Pins and things. Maybe earrings. I don't know. I've seen plenty of jewelry on people but never laid out like this.

The vertical pane goes from my knees to my waist, three glass shelves of items piled on top of each other behind it.

The heels of my hands land on the counter's metal rim as I bend down to look at the spread. Gold and silver. Glittery and smooth. All kinds of looks to them. All kinds of colorful stones.

The guy goes on. "You thinking earrings? Necklace? Brooch? Silver? Gold? Any particular setting? Diamonds on it? Rubies? Amethyst?" He rattles off a list of words I swear I've never heard uttered.

"I don't know what any of that is," I admit once he stops to take a breath.

The guy shrugs. "Different stones."

Shorty motions me aside. Puts a hand on my shoulder. "First time buying for a lady?" he murmurs.

I nod.

"Should have known."

"Sorry." Will Shorty ever get tired of schooling me? If he does, I'll be lost. Probably fall into a sewer hole and die.

"OK. Earrings and bracelets are good for making up," Shorty says. "Necklaces, you're getting a little more serious."

He points across the case. "Don't ever *ever* buy a woman any kind of ring unless you mean her to stick around forever."

"What, do I look like I was born yesterday?" I joke. Everyone knows not to buy a girl a ring.

Shorty laughs. Acts like he's appraising me. "Not yesterday. Day before."

I would laugh along with him, but I'm too distracted

166

by the many, many shiny things glittering in my face. I can rule out the rings, at least. Keeping Sophia forever doesn't sound like such a bad deal, but right now I'm just aiming for enough to get another couple of dates.

"How much are you looking to spend?" the jewelry guy asks. "That usually helps narrow it down."

"Um . . ."

"Low end," Shorty says. "What, Red, like twenty dollars?"

Twenty dollars seems like a huge amount of money to me, but Sophia is a fancy sort of woman. "I don't know about that," I say. "Can I get something nice for, maybe, five?"

The jewelry guy shrugs. "Sure." He reaches behind him, grabs a rack the size of a shoe box stood up on end. Necklaces and things dangling from it. They sway as he lifts it over to the front counter and places it in front of me. "Any of these will run you three to five dollars."

"Is it OK to touch them?" I ask.

"Sure," the jewelry guy says. "They're all different. Pull them out and look."

"A necklace, I think." I'm fingering a smooth golden locket. I imagine that gold will look nice with Sophia's silken blond hair.

Then I look down into the glass case, with its big hefty padlock on it. All those things, all locked up, and then these just get handed to me. Three to five dollars must seem like peanuts to the jewelry guy.

167

The bell above the door jangles. My suspicions are confirmed when the guy walks away to greet the new customers, leaving the rack of jewelry in front of us. Unattended.

My fingers flit over the delicate chains. "Five dollars?" I tell Shorty. "I don't know if I got it." Five dollars is my weekly payment on my zoot suit. If I got the necklace, I'd have to miss a week, maybe. Or else cut back on something else.

"Just lift it, man," Shorty whispers. "Who's gonna know?"

A pause.

There are a dozen necklaces on the hook. All swinging slightly, from when I touched them. Anyone looks, they won't notice one gone.

I reach for the locket I liked. Let my fingers rest on the back of it, feeling its heft. Not much to it, really. Very lightweight. Dainty, you might even say. Not the sort of thing that would bog you down.

Shorty watches the clerk over my shoulder. "He ain't looking."

"You gotta understand," I tell him. "I can't lose her."

"I hear you, homeboy," Shorty says. Blink of an eye. He reaches up and flicks the chain. So swift, I almost missed it.

The small gold circle falls into my palm, nice and easy, followed by the coils of chain, and I fist it up, fast. With my other hand, I trace a slow line along the cool metal lip of the counter. The line I'm crossing, maybe. I studiously gaze down into the case like I'm still considering something fancier.

Smooth, I think. Like we've done it a thousand times. A hot rush surges through my chest, spreading outward. I slip my fingers into my coat pocket. The locket slides down, out of sight.

"Let's go," Shorty murmurs. "'Fore he comes back over."

He doesn't need to tell me. I'm already moving.

"Did you decide to go with the locket?" the clerk asks. He glances at the necklace tree we've left behind. I falter in my tracks. Hold my breath.

Shorty claps my shoulder. "Big decision, eh, homeboy?"

His cue prompts me that I ought to say something. I loosen my fists. Casual-like. Give the clerk a sad little shrug.

"I gotta save up," I tell him. "Get her something real."

"You got something in mind?" the clerk says, leaning in. "You pay half now, I'll lay it away."

"Naw, man." I lean in to mirror him. My coat pocket brushes the counter display. I imagine a tinkling sound, the locket striking the glass, even though the fabric in between makes contact impossible. I conceal my cringe behind what I hope is a wry smile.

"See, I never bought real jewelry before. I wanna come in with the cash, walk out with the thing in my hand. I never done that."

"Sure, Red," says the clerk. "I'll be seeing you, then."

I tap two fingers off my forehead, like tipping my hat.

Then Shorty and I stroll right on out of there, heavy one fake gold locket.

In the street, down a ways from the jewelry store, Shorty slaps my hand. "You're real cool, man," he says. "First time out, how'd you get to be so cool?"

I roll my shoulders. "What makes you think it's my first time out?" I'm thinking about all the shenanigans Philbert and I used to pull back in Lansing. How we'd celebrate, slapping hands and devouring apples, or whatever we'd scored.

"*Whoo,*" Shorty hoots. "I'm gonna have some fun with you. I can see it a mile off." He sweeps his hand across an imaginary horizon. It's like he paints a picture in the air. Some kind of magic at his fingertips. I can see it.

I shake off the thoughts of Philbert.

"Look, I gotta go," I tell Shorty. "Let me find Sophia and see if I can buy me some goodwill." I pull the locket from my coat and dangle it over my middle fingers. The pendant settles on my wrist. It glints in the sunlight. It's gonna look real nice on Sophia.

"You ain't got to *buy* it," Shorty quips. "It's yours for the taking."

I grin, pocketing the necklace again. "Let's hope."

"Good as gold," Shorty says, slapping my hand again.

Walking home, Philbert floats into my mind once more. It's weird, I guess, that the thing I used to share with him, and only him, I now share with Shorty, too.

Hands in my pockets, I clutch the locket in a tight fist, until the edges of the metal start to hurt my skin. I wonder if, right this minute, all those hundreds of miles away, Philbert's fingers might be tingling. If he somehow knows. If what I just did might be a way of bringing us close again, like we used to be.

Lansing, 1938

As I slid closer to the barrel of apples outside the door of Doone's Market, my stomach was growling, hot. I felt the acid in my throat, my body dying to digest something.

Not so much as a nickel in my pocket.

I leaned up against the side of the building, watching the people come in and out. It was busy. Not much time between customers. I waited for the right window.

I crossed my legs, stuck my hands in my pockets. I was all but whistling. Innocent.

Edged closer to the barrel now and then. Eyes on the highest, nearest apples. Red skin glinting in the sunlight.

I knew how they were gonna taste. All slick and sweet and crisp. Like an autumn sunset.

I wiped my hands on my pants, getting ready.

The white woman walking in from the parking lot now was Mrs. Stockton, one of our neighbors down the road. No one behind her.

"Hello, Malcolm," she said, nodding.

"Good afternoon, ma'am." I pulled it off nice and polite. Let my shoulder turn, tracking her walk to the door. It was propped open, trying to let in some breeze. Inside, the clerk was at the register, weighing cabbages for a small old woman with a coin purse clutched in her hand. He bent to jot the price on the receipt pad. Mrs. Stockton passed through the doorway, between us.

I swiftly scooped up three apples. Spun. Lobbed them as hard as I could.

Waiting at the corner of the building, Philbert snaked out his arms and caught them. One. Two. Three. He bobbled the third but kept hold of it. He slammed his arms together as it rolled toward the crook of his elbows.

My aim was getting better. I slipped my hands back in my pockets. Leaned. Tipped my head toward the open doorway. Mrs. Stockton was out of sight. The clerk raised his eyes from the receipt pad. Glanced out at me. I gazed back. Calm. Innocent.

The clerk turned away to open a brown paper sack for the cabbage woman. A split second was enough. The parking lot was still empty. I grabbed an apple in each fist and tore off running.

Philbert had a head start. We dashed around the building, into the woods, running until we were sure we wouldn't be caught.

My teeth sank into the crisp flesh of an apple. It tasted

like freedom, like heaven. I stripped it down to the seeds, then started on the next one. Philbert chewed loudly, walking beside me.

"Mmm." He sighed around a mouthful.

Dinner the night before had been nothing but old bread soaked in small bowls of watered-down gravy. There was never enough food on hand to fill all eight of us.

"Split the last one?" Philbert held it out to me. We couldn't bring an apple into the house. Mom would demand to know where we got it.

I grabbed it out of his hand. "No way. I did all the hard work to get it." Philbert always wanted to go in, all brazen, and just take stuff. I knew how to bide my time. Never got caught—until the chickens, and that was just foolish to begin with.

I started gobbling the apple. I wanted to take my time, to actually enjoy it, but I knew what was coming.

"No fair," Philbert screeched. "I was there." He slugged me over and over on the arm holding the apple, trying to knock it loose.

I braced myself for a knock-down, drag-out fight. I let my teeth crunch deep into the apple, right down to the core, locking it there. Raised my fists. Philbert launched himself at me. I shoved him off. Hopped around like a fighter, fists up and ready for round two.

But it didn't come.

"Malcolm," Philbert said, suddenly still.

I pulled the apple from my mouth. "What is it?"

We'd reached the edge of our property. My brother stared past me, across the half-planted garden to the house. Following his gaze, I saw it, too. The long car parked in front of the house. I knew that car. The welfare man's car.

I took one more huge bite, then handed the rest of the apple to Philbert. He scraped it to the core, quick and clean. No questions asked. It was fine to fight when it was us against us, but it was about to be us against them. And that changed everything.

Boston, 1941

It's still us against them, I think. The government people might have beaten our family, but there were lots more people out there against us. The type of people who would try to hurt Sophia and me for being together—assuming she still wants to be together.

I lie on my bed, stick my foot up in the air, and dangle the locket off one toe. I try to imagine how nice it's going to look hanging around Sophia's neck, try to push the way I got it out of my mind.

It's never bothered me to take. But I've only ever taken things I need. Before, I always thought Papa might even be a little bit proud of me for doing what I had to do to help the family. Papa wouldn't be proud of me today.

The locket dangles over my face. This is something I wanted, not something I needed. Something I could have rightly paid for. But why should I? When it's us against them, anything goes. Maybe you could say I'm being denied so much as a Negro in America that I deserve some of it back. Gotta take a little. Can't just let it all be taken from me. Why should I always be the one to go without?

Mrs. Swerlin used to lecture me about all the wrong things I had done. "Mistakes" she called them, as if I'd accidently stolen some chickens while I meant to be doing something else. She was always talking about how I could recover from what I'd done up until then, but that somewhere up ahead of me there was a line. A line there'd be no coming back from once it was crossed.

I liked how she didn't just talk about some things being right and some being wrong. She could see all the shady lines, the way I could. Like how stealing could actually help someone, could maybe be worth the risk. She knew there was a line between a little bit of trouble and real danger, and many, many lines between getting caught and getting off scot-free. It surprised me that she saw all that shady stuff. She was more than a schoolmarm with a ruler, trying to nudge me to the straight and narrow, which could never work. I'm bigger than that.

"You have to be careful," she'd say. "You don't want to cross a line you can't come back from." But it's hard to know which line is the one that counts. Or maybe there's only one line, but it isn't a sure thing, solid in its place. Maybe crossing isn't what I do.

I'm pushing the line. Moving it. There's always another side. The line moves. It moves and it moves.

Chapter Thirteen

Boston, 1941

I ring up Sophia. Hold the necklace in my hand, like a good-luck charm. *Answer,* I plead silently. *Be there for me.*

"Hello?"

"Hi, baby. It's me."

"Red," she says, low and sultry. "Take me dancing?"

My heart exults. I try to play it cool. "Sure, baby."

"Tonight?"

"That's perfect. We'll go to the Roseland." It's Negro dance night. Coming back around to where it all began. Maybe it will remind her of how we connected, right from the start.

"Wear the sharkskin," she says. "That's my favorite."

"Always." She coulda said, *Walk across coals*. My feet would be burning. "I got a present for you."

"For me?" she says, real coy.

"None other."

A light, breathy laugh. "I'll see you soon, Red."

I pace a rut in the living room, near the front window, watching for Sophia's headlights. I'm thinking about waiting on the porch, despite the chill, but I don't want to seem too eager. That was Shorty's advice. Play it cool.

Ella comes down the stairs, bundled in her housecoat and slippers. She shakes her head at the sight of the zoot, as usual. But she's learned not to comment. I already know what she thinks, and I'm still wearing it. Classic impasse.

"You're going out?" she says. Seems like a dumb thing to say. I'm always going out.

"Yeah. Someone's picking me up."

"This the same 'someone' who picked you up last week?"

"Yeah."

Ella's nose wrinkles. Maybe she caught a whiff of her own disapproval. It's ripe and wafting all over the room.

"In a flashy car, as I recall."

"Yeah," I say. "She lives on the Hill. You ought to be happy about that."

Ella's eyebrows perk up. From the kitchen, the teakettle sings. Must be what she was coming down to attend to in the first place. "Oh, does she?" Ella says. "See, I knew you'd meet nice girls at Townsend's."

If only she knew.

I smile. Let her draw her own conclusions that fit the picture frame she wants me to fill. There are times when it is best to say plenty and times to leave well enough alone.

"Your tea's ready," I remind her.

She moves into the kitchen as Sophia pulls up in front. Close call. I duck out of the house and rush down the walk to meet her.

It's much too cold to have the convertible top down, but it's down anyway. I don't even open the car door. I rest my hand on the rim and leap over, bending, then quickly straightening my legs into the space beneath the glove box. Not too bad. Fairly dashing, I might even say.

Sophia has her hair wrapped in a kerchief to protect her style from the wind. I sweep her into my arms, going for dramatic, romantic, larger-than-life.

"Has it been just a week?" I tell her. "It feels like a lifetime."

We kiss.

"I'm glad to see you, too," she says. Then she drives us off down the street.

Dawn is lightening the sky by the time she drops me home again, a whirlwind of Lindy and reefer and whiskey at our backs.

She slides the gearshift into park and faces me. "You said you had something for me?" She pauses. "Or did you already give it to me?" She squeezes my thigh with a sexy smile that makes me want to give it to her again, right now.

"Yes, I do." I've been saving the necklace for the end of the night. I want to leave her with a memory of me to carry with her, so she won't forget. So she'll take more of my calls. I want to see her every day. Be seen with her every day, too. I haven't found another high that gives me the kind of rush Sophia does.

I withdraw the gift from my jacket pocket and present it to her. I hadn't wanted to give it to her plain, so I swiped a nice hinged case from the bureau in Ella's bedroom. I took out the necklace that was in it and just left it in the drawer with the others. I figured she wouldn't miss the box, or at least if she did, it wouldn't occur to her to blame me.

Sophia takes the case in her hand. Offers me a surprised glance. "From E. B. Horn?" She sounds impressed. "Well, well." The logo on the case must be from a fancy sort of place. An unexpected benefit.

"Do you like it?"

She opens the case. Strokes the gold locket with a single manicured finger. Nods. "It's lovely. Thank you." She kisses my cheek.

As she pulls away, I whisper, "See you tomorrow?" The question mark just kind of creeps in there. I meant to say it straight up, real confident. Not to give her a choice.

Sophia hesitates. "No, not tomorrow."

"Oh."

"I have plans tomorrow." She looks away, out the windshield. "You're not the only fellow I see. You know that."

I didn't know, but it doesn't overly surprise me. I look away, too, out the window on my side.

Up in the house, a curtain ruffles. Ella, checking up on me, no doubt. Fortunately, the top is up now, so I doubt she can see us very well.

Play it cool. "I'm not the jealous sort of cat," I tell Sophia. I remember how she liked that about me at the first dance. "You do what you do. I'll do what I do. When we're doing what we do and it happens to be us together, all the better."

Sophia slides closer along the bench. "I knew you'd understand."

I understand. I understand what it will take not to lose her.

My arms loop around her. While she's here, on my street, in my reach, she's mine and mine alone. I whisper, "You and me, baby. We've got to be free. I dig that."

Then I grab her close. Smooth my fingers over her neck in the way she likes.

I kiss her passionately. Stamp myself on her, so she won't soon forget. I might not be the only guy in her life—and probably not the oldest or the smartest or the richest or the best looking—but I'm bound and determined to be one of her favorites. The one who gets her. Who just lets her be. A no-hassles guy who twirls her and dips her and rocks her. The one she wants to come back to again and again.

I watch from the front stoop as Sophia drives off down the street. I linger, my breath fogging the air.

I've got a cold premonition that I know what's waiting for me inside. It's not very dark at all anymore. Surely she's seen us. Surely she's mad.

No choice but to step into it. It's too cold, I'm too tired, and anyway, this is where I live.

Ella springs up from the sofa like her tail is on fire. "Are you serious with this?" she screeches. "A white woman? Lord," she moans, "you are making one mess of your life."

Yeah, that sounds like me.

"There's nothing wrong with it," I say. Ella doesn't have a problem with other couples mixing races. I know for a fact she has friends on the Hill who've done it.

"Wrong's not the point," Ella snaps. I stay quiet.

"That kind of woman is no good," Ella says. "She's loose. She's dangerous."

"She's not," I protest.

Ella shakes her head. Her whole body quakes, in fact. "She's going to bring you trouble. You don't even know the kind of trouble."

I can't pretend I don't know. That I don't understand.

In my mind's eye, a shadow. Something swinging from a tree.

"It's OK here," I yell at her. "So get off my back!" Ella

182

flinches in surprise at the volume of my voice. I've gone from silent to screaming in a matter of seconds. It's just that I'm much too fried to have this fight. I've been up all night, dancing till my feet ached. They still ache. My fading reefer buzz is no longer enough to sustain me. Sophia has fallen out of my arms, her return uncertain, and all Ella wants is to rip her further away.

Ella launches into a lecture about the trouble I'm bound to get into, but I can't stand to hear it.

"I'm going to bed," I say over her. I don't even wait for her to admonish me. Just walk off and stomp up the stairs.

Ella shouts after me.

I don't care. I keep on climbing.

"I can't take it anymore," I tell Shorty. "Every tiny thing I do, she's got something to say about it." I pace through his living room. It's not a large place. I go corner to corner to corner. I've got a route all worked out, dodging the sofa and chairs, skirting around the folding table that Shorty calls the dining room.

"Red, man." Shorty's been listening to me rant for going on an hour now. He talks around the toothpick he's been gnawing on. "Your sister's just doing what women do."

"Half-sister," I correct.

"Uh-huh." Shorty fingers his sax. At some point, he must've pulled it out of the case. He's done this before, practicing scales or something while we're talking. Calls it being efficient. The keys make little clicking sounds.

I pace. The boards creak in certain places.

"'Opportunity' this, and 'expectation' that. But then every other word is 'you can't, you can't.'" I throw my arms out. "Who does she think she is?"

"Your mama," Shorty quips.

"Well, she's not." I bark it at him, glaring fierce. Mom is locked up right now, for being strong and proud and, heck, for being exactly what Ella wants me to be. "Opportunity" and "expectation" got Mom locked up. Got Papa killed. And Ella still wants to preach? I don't have to listen. "She's *not* my mother!"

Shorty's brows go up, but he looks down, away. "I know, homeboy. I know." He's got his quiet voice on.

I pull the comb out of my back pocket. Run it through my conk. Take a second to pull myself together.

"Maybe it's nice," Shorty says. "Having someone around who looks after you."

"Maybe it's a pain in the butt."

Shorty shrugs. He's slouched all crooked on the couch, one leg bent up, the sax splayed across him. "You gotta take the good with the bad on a thing like that."

I can't see any good, and I say so.

"She cooks good, right?" We've had Shorty over to dinner a time or two. Ella isn't much of a fan of his, either. I can't do a damn thing right, far as she's concerned. Not even make friends. She hates Shorty. Hates Sophia. She liked Laura the one time she met her, and I can see why.

They're cut from the same righteous Hill cloth. The kind I want to shred with my teeth.

"Yeah, she cooks."

"That's a big deal," Shorty goes on. "Having food put on the table for you."

The food is nice. But I can eat some at Townsend's. And anyway, I can get by with less. When you've lived on dandelion greens, everything is uphill from that.

"Nah. I'm getting out of there."

"You sure?"

"Heck, yeah." I'll sleep in the back room at the Roseland if they'll let me.

Shorty sighs. "Well, here's something you might want to know."

"What?"

"My cousin's moving out," Shorty says. "I've got a bed open and half the rent to account for."

I perk up. "Oh, yeah?"

"You interested?"

Interested? I'm falling all over myself as I stop pacing long enough to collapse in one of the chairs. "Heck, yes."

"You gotta be good for half the rent. Every week."

"I can cover it."

"Toilet runs. You gotta jiggle the handle."

"Sure." I'm on the edge of my seat.

Shorty moves the toothpick to the other side of his mouth. "Yours if you want it."

"How soon?"

"Starting next week."

"I'm in." Couldn't have been more perfect.

Shorty studies me. "You sure? You gotta think twice before you ditch a good home like you've got going now."

"It ain't home," I tell him straight up. "Ain't nothing like it." But I take the second to think. Only because he's making me; I already know. Live with Shorty, my best pal? In our own place? No sneaking in and out? No having to answer to anyone about where I've been or what I've been smoking or who I've been seeing? Only options, no rules? There isn't a single thing to second-guess about it.

"Yeah, I'm sure," I tell him. We slap palms. Done deal.

My bags are packed and stacked beside the door. Ella motions me in and hugs me. I stiffen in the circle of her arms. She releases me.

"You don't have to go," Ella says.

But I do.

"I haven't been happy with some of your choices, but we're still family." In our last week, Ella has been all the things she ever was. Wise and warm and willing to hold me close.

"Thanks for bringing me here," I say, and I mean it. I'd be crushed dead by now, stuck in my old sadness, if I'd had to stay back in Mason. Boston has made me a new man, and Ella was the first doorway out of that past.

There are new doorways opening now. And the new me is going to walk through them.

"I don't know what you see in him," she says of Shorty. "Are you really going to live with him? I just don't like that man."

I laugh. "You don't like anyone," I say. It's OK to laugh together now. Now that what we've shared is ending.

"Seems that way, huh?" She strokes my face. "I like you."

That doesn't seem very true at this point. Ella likes the old me. The Little me. Now I'm Red.

I feel like a man, out in the world finally, with my own pad. I lie in Shorty's cousin's bedroom—my bedroom—taking it all in.

The vibe here is different. It's all Shorty and me, like we are. No one to answer to. No fine furniture to keep unmussed.

The first time I check the mail, I get a shock. All the bills are addressed to "Malcolm Jarvis."

"Hey," I tell Shorty. "They gave me your last name."

"That's me," he says. "I'm Malcolm, too."

"Really?" All this time, I've never known him by any name other than Shorty. I guess I knew it was a street name, but at the same time, it seemed like he'd always had it. "That's some kind of fluke."

Shorty just shrugs. "Things happen for a reason."

"No reason I can think of for a thing like that." Two Malcolms, both from Lansing? Maybe Shorty and I were meant to be friends.

We eat off thick, chipped ceramic plates. Drink from

mugs stained in blotches or in rings, brown from coffee and red from wine. No fine, fancy china like Mom's or Ella's.

"This is good," I tell Shorty one night, scraping my plate clean. It's some kind of beef stew. He made an enormous pot of it, enough to feed us for a week.

"You think?" he says. "All right."

"Over-the-top delicious," I say, going in for another scoop. "What's the secret?"

"It's just beef and vegetables, salt and water. And a ham hock."

I slow my eating. Ham hock? "There's pork in this? In a beef stew?"

Shorty shrugs. "My mom always put a ham hock in everything. The bone flavors the broth, and you don't have to put in as much meat. Meat's expensive."

I rub my tongue on the roof of my mouth as if to clean it. My whole life, I never ate a bite of pork. I thought I wasn't supposed to. Mom said God put it on earth to eat the garbage and it wasn't made for human consumption. But I can't think of any good reason to hold to that rule now.

"Ham hock, eh?" I bring the spoon to my lips again. Pork. I didn't know what I was missing. This stew might very well be the best-tasting thing I've ever had my mouth around. "Tastes like freedom," I tell Shorty.

He laughs. "You better learn to cook something, too. Freedom gets old after a while."

"So where are we going tonight?" I ask.

"Tonight I'm getting together with some other cats to

jam a little," he says. "Count me out." Turns out my impression of Shorty as always out in the street isn't quite accurate. He has a lot going on. I'm the free one, the one without a care.

"Come on, man," I groan. "Didn't you just jam with them the other night?"

"We're hoping to catch a gig together soon," he explains. "We're getting pretty good."

"Maybe I'll catch up with you later?"

"Maybe." Once he gets to playing, it's hard to tear him away.

Shorty has all these goals and plans, and it starts to seem that those things are bogging him down. Can't go out Tuesday night—got a saxophone lesson. Can't buy another bag of reefer—gotta pay for the lesson. He has a boring kind of drive underneath him. I guess all along he's been showing me this one side of him, letting me think it was his all. The way it's mine.

He stands up to clear the table. "Call Sophia," he tells me. "It's not like you'll be bored."

"Yeah, I will." Call her, that is.

Sophia comes around more often these days. Now that I have my own place, I can bring her inside. That raises my stock for her more than a little.

She has plenty of money to burn. We drink and smoke our way through it. I don't even need to keep my slave at Townsend's. Now that I don't have Ella looking over my shoulder, I can work anyplace I want. Or not.

Chapter Fourteen

Boston, December 1941

I haven't missed the job at Townsend's for a second. But I'm missing credit payments left and right, and I still have to make rent, so I catch a slave at the Parker House, a big restaurant downtown. I have to wear a white coat, but I'm not a server. I carry trays of dirty dishes from the dining room back into the kitchen so the dishwashers can spray and scrub them clean.

It's a mindless kind of work—no need for grinning and cheerful chatter to please the customers. I keep my head down, move the trays. Even though I'm back to dishwashing again, it's still a step up in the world from Lansing.

Every free minute, I spend with Sophia. It never gets old, taking her around the Roxbury night spots. We always turn heads. She's with me almost every night now; every night we take some dance floor by storm.

I wake up late for work, running on maybe three hours' sleep. It's a Sunday, and last night the dance went until all hours. I rub my eyes and kick myself into gear. By the time I get there, I'll be so late they'll probably fire me.

I hurry toward the Parker House, hoping I can get downtown and into the kitchen before they notice me missing and penalize me for being late. Not likely.

I burst in the door, only to find the main kitchen entirely empty. It shocks me into stillness. No dishes getting washed. Food laid out in pans on the fired-up stove, getting burned. The sharp smell of overdone meat starting to stink up the room.

Where is everybody?

From the back I can hear voices, so I follow the sound. I move through the kitchen, around the corner to the head chef's office. The door's open.

There's a voice on the radio, in the middle of giving a special report. All the boys from the kitchen and the servers are clustered around, listening.

"... *surprise aerial attack* ... *uncertain at this hour how many lives were lost.* ..."

My heart speeds up. "What happened?" I ask.

"Shh . . ." They hush me, patting the air with their hands.

"*. . . brave servicemen and sailors fought off the attack to the best of their ability. In the hours and days to come, we'll learn exactly how much damage to our Pacific fleet. . . .*"

Whatever the news, it sounds bad.

One of the cooks turns to me. "Japanese planes bombed the U.S. naval base at Pearl Harbor, in Hawaii."

"Bombed?" I echo.

He makes a sweeping motion with his hands. "Took the whole place out."

"We're under attack," one of the waiters says. He touches his forehead, chest, and shoulders in the pattern of a cross. "God help us all."

I look at him. Can't help but think it: *God checked out a long time ago.*

After my shift, I come home and find Shorty, half-out-of-his-mind drunk and wailing on his sax. The bottle on the table is the bourbon we like. Not the cheap one—the one we get when things are serious.

I want to ask Shorty, *What does it mean?* But I'm pretty sure I know.

"I guess you heard?" I say.

"We're going to war," he answers. "Drink up, home-boy. It's a whole new world tomorrow."

But it turns out, tomorrow and the next day aren't all that different from the days that went before. For us, anyway.

The newspaper is splashed with headlines about the surprise attack and the announcement that President Roosevelt has asked Congress to declare war on Japan. The government puts out calls for men to enlist in the service. All over Roxbury, posters go up.

Old-timers on the street have things to say about it. Memories of the Great War, back before I was born. Not all of them served, but they can remember, and they love nothing better than to sit on the stoops and spout off about the old days. The few veterans among them worked as cooks or janitors or ship hands. The black infantry recruits, they inform me, tended not to survive. Black units were always the first ones sent to the front in battle, to draw enemy fire and protect the white soldiers coming up behind them. Been that way since the Civil War, the old-timers crow. So what else is new for the Negro?

Next come the patriotic ads on the radio, talking about how all Americans must fight for good old Uncle Sam. The old-timers grumble, but I like those ads and the posters. The soldiers look noble and brave, willing to go out in the world and fight. With their broad, muscled bodies and determined expressions, it's clear that they are men, and everyone treats them that way. It must be nice.

"You thinking about joining the service?" I ask Shorty.

Shorty laughs outright. "They're not talking to us."

"They're talking to everybody."

"They think they are." Shorty looks at me sideways. "Shoot. When am I gonna be done schooling you, homeboy?"

"What are you talking about?"

"Yeah," Shorty says, half to himself. "I've been schooling you on the ways of the street. Negro ways. We ain't touched the white world yet."

I know the white world just fine. The white world killed my father. The white world calls Mom crazy. The white world tore us limb from limb and came back to feast on the chitterlings.

"They always take," I say, to show I know something.

Shorty laughs. "That is so, Red." Then he launches into a speech about the war ads, how they're trying to talk black folks into going to fight for the so-called freedom we don't even have on our own shores.

"Black folks died at Pearl Harbor," he goes on. "Bootblacks and janitors and cooks in the kitchen. But we ain't allowed to serve outright, alongside whitey. They just keep us around to build everything and then to clean up after him. Ain't that always the way?"

"I heard they were taking black soldiers," I say.

"Yeah, they call it soldiering," Shorty insists. "But then they arm you with a whisk, send you to beat the crap out of some eggs. Or they put you on the front lines as their shield. Don't believe what they tell you." He slugs my arm.

"You got nothing to worry about, anyway. You're too young to go to war."

"Only for now," I say. I certainly feel old enough. I'll be seventeen soon. Eighteen isn't so far off.

"If either of our numbers come up, we'll find a way out," Shorty says. He sounds pretty confident, and he hasn't led me wrong yet.

I probably shouldn't be worried about the draft anyway. It's over a year away, and what would the army want with a conk-headed hustler like me in the first place? I'm not worth much to anyone, least of all to Uncle Sam.

Boston, spring 1942

Sophia picks me up from the Parker House after my shift. It's nearing midnight. "Let's go somewhere around here," I say. We never hang out downtown, and maybe it's a good night for a change of scenery. I know Sophia loves being downtown, because this is where she comes on the nights when she's not with me. No reason I can't come with her. Maybe I'll end up seeing more of her in the long run.

But Sophia looks at me askance. "Really?"

I slide across the bench seat and kiss her. "There's a place a few blocks away I heard the busboys talking about. Sounds happening."

"Have you been smoking?" she says. She pets my chest,

and I think we could have our date right here and it'd be all right.

I stroke her back. "Just a little."

"We should go to Roxbury," she says. "The usual places."

"No, baby," I whisper. "Let's do something special." We're at war, after all. We could get bombed. I could get drafted someday, and I need her to know she's the only thing that matters to me. The only thing I'll fight for.

"Maybe a walk," she says quietly. "Down by the water. I know a place."

"Lead the way."

It's newly spring, so strolling along the harbor seems like a good idea, but the night air soon catches up with us. My lips grow cold. I put my arm around Sophia and hold her against me to keep her warm, but she seems fine. She's looking around at everything over and over. Enjoying the view, I suppose.

"I think that's enough," she says. "Let's go."

"Are you cold? We should go inside," I tell her. "Let's find a place."

She takes my hand. "In Roxbury."

"Let's stay downtown," I insist. I'm hungry for something new and different. Exciting. "You love it downtown. I've heard you say it." I lean in and catch her lips with mine. They're surprisingly warm. But she jerks away.

"Don't kiss me," she whispers. "Not here."

Not here. In the echo of it, I hear everything she's said

tonight. I hear the hesitation. She's not having a good time. She's afraid.

"Hey!" The cry comes from over my shoulder. "Let go of her!"

I spin around. Three beefy white guys are running along the harbor toward us. Two tall, one shorter. All big enough to do some damage. My heart pounds.

Instinctively I back away. From them and from her.

Sophia steps in front of me. "No. It's OK," she cries, holding up her hands.

The three men stop, circling us. They look like they might have been working on a boat all day and just stopped off to grab some brews. Strong guys.

"Are you with this nigger?" the shorter one asks.

"Yes," she says, tossing her hair to the side. "It's OK. We're just friends." It hits me all at once, the curse of "nigger" and the blessing of being claimed by Sophia.

"Looked awfully *friendly* just now," one of the tall ones says. He's not quite my height, but he's over six feet.

"I don't know what you think you saw," Sophia says. I know that voice, flirtatious and coy. The one she uses to get men to do what she wants. "But my *friend* is just walking me home."

One of the men grabs her anyway. Two fists around her biceps. Sophia screams. "You should know what happens to bitches who keep company with niggers."

I lurch forward to save her. I don't see the hand coming. Story of my life. The side of my face suddenly burns, and I see bright light. I stumble against the railing. I try to rise, to fight back, but the next thing I feel is Sophia's hands on my chest. "Are you OK?" she cries. "Did they hurt you?"

"Did they hurt *you*?" I ask, blinking up at her.

Behind her the three guys are walking off, talking and laughing. As if nothing happened.

"No. It could have been so much worse," she says. Her face is tear streaked, so I reach up to wipe it clean. Her cheeks are a sticky mess, actually. It's more than tears. They've spit on her.

"Shit," I say. "I'm sorry."

She kneels on the concrete and fusses in her purse, extracting some tissues. "It's my fault," she says. "You didn't know. I did."

She thinks I don't know some people don't like a black man with a white woman? "I'm not stupid," I snap.

Sophia sighs. "I mean, you think all of Boston is like Roxbury," she says. "Well, it's not."

I get up and pull her to her feet. Papa used to say, *When you make them angry, that's when you know you've got to keep on.* I put my arm around her as we walk back toward the car, but she shrugs me off. "You need ice on your face," she says. "It'll help with the pain."

"Yeah," I say. *Ice. That's what I need.*

My cheek stings, and the ache of it vibrates beyond the handprint. A thin layer of pain across every inch of my body, as if I can feel the very color of my skin.

I close my eyes and see images of things, clear as day, much clearer than a dream. All kinds of memories.

There are so many rules for how to be a black person, things you cannot say and places you cannot go. In Lansing there was a signpost on every road leading in from the outskirts of town: NO NEGROES AFTER DARK. I've never seen such a sign in Boston. Maybe here you're just supposed to know.

I guess I do know. It's just that all the mixing of people in Roxbury and on the Hill made me forget. Made me think the rules didn't apply in Boston. Or that I was above them.

Papa never liked those rules, either. Went out of his way to prove them wrong. I remember when I was really small, we used to live in a different house, one that was inside the city limits, even though blacks were not allowed. I don't remember much else about the house, but I remember the night it caught fire.

Smoke everywhere. In the air, by the door, at the windows—in our very bed, it seemed. Hot and dark and choking. Someone's hands on me, dragging me up, then down. Stumbling over floorboards and furniture. Scooped up into strong arms. The first breath of the cool, fresh night.

We watched the house burn from the back of the yard. Papa said members from the Black Legion—a Ku Klux Klan splinter group—came in the night, stood right outside our windows, and set the place on fire. They were angry at us for living on prime land that was supposed to be reserved for whites. But Papa had bought it fair and square.

The house burned down to the ground.

We survived. Papa got us out: all of us kids and Mom. Papa knew how to fix things, even the really bad things. But once he was gone, it seemed like nothing could ever be made right.

Who's going to protect me now? I already know; the answer is no one.

Through the night I keep my eyes open, but it doesn't help. The wood walls creak in ways they never did before. The shadows on the wall now have fingers, like ghosts.

I try not to think about missing him. Try not to wonder what he'd think of me now, a high-school dropout with a conk on my head and a white girl in my heart. What would he think of me for trying to blend into a place I don't belong? Would he say I was building my house where I wanted, the law for Negroes be damned? Isn't this what he wanted—for me to turn my back on injustice by flouting the laws created for us blacks, no matter what might happen?

Up, up, you mighty race.

Why didn't he tell me the truth back then? There's always someone trying to bring us down.

Chapter Fifteen

Boston to Harlem, summer 1942

One good thing about the war, at least for all of us down in Roxbury, was that a whole bunch of white guys decided to hurry up and enlist, which meant that they all left jobs open, and some of those slots started going to us Negroes. Jobs we probably wouldn't have had a shot at before. Compared to how it was growing up, when jobs were like unicorns, now it seems like opportunity's always knocking.

I land a new job, working on passenger trains. It's still a dishwashing slave, but it pays better, and I'm always moving. I work the Yankee Clipper route, from Boston to New York.

There was a time when I wouldn't have thought I'd ever want to leave Roxbury, for even a little while. But things are different now.

"Why don't we cool it for a while?" Sophia tells me. She says she's not upset about what happened downtown, but I feel her pulling away from me anyway. I dial her up and she'll talk to me, but when it comes to going out, it's all, "Not tonight, Red." We're down to maybe once a week now. Dancing at the Roseland. Necking in the car.

"Come inside with me," I ask her, and sometimes she comes, but she doesn't stay long. Not the way she used to. I stop calling so often; it's no fun to keep hoping, keep getting shot down. The space she filled in my days and my nights is glaringly open.

And Shorty's got this band now, trying out for paying gigs it seems like every other day. If I run around to Ella's place, to grab some dinner or whatever, all I get is an earful of what I should be doing differently with my life. As if it's not all in my head and heart already; everything Papa ever said echoing like a chorus of little sentences that float through me in his deep, disappeared voice.

Up, up, you mighty race.

The Lord has great plans for you.

You can be anything, son. You're going to preach and teach like I do, but better.

The more time that passes, the more impossible it all sounds. A mouthful of lies; things not worth thinking about or standing still for. So I'm on the move now. The train gig is where it's at.

You have to learn to walk smooth, even as the train rocks back and forth beneath you. It's a kind of balancing act. All the turns around the dance floor at the Roseland made me ready. I'm good on my feet now. Real steady.

This gig is the best slave I've ever had.

The kinds of people coming and going from Harlem make me want to get off the train and stay there. They're the hippest cats I've ever seen, in nice pressed suits, looking sophisticated. And all the ladies look downright fine. Roxbury is old news, compared to the energy and excitement radiating from the Big Apple. I write home about how I've made it to the big time, with my hot new railroad slave and all the fancy people I rub elbows with.

Philbert seems especially interested in my travel gig. Troubled by it, I guess. *How are we supposed to know where you are?* he writes. *You're moving all the time.* I never thought about it like that. I always know where my siblings are. They're in Lansing. The idea that they think about me the same way is a bit funny, but I guess it makes sense.

I pull out my old map and carefully copy the outline of the states: Massachusetts, Rhode Island, Connecticut, New York. I mark dots for all the cities we stop in and label them, then draw two thick black lines like train tracks going through. I send Philbert the drawing. *Here I am,* I write, feeling real good about it. Funnily enough, the next time I'm on the route, I imagine my brother sitting at the dining table, staring at my rough-sketched map. I imagine his finger following me up and down the eastern seaboard, hovering right over my head the whole way. It makes me strangely happy.

My favorite moment of the train ride is going over the bridge into the city. The sprawling brick buildings of Harlem are laid out like a quilt beneath us. If you have a minute to spare, you can look down through the windows past the tracks and see people walking. Sitting. Riding. Sometimes they wave up at the train cars. I'm never sure if they can actually see me, so small in my high-up window, with the sun glaring against the glass to boot. But I wave back at them anyway.

Soon they promote me from dishwasher to sandwich guy. I walk the aisles every day with a tray of sandwiches, coffee, drinks, and snacks to sell to people at their seats.

Sometimes I can spend the night in Harlem between train runs. I whip off my uniform the second I get off duty. Slap on my zoot suit and head uptown.

Harlem is all that it promised to be. Music. Art. Jazz. A kind of celebration of blackness I have never seen or experienced. At least not since the days when Mom and Papa used to gather us in the living room and tell us things that Marcus Garvey and people like him had said.

I recognize 125th Street the first time I set foot on it. The Apollo Theater marquee stands out above the crowds, always announcing some exciting show coming up. I'd seen it in a photograph in the newspaper, the day after Joe Louis knocked out Jim Braddock and laid him on the mat to become heavyweight champion.

Lansing, 1937

That day Philbert and I raced home from school to listen to the match on the radio. It was only going to be the greatest boxing match in the history of the world: our favorite, Joe Louis, going up against the heavyweight champion of the world, Jim Braddock. Head to head. In the ring. To see who would be the new heavyweight champion.

Braddock was a hero in the ring, too. They called him Cinderella Man, because he starved through the Depression, like the rest of us, but somehow fought out of the darkness to become the champion. But Joe Louis was the Brown Bomber. The best boxer to ever step into the ring, and a Negro besides. Joe Louis was going to knock Braddock right out of his glass slippers, Philbert told me. Used to be, Negro boxers weren't even allowed in the ring with whites. And now, Joe Louis was about to dominate, on the biggest stage in the sport.

"Let's go, let's go," Philbert called. "The fight's about to start!" He pounded on my shoulder blades.

"Coming," I said. We sparred as we jogged up the lane.

Philbert got in front of me, trying to cut me off. Philbert was always the better fighter; it was all I could do to keep my fists in the right place.

"I can take you," I bluffed. "I've gotten good. You haven't seen it yet, but I've gotten real good."

"Oh, right," Philbert said. "That's likely."

I spread my arms out wide. "Who are you talking to?"

Philbert took the opportunity to deck me hard in the stomach. "My dumb-as-a-rock kid brother."

I groaned, doubling over. "Give me a break, man."

He started hopping around, all fleet of foot. "I'm gonna get real good," he said. "Then I'm gonna get real big, and I'm gonna follow right behind Joe Louis."

I laughed. "Well, yeah, the place to be is behind Joe Louis. So he can knock down anybody you might have to fight."

Philbert grinned. Couldn't help himself. He darted toward me and popped me lightly in the jaw. "You lug."

I rubbed my cheek. "Don't mess with this face."

Philbert snorted. "A broken jaw would be an improvement, bro."

"Hey," I protested. We skidded into the living room and tumbled onto the rug in front of the radio. It was a few feet to the side of the fireplace and half as tall, propped up on a small wooden table. We crouched in front of it.

Philbert played with the radio dial. The static blipped and focused as the stations turned. We caught a snatch of voices. Philbert slowed and got more careful with his finger.

"... *fight we've all been waiting for* ..."

"There! Go back," I said.

"I heard it, I heard it," Philbert said. But he scrolled too far, too fast. Static again.

I batted his hands away. "Let me do it."

"I got it." He inched the dial with just the tip of his finger.

"... *in the ring now* ... *Louis* ... *Braddock* ..."

"There! There."

"Yeah, yeah," Philbert said, making the final adjustments to minimize static.

"*First round getting under way now*...."

Good. We hadn't missed much.

"*Fighters circling*.... *Braddock gets the first hit in*...."

Through the speaker, we could hear the fighters' footsteps on the pads. The *thump* and *oof*s of contact. Skin and gloves. Smacking. Connecting. Pushing off to circle again.

The radio crackled over the voices and the murmur of the crowd and the occasional *ding* of the round bell.

"*Louis pummels Braddock* ... *left, right* ... *quite a beating*. ... *Braddock pops Louis* ... *a right to the stomach*. ... *Louis down!*"

We groaned loud.

"*No, he's up, he's up! Just a knockdown, more of a stumble, really*. ... *This fight is far from over*...."

Our ears were inches from the speaker. Philbert's breath on my neck.

DING.

We sighed and pulled back. I shook out my hands. How could I be sweating this much when I wasn't even in the ring? Philbert, too, was wiping sweat off his brow. Rooting for Joe Louis just put us out of our minds. He had to win this fight. He had to. "He's going to do it," Philbert said. "Just you watch."

Every punch, every jab, every time those gloves connected, it felt like we had thrown the punch ourselves. Like we were part of it. It was like somebody out there had to be fighting. Somebody had to have his fists up, because not everyone found it so easy—or even possible.

We hung on, on edge, through eight long rounds of the fight. Then . . .

"A left to the shoulder. Right to the jaw. . . . Braddock stumbles. Braddock's down! Braddock's down!"

We cheered. But briefly, silencing ourselves so we didn't miss anything. *"And the count is up. Two . . . three . . . four . . ."*

I held my breath. Next to me, Philbert moved his arms, replaying the fight. I'm sure he was playing Louis in his mind. Jab. Jab. Uppercut. Watch the other man fall. The white man.

"Braddock is stirring. . . ."

My fingers dug into the matted edges of the rug. Hold on. Hold on.

"Five . . . six . . . seven . . ."

Please. Please.

"Down for the count! Louis wins! Joe Louis is the heavy-weight champion of the world. Louis wins! Louis wins!"

We leaped up, screaming. "Louis wins! Louis wins!"

The announcement continued, but it didn't matter what anyone said after that. Victory! Louis wins!

Never mind that I couldn't dance to save my life. I was jivin'. We all were. A victory for Joe Louis was a victory for all of us.

In the morning, Philbert and I ran down to the news-stand to see the coverage. There was a big photo of Harlem people, cheering Louis's victory, on 125th Street that night. Right in front of the Apollo Theater.

Harlem, 1942

Five years later, and now I'm standing in that very spot. If that photo were taken today, I'd be in it. The thought astounds me.

When it's time to leave the city for a northbound run, it hurts to look out the train window. I can barely stomach the overwhelming longing I feel to return there. Like a beacon tugging in a way I haven't felt since . . . I don't remember ever feeling this way about a place. Like it's gonna be home.

* * *

Sophia calls me up one night, my night off from the train. "I miss you, baby," she croons. I hear her voice, and I know. She still has my heart, sure enough.

"I know I haven't called in a while," I say. "I've been busy."

"I could come over, if you want," she offers. "I really miss you."

"You wanna go out?" I ask.

"I just want to see you," she whispers. It makes my heart beat special.

"Well, come on, then."

She's in my arms like a flash. Like old times. "Let's not be apart anymore," she says.

"It was your idea," I remind her. *I would have loved you forever, through anything.*

"I'm sorry," she says. "That night . . . it really scared me, you know? But I do love you."

"I love you, too." Like a trapdoor. Like a box. Once you're in, you're in.

"I just want . . ." she starts. "Let's try to forget it ever happened, all right? Some people are just . . . Let's try to forget about them."

"OK." I don't see any reason to tell her that I have some experience with putting people out of my mind. You can try to forget, but some things get written on you anyway.

I light us a reefer, and we lie in bed passing it back and forth. "You should come with me to Harlem sometime," I tell her. "You'd love it there."

"Maybe sometime," she says.

"It's like Roxbury, but . . . more," I explain. "It's amazing."

She rolls over me, spreading herself against my chest. "People like us, if we're going to be together, we have to keep it to ourselves, you know?"

"I know." It just isn't how I wanted it to be. That's, I guess, what hurts. I convinced myself it was different. That we could be different. Or, at least, I could. Somehow, I got to believing that because Sophia loves me, we are the same. But I'm not like my mom, so light-skinned that a conk does the trick and you can go incognito. I'm a nigger if ever there was one. And everyone I try to love gets taken away because of it.

Chapter Sixteen

Harlem, fall 1942

The Savoy Ballroom is massive, even compared to the Roseland back in Boston: an expanse of waxed dance floor positively stuffed with Lindy Hoppers dancing elbow to elbow. Every one of them looks classy, dressed to the nines. I'm going to need something more classic than my snappy sharkskin zoot. A better hat maybe. And some of the newfangled, colorful shoes the guys are wearing, called Florsheims.

Lionel Hampton is playing, and the place is jiving and hopping. I'm lost in a swirl of pretty women, and I go on ahead and dance with as many as I can.

Then the singer comes out.

First we just hear finger snaps from out of the deep black stage. Then the fresh soft strains of jazz blues, like waking up from a long sleep. The single tone draws itself out like the stretching of arms. A ripple of notes, smoothly dissonant, with the *ch-ch-ch, ch-ch-ch* of sticks on cymbals. A cool blue spotlight captures swirling dust like visible chords. She steps into the light, beautiful and dark as ebony.

We should clap, I think. But no one moves to. The spell is already woven. She croons the lyrics. Her hips roll seductively in the tight blue-sequined dress. Singing the blues, yeah. Sing it. Swing it. My eyes keep wandering to the smooth brown skin of her leg, revealed by the slit in her dress that goes up to mid-thigh. The full sleeves glitter with each ripple of her arms. It's like she's the conductor and every sound in the air is part of her symphony.

It's smoky. It's wonderful. I'm transfixed.

At the Roseland, I'd seen about every hot band, every singer with a name to know. It all astonished me for a while, sure, but then it became part of the scene. I thought I was beyond being so impressed. So captivated.

I was right about Harlem. This is where I need to be.

Every chance I get to stay in Harlem, I do. There's always something happening.

Sometimes I just walk the streets and take it all in. The rough-and-tumble street life has an energy about it that's unlike anything else.

At a bar called Small's Paradise, I meet these guys who call themselves hustlers. Straight up. No pretense, which is funny since all they do outside these doors is pretend. The sly looks in their eyes remind me of Fat Frankie, hustling me out of my pocket money—only these Harlem cats are classy. They're fine, clean guys in straight, pressed suits—well-off cats who earned their bank on the slant. Running numbers, pimping ladies, slinging reefer, moving questionable products into the hands of questionable people. A guy called Sammy the Pimp makes a show of himself from time to time, telling stories about the great hustles of his day, which seems to be more or less today. There are old-timers, too, like Frisky and Sal, who've already made their bank and are basically retired. Not that you ever really give up the hustle, it seems, but they delegate certain activities to young hungry up-and-comers my age. Seventeen's old enough to grab a stake in something, sure enough. I just gotta find the right opportunity.

A lot of musicians hang out at the Braddock Hotel. Famous ones, like Lionel Hampton himself, great jazz artists like Duke Ellington, and many other familiar faces from back at the Roseland. Shorty would have been out of his mind, rubbing elbows with these guys, up close, just sitting around the bar. I hang with some of Lionel's band, a bassist and a drummer, and I'd say there aren't two better guys in all of Harlem to smoke reefer with.

I wake up every morning, buzzed and breathless, reminding myself that the night before wasn't a dream. I really have hustler friends and jazz musician friends—I'm becoming part of the two corners of Harlem that fascinate me most.

Getting into the street life is easy. I can just relax. Drink. Smoke. Walk around all loose. Speak my mind.

I have to keep showing up for work, or else I'd lose my constant rides down to Harlem, but selling snacks in the aisles comes easy. Like I'd learned way back as a shoe shine and behind the counter at Townsend's—with white people, good tips come if you entertain them. Snap that rag real loud. Do a little dance. Grin and act all cheerful. Pour some milk into their coffee with a flourish. Happy to serve.

Easier than pie. I can show up drunk or high from the night before and still manage. In fact, it makes it better. Makes the bowing and the scraping easier to tolerate. *"Yes, sir." "Thank you, sir." "Can I get you anything else, sir?"* A chorus of fake politeness, all the things I've grown to hate about trying to fit into that world. The raw brittle language of the streets makes a hell of a lot more sense to me. *"Whadda ya want?" "Here ya go." "Just take it, why don't ya?" "Gimme two bucks (and shove it)."* That feels better. Much better.

The train steward, my supervisor, calls me over one day during the southbound run. "Red, we're getting some complaints about you."

"Complaints?" I follow him back into the commissary, where he sits in a booth and motions me to sit across from him. He's a white guy, kinda scrawny. His uniform is always loose.

"Several customers have commented on your rudeness today."

"Is that so?"

"Now, Red," the steward says. "I think you know what I'm talking about."

Sure, I do. But that doesn't mean I'm going to make it easy for him.

"You've been my best salesman," he continues. "I think you like the job, and you're good at it."

I nod.

"You need to be more careful with your words, all right?" He looks at me, real earnest.

"Sure, yeah, all right." I give him a big grin, like I'm supposed to do with the passengers. "Yes, sir. Right away, sir. I'll take care of it, sir."

"I knew I could count on you." He smiles. Doesn't even realize I'm playing him, hard. It's just what white guys want to hear.

He sighs. Letting the air out like that makes him even smaller. He smacks the table, as if to say I was done and dealt with. "Great," he says. "Keep up the good work."

That heats me more than the whole conversation up until then. Just how small he is and still trying to tell me how to be. Maybe the reefer buzz I'm carrying doesn't help, but the talking-to just makes me want to beat on someone.

I get up from the table and walk away from him before

I say something stupid and get myself into trouble. He doesn't know. He's never walked these aisles. He just sits there in the back watching everybody else work. And why didn't he go off and join the army, like everyone else white who used to work here? Too small? Too weak? Too chicken?

I strap on my sandwich tray and start off on my rounds. Rude? These white assholes are the rude ones. Sticking their big long feet into the aisle and not even moving them when I walk through. I haven't fallen over yet, but I've tripped on them enough times to hate the way the men look at me afterward. Like I'd kicked them on purpose. I know what I'm supposed to say. *"Sorry, sir. Did I hurt you? Take a coffee, on the house."* It's enough to make me wish I really had kicked them on purpose. Maybe I oughta start doing that. Maybe it would wake them up to the kind of jackasses they're being. Walk down the aisle and kick every one of them as I pass by.

I push it down, though. I don't want to lose the job.

"Sandwiches, snacks, coffee," I call out as I walk the aisle. "Ham and cheese, cake and ice cream. Anything you're looking for."

My foot flops against something, and I stumble. Some asshole's foot is in my path. I've nearly tripped. Again.

The thing is, with the tray strapped around my neck, balanced against my middle and sticking out front, I can't really see where I'm stepping. I can see down the aisle, but by the time I get there, they've moved.

I didn't do it on purpose. I swear.

I back up far enough to see who the foot belongs to. Open my mouth to say the things I'm supposed to. *"Sorry, sir. Can I help you, sir?"* But nothing comes out. My mind stalls, steaming mad, as my gaze lands on a long booted leg extended across the aisle. No way he didn't see me coming.

The guy looks up at me. "Clumsy nigger," he says. "What do you have to say for yourself?"

I stand, silent. Anything I say is going to come out in red-hot rage.

Guy gets up. He's an army man, with some kind of big coat on. Hefty guy. Not as tall as me; not many people are. But he's as thick as a bull.

And drunk. He's bobbing and weaving, looking none too steady on his feet above the rocking of the train. His scrubbed-looking cheeks are bright red, his pink eyes half focused and blinking.

"I'm about to fight you, nigger," he says. "What are you going to do?"

I'm gonna bust your ass, that's what I'm gonna do! My mind screams it.

He puts his fists up. I've got the sandwich tray strapped to me, and I'm thinking.

Thinking, *Gotta get out of this situation.* This guy is nuts. I try to calm myself down off the edge. Thinking, *Just get past him. Finish your route.* Thinking of all the times I've seen fists flying at me, and how I always end up flat on the ground.

Philbert, trying to teach me. Richie Dixon, all in fun. Those guys at the dock, dead serious.

"What are you gonna do, nigger?" he repeats. Dead serious.

I'm going to get fired for this. This asshole is going to cost me everything. My eyes narrow. I try to hold on to it—the part of me that's calm and sober and willing to walk away.

"I didn't mean anything by it," I say. "Really."

"I'm coming for you." He takes a lurching step forward. Every face in the train car is pointed at us. A couple dozen white guys are about to watch me get handed my own ass.

Fight with your words, Malcolm, Papa's voice says.

"You gotta take off your coat," I suggest, stalling for time. "How am I supposed to fight you wearing that? You can't even get your arms up."

Guy pauses. Looks down. Shrugs himself out of the coat. Tosses it on his seat. Under the big coat, he's wearing a serviceman's jacket.

"Really?" I say. "In your army jacket? All right, but I hate to get your blood on it."

Guy starts pulling his arms out of his sleeves. He stumbles to the side with the momentum of the train. Other guys in the seats around us start grinning.

Now he's standing there in his white jersey under-shirt. I'm feeling like I'm on a roll. I shrug. Tell him, "OK. That one's at least replaceable."

I didn't think it would happen. But now the guy's all

confused, twisting and turning and rocking in the aisle. He pulls the undershirt up out of his belt and tugs it over his head, exposing his bare furry chest to the entire train. He holds the cloth high, triumphant, and charges toward me, then stalls. Looks down, like he's realizing just now that he's half naked.

The entire train car erupts in laughter. I try not to grin too hard myself. Don't want to make it too obvious that I outsmarted him.

One of his buddies steps up and gets the guy to sit back in his seat. He puts his clothes back on, cheeks even redder than they had been. I have all kinds of names for him in my head, but I keep them to myself. Keep moving along my route.

"Sandwiches, coffee, ice cream," I hawk.

As I make my way past the big guy through the train car, I sell a whole bunch of sandwiches. Best tips I've ever gotten on the Yankee Clipper. The steward might not be too happy about the result, but at least I'm watching what I say.

At the Braddock Hotel, I sit down beside a girl called Jean, a hopeful lounge singer. Our paths have crossed before. Sometimes she's good for a little company in the evenings. I like her well enough, and she takes my mind off Sophia and the distance between us.

"Look," Jean says. "That's Billie Holiday."

Sure enough, the famous jazz singer is sitting at the

bar. "I've seen her here before," I say, real casual. Trying to sound impressive.

"She's singing at the Cotton Club tonight." Jean looks at me through her lashes, on the slant.

"You want to go?" I can pick up a cue as well as the next guy.

"Well, sure," she answers.

So I take her on down there, and we have a few drinks and share a tray of snacks while Billie's voice floats its magic over the room.

I try to catch the waiter to bring another round, but he disappears into the back just as I signal to him. The lights click down. The room plunges into all black.

A single spotlight comes up. Billie's smooth, wide face is all that can be seen. It seems like she's wiped the rouge from her lips. Or maybe it's an effect of the stark white light, illuminating just her face. Her eyes are closed.

Slight rustles of anticipation among the crowd. The first mournful strains squeeze out. She's known for this song, "Strange Fruit." It's a slow, haunting melody about the horror and the senselessness of lynching innocent Negroes. She sings of the swinging bodies, how they hang among the branches like unnatural, disturbing fruit. Negro men, women, and children hanging from the tree limbs, blowing in the wind.

Amid her words, I'm caught in a flashback, to the image of a body dangling from a tree in rural Pennsylvania.

Avert your eyes, son.

I avert them now. Gaze off into the darkness. The ache and the beauty of Billie's words captivate me, despite the ugly images they bring to mind.

When the song ends, Billie strides off the stage in the dark. She doesn't return for a bow or a curtain call or an encore.

We all sit in motionless silence. Stunned by the power of her words and the haunting melody. So spare. So stark.

After a moment, the audience stirs enough to clap. Light taps at first, then full-fledged stomping and whooping. The cheers go on, rousing, hoping to urge Billie back for just one more song. But the stage stays dark.

Got to have some reefer after that. A little whiskey. Something to counteract the shakes and the cold. The song stays with me through the night. It evokes, really evokes, the lynched body I saw. The lifeless bodies Billie sang about. Hanging there, blowing in the wind. The song never says why they were lynched. There is no why. What did they do? Blackness is reason enough.

It was some time ago, my bus ride through the night, when the sun came up to that dreadful sight. But at the moment it doesn't seem like that long ago. Certainly not two whole years. It seems like yesterday. I can feel the rough sleeve of that cropped green suit, like an emblem of the green boy wearing it.

Look at me then. Look at me now. How far I have come.

The music starts up again, off a record this time, and couples take to the floor. "You wanna dance?" I say to the girl I'm with. Jean. The whiskey is flowing, and I'm definitely in the mood to just shake off my thoughts and let my body loose.

She shrugs. "Sounds good."

So I take her hand and lead her right to the middle of things. I'm no sideline dancer anymore. I want people to see my moves, my skills. And for the first time in . . . maybe ever, I'm glad it's not Sophia with me tonight. I don't know if I could shake that song off so easy if I had to look into her beautiful white face and remember what almost happened to us. As it is, I throw back drink after drink to take the edge off.

We party till they close the place down, and we find ourselves stumbling into the streets, half out of our minds on reefer and drink.

Soon enough we're kissing in the parking lot, down the block from the place I'm staying. I want to take her up for the night, but she's thinking about calling it time to go home. Luckily her pad is close by, so I start to walk her, but I've still got my moves going, because the night's not over till it's over.

I lean her against a railing, in front of somebody's brownstone stairs. "How much farther?"

Turns out it's her place we're in front of. That would

be as good as mine, so I start walking her up the stairs.

Jean takes my hand. "Billie was amazing tonight, don't you think?"

"Sure, sure." But my mind is on the feel of Jean, soft and right up against me.

"The way she walked off, in the dark."

It's not happening tonight. So I push her away. "You're home, right?" I tell her. "And you're not asking me up?" My tone is sandpaper rough. All this time, trying to get away from the heaviness. The song. The picture. She wants to bring me back. I ain't going back.

"Aww, Red," she whines. "You know I'm not like that."

She tries to kiss at me again, but there's only so much that a guy can take. "Catch you later," I say. Jog down the steps. Light a reefer for the walk back to the rooming house. I suck down the smoke, skip on faster, like I can outrun it. Knowing that the road behind me is littered with strange fruit. In the trees. By the harbor. On the tracks.

There's some little voice in my head. *Just buzz it off, man. Just buzz it off.*

I turn up my collar and scoot along as fast as I can.

I carry that high as long as I can, through the night and into the morning, till the voices and the image and the music fade to a dull buzz in the background. I show up to work maybe more buzzed than I've ever been. This slave's easy. I can do it in my sleep.

We're halfway back up to Boston. I stand out on the

tailgate at the back of the train during my ten-minute break, grabbing a bit of fresh air to clear my head and keep awake.

"Do I smell marijuana?" the train steward says when I come back in.

I usually have a reefer in my pocket, but I don't make a habit of lighting up on the job. It must just be wafting off me from earlier.

The steward sniffs the air. "Have you been smoking, Red?" Looks me close in the eye. "Are you high?"

"I'm fine," I tell him. But there's no fooling him. Not anymore.

"I can't keep you on if it's going to be like this," he says. "You're shirking. Have been for a while now."

"Really, I'm fine." Little stabs of terror. Without the train, I'd be stuck in Boston again. No trips to Harlem.

"You're fired, Red," the steward says.

"I don't need this slave," I snap, to cover the sting. I lie down in the back of the commissary—I figure they aren't going to pay me for the end of this shift, anyway—and grab some shut-eye.

When the train rolls up in Boston and I have to get off for the last time, that's when it really starts to hit me. No train. No Harlem. No Braddock, no Small's, no Cotton Club, no Savoy. None of it.

I head home to Shorty's place. Maybe if we can go someplace together, it'll be like old times. Maybe he can shake things up and remind me how much fun Roxbury can be. But when I get to the house, Shorty's already out.

I smoke and I smoke, and I dial Sophia. Her phone rings without an answer, and I wonder if she's out dancing with some other Negro.

I don't want to stay here; I want to pack up. Hit the road. If I skip a day playing numbers—or maybe a zoot payment or two—I can scrape up a train fare. Harlem's where it's at, for sure. I can find a new gig there. No problem.

I flip through my small pile of mail. Open the most recent letter from Philbert. I squint through the smoke haze to catch every word. Then I hold it to my chest as if I can pull it into me. As if maybe it can fill this gaping space I feel. The last line stands out to me like a directive.

Get on a bus, Malcolm. Come home.

Chapter Seventeen

Lansing, December 1942

The bus rolls onto Lansing soil, and I don't feel the tug I was expecting. No measure of longing, no hint that this is a place I've been, a place I could've stayed, a place that might have missed me. It's just a road.

The bus shudders to a stop, and I take up my bag and look out at the car, where my brother and sister stand waving. I have a vision of the day I left, all of us hugging awkwardly, not able to imagine being apart for more than days.

I almost laugh aloud. So much has changed.

I jump off the bus and rush straight toward them. They won't know me to come running, I figure. My conk. My zoot. The hip new cat that is me.

"Malcolm?" Hilda says. She fingers my hair right off. I'd sent them a picture right away, after my conk, posing in the zoot. But it still must be a surprise to see it in person. "What have you done to yourself?" When her face furrows in disapproval, she really looks like Mom.

Philbert claps me on the shoulder. His expression, too, is a study in unrecognition. "Long time," he says, and draws me into a hug.

They haven't changed, but everything else is smaller. The bus station. The houses we go by. The whole of downtown Lansing passes in a moment. How had this place ever felt big enough?

Philbert takes me up to see Mom in Kalamazoo. It's still a long ride—it feels even longer than the bus to Boston. It's like we're on a slow-motion train or one that's moving backward, into fog, against track warnings.

"When did you learn to drive?" I ask Philbert.

"When did you buy that getup?" he answers, glancing at my sharkskin zoot.

"Soon as it hit the rack," I declare, feeling proud. "And I still got credit to spare."

Philbert sucks in his breath like I just said a curse word, which I actually have been somewhat careful not to do in front of him. I don't need a lecture. For a second it feels like he's going to launch into one. But he only sighs.

After a minute's silence, he goes, "I don't know when I learned to drive. Sometime." He taps the wheel. "It's fun. Want me to teach you?"

Underneath it I hear him saying more. Something about how we would have learned together if I was here. Something about how even though we're driving on the same road now, it isn't enough.

"Naw," I say. "I know how." Bald-faced lie. It just rises up and comes out. Unexpected. I'm the city guy. My country brother's not supposed to have to school me. In anything.

"You still boxing?" I ask. I know from the letters that he is. That's his thing. Talking about it makes me feel better about putting him off on the driving thing. Didn't matter how good he got; he never could teach me boxing. None of his skills ever rubbed off. Why would he be able to teach me to drive?

Philbert parks out front of the hospital. We go in to see Mom. I catch sight of her down the hall as we're walking in.

She looks so different from how I see her in my mind. How I remember her. So very, very small. I can't help the gasp. It comes out loud.

"She's fragile," Philbert tells me. "Just know that."

I can't quite wrap my head around that. After everything, what I know is how strong Mom is.

She hugs me, but there's nothing there. No sense of Mom as she should be. Instead of holding me tight and safe, her arms are porous. Like a drain, swirling me. Sucking me dry.

She pets my skin like it's foreign to her. "How are you?" I ask, but she doesn't give an answer.

We sit with her and talk awhile. I tell her about Boston and Harlem, making my exploits out to sound like I've taken the whole eastern seaboard by storm. Mom nods along and smiles, but she seems to me only partly there. I can't believe how much her time in this place has diminished her.

As we go, I kiss her cheek, realizing how brought down by this I really am. Don't want to sit here and think about the warm way she used to smell, or how soft the arms were that used to hold me. Don't like how my tongue starts longing for chicken and gravy the way she used to cook it in the old days. The homemade biscuits she'd make from scratch, while telling us great stories of when we were kings and queens ruling the lands, running free. I downright hate the bland green flavor of dandelion broth, the taste of which rises in my mouth without warning.

I especially don't like how faded she seems, even outside of the pushed-back corner of my mind where she resides. She's not in my mind now—she's right in front of me, and yet I miss her more than ever.

The Swerlins' house looks the same as always. Not a thing changed, as far as I can see.

I knock, and Mrs. Swerlin answers the door. I'm a

surprise guest. She looks just as I remember her. Her big arms sway, loose, and her mouth pokes out into a small O.

"Hi, Mrs. Swerlin."

"Malcolm Little?" she says. "I barely recognize you."

"I got a new look," I tell her, brushing my collar and turning sharp.

She's nervous. Not really glad to see me. Why did I even come here? I don't know. I'm visiting the old haunts, making the circuit, and she's part of it. The only place I didn't try to go was the old house. Wilfred's away at school now, and Hilda's taking care of the rest of our family. I didn't suppose there would be anything to see there.

Mrs. Swerlin invites me inside. She looks at me like I'm a foreign object, which strikes me as both the same and different from how it used to be.

I remember how I used to walk from room to room in that house, people talking about me like they couldn't see I was there. Like I didn't matter. I remember coming in to dinner the first night and hearing one of the other boys say, "Neat. We've got a nigger now." It wasn't a mean voice, just blandly matter-of-fact. Like I was a mascot or some kind of prize. I sat down at the table that night feeling practically invisible.

It's a far cry from how I am now. Zoot suit bagging around my limbs. Loud street jargon flying. With my slick-top conk in her face. She's seeing me now.

* * *

I stand on the streetcar tracks, looking up and down to make sure nothing's coming. Maybe this is the very spot where it happened. I don't know. No one ever told me the specifics. I look at the tracks and the pavement and the way they go together, and it sinks in deeper than it ever has before.

No one falls in front of a streetcar. Especially not Papa, so sure on his feet. Why would anyone ever believe it was an accident?

Sophia would call this morbid thinking. She knows about Papa now. Sometimes, when I'm high, things slip out. Usually right when I'm feeling high enough not to have to think or to remember.

It's a cold world, she says. *That's why we have to keep each other warm.*

I don't want to be away from her. I don't know why I've come back here. Everything I want is ahead of me. No sense holding on to what's behind.

The streetcar's coming now. I kneel in the space between the tracks and press my hand against the ground. Feel the rumble in the road. Hear the bells ringing. Think: *Anyone who had fallen would move right about now.* Think: *Anyone even close enough to the tracks to fall on them would move right about now.* Think: *His last sensation.* Think: *I've tried so hard not to touch this.*

But here I am.

I step out of the way with time to spare. Plenty of time. Keep on walking. Don't look back.

The farther I get, the harder it is to hear him. The less my fingers vibrate, the quieter my heart.

I never rode the streetcars in Lansing again after Papa died. I'm not about to start now. But that rumble is familiar. Working my train slave this past year, I felt that rumble all the time. Maybe it was never destined to work out. I should have realized that no train slave would suit me long term. Trains run on tracks, too.

There's a good bar near where Philbert works. He agreed to meet me there, though he didn't like the idea. They have pool in the back, which I'm not in the mood for. I just wait there for him, taking down shots of whiskey and whatever they offer me that's cheap. They've got something called a pocket-friendly pint, and so in between the shots, I sip this dark, bitter brew.

It's good enough. I try to pretend I'm in the South Side Tavern or someplace down in Harlem. They're pumping a bit of jazz from time to time, which helps.

Philbert arrives, takes stock of my table of glasses. "How long have you been here?" he says.

"Not long." I motion for another round. Point to my brother to include him in the mix. I can buy him a drink or two and feel like a big spender, since everything's a little bit less around here. It's no different from scoring a bottle at the corner store or some reefer from the street. One night's high, on Red. 'Cause that's what brothers do.

Philbert takes a seat at the bar stool across from me. "What are you doing?"

"Feeling good."

He toys with the edge of an empty glass. "You know, you could hang around here in Lansing for a while." It feels like a sharp change of subject.

"Not likely," I tell him.

"Why not?"

I snort into the pint of beer. "In this hick town? Please." I offer some of my beer to him.

My brother says, "I don't drink."

More drinks for me. I guzzle it down. It's too hard to be here. Too hard to look back. It feels like looking in a mirror and not liking what you see. A cracked mirror, to boot.

"You're different," Philbert says.

"Everything's different," I answer.

"You don't have time for your hick family anymore?" He lowers his chin like *Aww, shucks.*

"Shit," I tell him. "You don't have to be a hick if you don't want to be. You can go anywhere."

Philbert shakes his head. "There's nothing out there for me."

"Everything's out there. Whatever you want."

"I sure don't want to end up like you," he says.

That slices. "You wish you could be like me." I puff up my chest. "They call me 'Red.' I run things over there."

"I'll bet." There's bitterness there. And distance. Layers of frustration and anger. The silence hangs between us, empty of all things good.

We glare at each other. In a second, maybe, he'll lunge at me. We'll be tussling on the floor like six-year-olds. My heart beats faster, waiting. Waiting.

Philbert and I have fought a thousand times. Hell, back in the day, we would be whaling on each other a dozen times a week. But it was always in fun. Always clear that we were on the same side, no questions asked, out in the real world. This feels like we're no longer with each other; we're against each other. And that punch hits deeper than any of the fists I've ever felt on me.

Slowly I reach for my wallet. Lay out some bills. Enough to cover the cost of the drinks plus tip—not too much, but enough to look like a big spender. I even kind of fan the bills out. Like a calling card or some nonsense.

Outside, I turn around swinging. Philbert's ready. He has his hands up and blocks me. Gives me a body blow that sets me back a few paces. I jog in place. He circles.

"Really?" he says. "We're going to do this? You know I'm gonna smoke you."

"Maybe I got better."

Philbert just smiles. Throws a couple punches. I don't even see from where, but I feel it. Shoulder. Hip. Jaw. My fists are flying, too, but I can't even touch him.

In an instant, it isn't a fight anymore.

I drop my hands and laugh. Seems easiest. "Hell. You still got it."

"You still don't." Philbert claps the side of my neck. Kind of hugs me to him from the side. "So don't start anything."

This is how we always were together, but it feels different now. I hate it. Here I am in my zoot suit, thinking how country everybody looks compared to me. Thinking, *How small is this place that I came from, and how'd I get so big that I can't fit?*

We walk back inside.

"I still don't get it," he says. "Why you went away. How you turned into . . . whatever this is."

"Why're you talking like that?" I ask him. "I'm here now."

As if on cue, the barkeep walks up to our table with my next round: a beer and two shot glasses of whiskey.

"No, you're not," Philbert says quietly, staring at the libations in front of me.

I raise one shot in a mock salute. "We're still family."

Philbert acknowledges my comment with a nod. "We're always going to be family, Malcolm."

Doesn't feel like it right now. I down the two shots of whiskey. "I wrote you." Maybe he needs reminding. "I wrote you all the time."

"I know," Philbert answers. "I'm talking about more than that."

"What?"

"The way you're dressed. Your attitude. Do people really behave this way out East?"

Philbert can't understand what it's like. His stare, so heavy with judgment.

"Lay off me."

"Why don't you just come home?" he repeats.

It's all I can do not to laugh. "Home?" The word echoes, like the empty cavern it is. "What does that even mean?"

Sounds to me like a thing long buried. Sounds to me like wooden planks someone kicked in, on a porch I used to walk.

"Forget it," Philbert says. And the door closes on a thing he could see that I couldn't. Some image of home, I guess. *"Forget it," he says? I'm doing my best.*

That night we gather for dinner. Hilda cooks a familiar meal, and the whole house smells like our childhood. So strange, to sit around the table and feel like everything and nothing has changed all at once.

We eat the chicken and vegetable stew—Mom's recipe—and everyone talks and laughs like it's the good old days. Only difference is I smoked a reefer before I came in here to take the edge off and keep the memories at bay.

Reginald tells of some traveling he's done, but I rival it all with stories of Roxbury nightlife, not to mention my recent forays into Harlem. I don't hold back. I want them to be impressed by my adventures, but I get a different kind of reaction.

"You didn't really sell marijuana cigarettes at the Roseland, did you, Malcolm?" Yvonne says, her eyes wide. Sure, I did.

I tell them about Sophia. Wouldn't any guy be proud to squire a fine-looking woman like her?

"You date a white woman?" Hilda asks. "What happened to that nice pretty Negro girl you wrote me about? Laura?"

"That's dangerous, Malcolm," says Reginald. "What if you're seen by the wrong people? You know what can happen!"

"No, it's cool," I tell him. "Lots of people do it." I don't mention that night on the docks.

Next I talk about the train work and how good I got at keeping on my feet, even wasted. "You were using drugs?" Wilfred says, his lips pursed in disapproval. "No wonder you got fired."

I can't take it. I stop trying to tell them what's what. They don't know what it takes to get by in the city. They haven't been where I've been. They can't understand.

Once I shut my mouth, the others take over. They talk, real familiar, about Wilfred's new job and how well Wesley's doing in school and the girl Philbert's probably going to marry. Every story is good, every story is new to me, but they go back and forth like it's normal to just be chatting. No one's trying to impress anyone, except me, and it isn't even working.

"Did you put a ham hock in this stew?" I ask Hilda, to change the subject. "It tastes amazing."

"We don't eat pork, Malcolm," Hilda chides. "You know that."

"Shoot. You don't know what you're missing." I lick my lips. "Pork is delicious."

My siblings pause their laughter to look at me. *"Mmm, mmm,"* I groan. "Bacon. Ham. Sausage. You should try it sometime." Mom's not around to scold me. I can eat whatever I want.

The others glance around, unsure what to say. I'm making them uncomfortable. Good.

"This chicken is delicious on its own," Reginald says.

"Yeah," I agree, letting them relax again. But the taste brings back a few too many memories. It's almost like it used to be, in the long-ago days, in the old house. Almost.

We're grown in some ways. I'm seventeen and living on my own. Wilfred, Hilda, and Philbert are on their own, too. Reginald and Yvonne look so different now; just in these two years they've become teenagers. But the youngest, Wesley and Robert, are still very much children. If we walked down the street together we'd probably look like a family—Wilfred as the father, Hilda the mother, with all these children. To look at us, to listen to us laughing, you'd think we had it perfect. But our circle is incomplete.

Chapter Eighteen

Boston, March 1943

Staying in Michigan is out of the question. I hop the first bus back to Boston. I pick up the train connection in Toledo. It gets me home much faster than the old bus route, which takes the back roads and stops in every small town.

I feel better almost immediately. The old rough streets that love me welcome me back. Back to Roxbury, hanging with Shorty and Sophia. Back to the worlds of Lindy, reefer, and jazz.

Being in Roxbury is better, but it isn't quite enough. Everywhere I turn, things pop up. A fruit vendor dressed up in a big apple suit. A new tune popular around the

Roseland called the "Harlem Hustle." A magazine advertisement with a picture of the Empire State Building.

The siren call of Harlem is too loud. I can't ignore it.

"You're leaving?" Sophia pouts. She rolls onto my stomach, trapping me beneath her supple warmth.

"You can come visit me," I promise. "As often as you want."

I'm not sure what to make of this sudden bout of closeness. We've been mostly apart for months now, because that's the way she wanted it. My brown skin, which she says she loves, suddenly became too brown for her to handle, I guess.

Well, I'm still brown.

"You won't go," Sophia whispers. "Not really. You don't want to be without this." Her mouth takes hold of mine. I'm used to leaping at her beck and call. She's right about what I want—but only half right.

I can always get a girl. They flock to me. They call me good-looking. I know how to dance. And my mother sure enough taught me how to treat a lady right. I do want Sophia, but I can't have her completely, and there are other things I desire.

It's her turn to want.

She kisses me deeper, and I almost change my mind. When we lie like this and I can feel her against me, I don't want to ever move, or leave, or think, or act.

But she won't stay. So I can't, either.

241

Shorty's more matter-of-fact about it. "I'm not gonna save your room," he tells me. "I gotta make rent."

"I'll miss you, too, buddy," I say, making a face at him.

Shorty grins, but there's a sadness behind it, like he really will miss me. "Just want to make sure you're serious."

"Yeah," I tell him. "It feels right to go there."

"Hey," he says with a shrug. "Then you gotta follow that."

"Come and visit," I tell him. "Trust me. Harlem is the cat's meow."

We slap skin. "You always got a couch to crash on here in Roxbury, OK?"

"Likewise," I assure him. "Soon as I've got a place."

Ella can't understand it. "What's wrong with here?" she asks. "You're doing just fine here, aren't you?"

"Yeah, I guess," I say. "But Harlem's so . . ."

"I know. You want the big city and the lights." She sighs. "I suppose I started you on that. Bringing you here."

True enough. But Roxbury, Sugar Hill, and Boston aren't where the action is anymore.

Ella reaches over and rests a hand on my arm. "You could achieve so much," she insists. "The minute you stop going down the Hill, into whatever it is you do there."

I shrug. She's like a broken record, playing Papa's old tune. The same damn story.

"Why can't you see how intelligent you are? You could

do anything. Right here in Boston. You could have every-thing you ever wanted."

I find the volume knob in my mind and turn her down. I don't have to hear it. I'm my own man now.

I stir in my seat. Don't even want to be sitting. Want to walk out the door so fast . . . but Ella has been good to me. She's blood and kin and the closest thing to home, yet it's making me crazy to stay. She radiates this dark-black pride, but not the way I want it. All that stuff she's saying, she's just trying to hold me back. Keep up the lies and keep me in my place. But I'm my own man now.

"I like it there," I say. "I was born for Harlem."

I simply know it to be true. Everything I've dreamed of and imagined is right there in the New York City skyline. There's a me-size slot waiting somewhere in the streets of Harlem. I can feel it. Calling me.

Harlem, 1943

Soon as my feet hit the ground in Harlem, I start making the rounds. Stop by the Braddock Hotel to see which musi-cians happen to be in town. Swing by Small's Paradise, fold myself in among the hustlers there.

On the road in between, everything I see is like a vision. There's new magic in every sidewalk crack, in the traffic rush, in the lurch of beggars on the corner. Every piece of this world is fresh and exciting. And unlike before, I'm here to stay. I never have to leave.

Small's Paradise is the place to be, I think. I love the worn wood walls and the low light, and the quiet old men who sit around the bar in their nice pressed suits and talk about their street days.

The high wooden bar forms one long *L* down the length of the room. The leather covers on the round bar stools are worn to tearing from use.

"Hey, Red, long time no see," says the bartender. "Where've you been?"

"Out of town," I answer. "But I'm back now."

I let him know I'm looking for a slave.

"We've got a waiter gig open," he says. "Talk to Charlie."

Charlie Small runs Small's Paradise.

"Really?" I say. That would be perfect. I can't imagine a better place to work than my favorite place in all of Harlem to hang out.

The bartender nods me toward the back. I walk into Charlie's office. Walk out five minutes later with a freshly minted slave.

Working at Small's is a dream come true. All the hustles and the talk and the suits and the laughter. Now I'm not just stopping by, watching it all happen; I'm a part of it.

The old hustlers sit around the bar, and I bring them food from the kitchen.

Even though all the regulars are hard-core old-time hustlers, Small's carries on as an upstanding, respectable place. People from downtown stop in for a drink. White people. Out-of-town people. Servicemen, especially. All of them thinking that this is the safe place in Harlem. Clean and straight up. Meanwhile they're sitting across the bar from the biggest-known pimps and numbers runners on the island. It's like an untold joke that everyone around the place is in on.

I carry a tray of drinks and appetizers over to a table, where three servicemen are sitting around with the guy called Sammy the Pimp, a Small's regular.

". . . everyone except Red here," says Sammy as I approach.

What about me? I wonder. But I don't say anything.

Sammy's known around Small's—around Harlem, really—for the women he can get for a fellow. He's a real clean, good-looking sort of guy. Women are on him like flies on honey, and he takes them and turns them so they work with their bodies. There's a whole crop of downtown white guys who will come uptown for the most beautiful Negro women, then head back home to their wives. Connecting them is Sammy's bread and butter.

I pause beside the table. Sammy and the servicemen have been laughing and joking for going on an hour now. It's the fourth round I've brought over in that time. I start laying out the drinks in front of each guy.

"You got a girl?" one of the servicemen asks me. "This guy says you're so wet behind the ears, your lobes are dripping."

I can see why Sammy might think so. When would he have ever seen me with a woman? Around Small's, I'm always working or hanging around listening to the hustlers.

I glance at Sammy, who's looking up at me with this half smile, one shoulder tipped up. Maybe he's just making fun of me. No big deal. I can take it. The customer comes first, is what they always tell me. But that's not quite how it is, I don't think. I read Sammy's expression like a dare or something.

I grin at the soldiers. "He's just having fun with you," I tell them. "Sure, I've got a girl. It's his sister."

The servicemen howl.

Sammy smacks his palm on the table. "You ain't laid off her yet? I'm warning you, Red."

"I'm just trying to make do with what I can get," I say.

"Red, I swear," Sammy cries, feigning anger. The servicemen are in stitches.

"What are you gonna do?" I clamp my empty tray under my arm and point at Sammy. "This guy's got the finest lady friends you've ever seen," I insist, putting on a half pout. "But does he ever put in a good word for the likes of me? Oh, no."

"What would a real woman want with your lanky ass on stilts?" Sammy retorts.

"Your sister doesn't seem to mind," one of the soldiers chortles.

Sammy rubs his forehead and cringes, as if realizing he walked right into that one. "Get outta my sight, Red," he says.

I shrug, backing away. "It's like I said: sometimes you gotta make do."

"And sometimes you just want someone for the night," Sammy says quietly, beneath the laughter. He places three thin slips of paper on the table without saying another word about it. Real smooth.

"Can I get you gentlemen anything else at the moment?" I say. But the servicemen don't answer. They chuckle themselves into silence. Sip their drinks. I back away, surprised at the sudden rush I got from that quick minute of banter.

I circle the room, checking on my other tables. Then I return to lean against the bar, facing the room, so I can see if anyone motions to me.

From a distance, mid-sip, Sammy raises his glass to me, ever so slightly. If I hadn't been looking right at him, if he hadn't been meeting my eyes right then, I would have missed it altogether.

Fifteen minutes later, Sammy's still sitting there. The servicemen are gone, and so are the slips. I walk over and pick up the cash they've left on the table to cover their tab. Sammy's bourbon glass is down to several chips of melting ice.

"Another?" I ask him.

"It's not what I was expecting," he answers.

"You want to settle up now?" I'm surprised—usually he stays much later.

Sammy shakes his head. Taps the rim of his glass, universal symbol for "Get me a refill."

"I meant you," he adds.

Oh. "Did I do something wrong?"

"You're a pretty smart guy," he tells me. "Real quick on your feet. Not everyone can keep up with my kind of hustle. So what are you waiting for?"

Coming from someone as seasoned as Sammy, that's pretty high praise. "What are you saying?"

"Red, you're too good not to be in the game."

"The game?" I echo. "Which game is that?"

Sammy goes, "Any one."

I grin. I'd sure enough like to get a stake in something. Listening to the old cats around Small's, I've learned a thing or two about hustling. I'm a quick study.

"Cool out awhile," Sammy says, pointing at the seat across from him. "Have a drink with me."

My shift is about up, and I'd just as soon stay. It's cold and a bit snowy outside, and I have nowhere to go but back to my room, alone.

We order drinks from the guy who comes on after me. The thick of the night rush is on now, and he flits from table to table, no time to stop and talk. I'm working my way up to the late-night gig that he has right now. Tipsier patrons, and more of them, means thicker tips. But I'm the new guy, so I work early.

Sammy's fairly drunk at this point, and he starts spouting off about the various hustles I could be doing. "You can sell—I know that," he says. "You're not the right style for what I do in the long run. But there's some small-time stuff. . . . You could just blow it out," he says. "No contest."

I listen closely to his advice. He tells me all about buying and selling, moving and shaking, numbers and pimping and every kind of hustle, small and large. But a lot of it sounds like time-consuming full-time work, and I'm liking the Small's job.

"So you pick up something on the side," he says. "Everyone in Harlem has a hustle. You gotta find yours, or you'll never break even."

There's a lull while we order a fresh round of drinks.

"I do have a girl, you know," I tell Sammy. "She lives in Boston."

"What's she like?" he asks.

I shrug. "Blond."

Sammy raises his eyebrows. "White woman?"

"Sure."

Sammy laughs. Loud enough that the people at the tables beside us glance over. "Well, my mistake. I underestimated you, Red. Boy, did I."

* * *

Sammy starts quietly using me in his hustles. Kinda like how we did that first night. He starts conversations, I come over and drop a line or two that helps him make his point, real subtle.

"Listen, Red," he says to me one night. "If we're gonna stay associated like this, we've gotta get you another name."

"How come?"

"People might confuse you with one of the other Reds around."

I've heard some other guys being called Red, but I don't really see the problem. It's not like Sammy is the only "Sammy" in Harlem, either. But when I think about it a second longer, I realize that he is the only one they call "Sammy the Pimp." Half the point of a street name is to make yourself stand out from every other Tom, Dick, and Malcolm.

"What do you want to call me?" I ask. Shorty was the one who named me Red in the first place, and that was good enough for Boston. I already know I need Sammy to help me get good enough to hustle in Harlem. This was just part of becoming who I needed to be next.

"We already got Chicago Red and Philly Red," Sammy says. "Where you from?"

"Michigan." I don't even bother saying Lansing. Who's ever heard of that backwoods place?

"Detroit?" Sammy says.

Close enough. I nod.

"So we call you Detroit," Sammy continues. "Detroit Red."

I can get on board with that.

I sweep behind the booths during a slow stretch. Midafternoon—only two customers in the whole place.

I move the broom real slow and steady, making my way toward where they're sitting. I can sweep faster, but the longer it takes to get over by them, the longer I can linger in their area once I get there. I've learned to listen close to the guys around Small's, because the old hustlers talk about anything when they're just among themselves. I've picked up valuable pointers from things I'd overheard.

I'm close enough now to hear. They're not hustlers, though. They're straight businessmen. I can tell by the words they use. No slang, no undercurrent of secrets. Just straight talk from a couple of Harlem's old guard. A big guy as dark as midnight and a slighter guy, also dark black. *Like Papa.* The thought slips in. They're dressed in fine suits and drinking the sort of whiskey that doesn't come cheap. Tipping me decently after each round.

I've seen them in here before, but later on in the day, when the place is busier. I've never talked to them or gotten their stories.

The smaller man's in the middle of a long monologue about Negro improvement. It's nothing I haven't heard before, between Papa's preaching and Mom's lessons, not to mention Ella talking it all back to me day in and

251

day out. Waste of time now. All of it. Negroes don't need improvement.

Real Negroes don't sit around and talk about how things *should* be and what they *should* have. Real Negroes—real *men*—go out and get some of their own. Get it good. Like every hustler in this place. Like Sammy. And me. I'm making decent bank, between my wages and tips and my take in Sammy's hustles. The zoots lined up in my closet are so fly, they nearly have wings.

"It's like Garvey used to talk about," the big guy answers, interrupting the small guy's rant.

"Up, up, you mighty race," I murmur, working the broom. It just slips out. I don't mean it to.

Both guys spin around to look at me.

"Detroit, you know Garvey?" the big guy says, not bothering to hide his surprise.

Put me on the spot, why don't you. "I didn't mean to interrupt."

"No, no," they both say, on top of each other.

"You know of him?" the big guy repeats.

"I guess," I say.

"From where?" the big guy says. "I would think he was a little before your time."

"My father," I hear myself saying. Don't know the last time I said those words. But it's quiet in the room. No distractions, nothing to stop myself from blurting the things that come to mind.

"A fellow Garveyite!" the small guy exclaims. "I tell

you, it's good to know that the message hasn't been entirely lost in your generation."

I don't really know what message they're talking about. *Up, up, you mighty race?* The things Papa used to preach about sounded good at the time, when I was too small to know better. But since then I've been up the Hill, as they say, which is about as far up as Negroes ever get to go. I've felt the emptiness, seen everyone's mask. There's nothing real up there. Down the Hill, down in the streets, that's what's real. "My father was beat up for selling Garvey's paper." I don't say Papa was one of the leaders of the Movement or that he was instrumental in getting Garvey out of jail for supposed mail fraud. Or that he actually circulated the petition against the government for violating the human rights of Negroes in the United States. I definitely don't say that Negro improvement is what Papa died for, either. That'd be saying too much. In the end, all their kind of talk gets you is run over. Better to dodge. Hustle just enough to stay alive another day.

"Come sit with us, Red."

"Naw." I glance back, toward the office where Charlie works. I feel a little sick to my stomach. I haven't thought about Garvey and Papa's lengthy history of shaking the status quo in years. Forgot I even knew about them. In my mind he only lived six years, only did the things I saw him do. Now he seems so much bigger than he ever has, his presence stretching far before me and far after, coming at me from all directions.

"Join us for a minute." The two guys look at me; their hopeful invitation lands on me with the weight of expectations I can't meet. They're old, like the hustlers, and their gaze is just as sharp. But different. Way too much like . . .

The bar's front door creaks open, admitting a gust of fresh air and a new customer. One solid old hustler I recognize.

I stir the broom, grateful for the distraction. "Can't sit. I'm on duty. You want another round?"

"No, son, we want to talk to—"

"All right, then." I sweep away, faster this time. Feeling their eyes on me. Hearing them say things meant to draw me back until I'm out of earshot.

The customer who just entered hefts himself onto his usual bar stool, leans his forearms on the polished wood. He's a thick-bodied sort but not too tall. It's such a relief, walking over to him, knowing what I'm going to get. No Garvey talk from this cat. He's a hustler through and through.

"Good timing," I tell him. "In another second I was going to have to sit down with those guys. I think they're trying to recruit me," I joke.

He turns partway toward them and slightly lifts a hand in a half wave. The Garveyites half wave back. Sometimes it seems like everyone knows everyone in Harlem. Or maybe it's just that everyone knows West Indian Archie.

"Nah. They're all talk," Archie says in his strong, quiet voice. "You look like a man of action."

"Yeah," I agree. "That's what I've been thinking. What can we get you?"

"Pint of ale," Archie says. I lean the broom against the end of the bar and scoot around behind it. Archie glances at me, clearly amused. "You tending bar now, kid?"

I grin. "Charlie's in the back." I'm supposed to call him out to mix the real drinks, but I can pull a tap handle as well as the next guy. "But I didn't want to keep you waiting."

Archie nods. "Man of action."

I can't stop grinning. "Right on."

The bar has four taps, but I know which ale West Indian Archie likes. Everyone knows. I tip the glass and let the foamy head flow off into the drain. I top it off and slide it across the bar to Archie.

"You're a natural," he says.

My grin starts to almost hurt. I can't understand why I feel so good right now. West Indian Archie's known to be the meanest, most powerful numbers runner in the racket. His turf is enormous, his power practically unlimited. I've seen him get a look of anger on his face that could make the toughest sort of hustler fear for his life. If the bar was full, he could command the room. No question. But in the dim light of the afternoon, with no one really around and Archie saying nice things about me . . . there's actually something comforting about him.

Chapter Nineteen

Harlem, 1943

I'm ready to start up my own hustle. I'm not going to watch
and wait anymore. I've been schooled by Sammy and by all
the hustlers in and around Small's. I can spot an opportunity as well as the next guy. I'm a man of action.

I approach the lone black serviceman at the far end of
the bar. "Hey, mister," I say, real low. "You thinking about
finding a woman?"

He cuts his gaze to me. Says nothing. Just fixes me with
the kind of glance that invites me to keep on talking. I've
seen Sammy do it a hundred times. It's all real subtle, and
you both just know.

"This is where you wanna go," I tell him. And I write down the intersection. "Building on the corner."

After a beat, the soldier reaches into his wallet and pulls out a dollar. Puts it between two fingers and offers it to me as a tip.

I almost take it, but for a strange tug in my gut. I wave off the tip. "Nah," I say. "Just helping out, you know?"

I walk away, and he leaves a minute later. No doubt off to find a girl, but as he goes out the door, he looks over his shoulder, back at me. I get a shiver down my back off that look. There's something in the way he pauses and turns.

Mistake. That's my next thought. I've made a mistake, approaching him. My mind rolls forward and backward, running over the things I've been told. Servicemen are always looking to get laid, I know. So what's the problem?

Like a flash, I remember the problem. The uniform is also an easy cover for cops. Cops in plain clothes are easy to spot, because they still walk like cops and talk like cops, no matter how much they try not to. You don't notice it as much when cops dress like soldiers because real soldiers carry themselves kind of like cops—the buttoned-up style, that righteous sort of edge.

I'm shivering now. Not just a quick wave down my spine, but my whole body. Like I've just stepped out into the cold.

I might have just blown my whole life in one shot. I might have just sent a cop into a handful of prostitutes. He might be back for me.

I set down my tray and walk to Charlie's office in the back.

He looks up from some paperwork when I cross into his line of sight. "Hey, Red."

"I screwed up," I tell him.

Charlie's forehead wrinkles. "What happened?"

I blurt out the story. Charlie listens to my confession, then sets down his pen and folds his hands.

"Yeah," he says. "You screwed up."

He sends me back to work without further ado. An hour later, the front door pops open, bringing with it a gust of winter and a uniformed detective, the combination of which curdles my stomach.

He marches straight toward me. "They call you Detroit Red?"

My voice is small. "Yes."

I recognize him. He's Joe Baker. A hard-ass detective who has it in for every pimp and prostitute in Harlem. I'm neither, but today's events don't exactly support my case.

"Come with me," he says. "We have some questions for you down at the station."

Swallowing hard, I pull off my work apron. I glance at the bartender, like he's going to back me up, but he's studiously wiping down the bar. Acting indifferent.

I have no choice. I follow the cop. He puts me in the back of his squad car and drives off down the block.

It's a short, tense ride to the precinct. I've walked by the building before, although I prefer to skirt this block altogether for obvious reasons. Sammy's convinced they photograph everybody who walks by. I can't imagine what would be the point of that, but Sammy says cops don't always make a lot of sense. They just make a lot of trouble.

I've never set foot inside this building. Hoped never to have to. Detective Baker leads me into a room with a small table and sits me down.

Through the wall I can hear someone else being questioned. Someone who did something way worse than what I did—or at least I hope so. I hear thumps and groans and scrapes. The sound of someone not cooperating.

It feels like forever. The pounding next door. The silence in my own room. The nervous slick of sweat that covers me head to toe. What are they going to do to me?

"It's just a misunderstanding," I tell the detective as soon as he comes back. "I'm just a waiter."

"You understand what you did wrong?"

"Oh, sure," I promise. "I just thought, I mean—I won't do it again." I'm tripping over myself to appear innocent.

No money changed hands, so it wasn't really a hustle. It was just a little information dropped. The cop must realize that, too. "Consider this a warning," he says. "We'll have our eye on you, you hear?"

I nod. He opens the door and I split, quicker and slicker than a banana.

"It wasn't so bad," I report to Charlie. "They just gave me a warning."

He riffles the edges of his paperwork and gazes at me sadly.

"What?" I say. "It's fine now."

"You're banned from the bar, Red," Charlie says. "Just so you know, I'm real sorry to have to do it."

It's like I'm hearing static. "What?"

"Banned," Charlie repeats. "I don't want to see you back in here again."

I expected I might be fired, but . . . banned?

"It was just one time. I'm never going to do anything like that again." I thought being hauled into the police station was the worst thing that could happen to me.

"Once is all it takes," Charlie says. "You're going to be on a list now. Someone's going to be watching you. I don't need that kind of heat on me."

"It was just a warning," I insist. "I'm not in any real trouble."

"Doesn't matter, Red. Like I said, I'm sorry."

The streets outside are colder today than usual. I'm utterly flattened by the knowledge that one stupid moment could bring down this kind of curtain. One impulsive thought. One whisper.

I tuck my coat tighter and walk. Shivering. My skin is like ice, while the core of me burns and trembles. I'm mad at Charlie for being unreasonable. Mad at myself for being so stupid. Hustling is always a risk, I know. But how could I have ever imagined this? Kicked out of Small's, the hustler paradise incarnate, for hustling? It had to be some kind of joke. Except it wasn't.

I go over to Sammy's place. Returning to my own rented room seems too frightening, too lonely. Too much of a dead end. I explain to him what happened, but he just smiles.

"Now," Sammy says, "this is your chance. You're out from under that job, so you can get your hustle together."

"Yeah," I tell him. "That's what I've gotta do." It's the only piece of Small's I can carry with me.

"What's it going to be?" Sammy asks. "You've got options, you know?"

"Numbers, I think." I've been playing numbers for two years. Big amounts and small, though I've only ever won a little. I usually play my tips, which might be ten dollars or up to twenty-five on a good night.

Sammy sort of shakes his head. "You don't want to start there," he says. "Takes a while to get yourself going with that."

"How come?" It seems easy enough. You just have to connect up with one of the runners who control a space of blocks, and then you can take bets. Because the runners own their territory, you have to pay them most of the bets you collect, but you get to keep a cut. Out of Small's, I already know some of the big-time runners in the area: Bub Hewlett, King Padmore, and West Indian Archie. "It's just numbers. You don't think they'd stake me?"

"Sure, sure. Thing is, it takes a while to build a client base."

"Why?" Isn't it as simple as going out and taking bets?

"Let me put it this way. You like numbers, right? You want to lay a bet with me right now?"

"No," I say.

"Why not?"

"I lay my bets with Carl."

Sammy smirks knowingly at me. "See? Everyone who plays has got a guy already. You can't just walk into it unless the time is right."

"What am I going to do?" I ask.

"You like reefer, right?"

I laugh. Who doesn't like reefer?

"I'll front you twenty bucks," Sammy says. "Just to get you started."

"Thanks."

He tells me where to go to get the reefer. He's not about to start supplying me direct, but he vouches for me with one of his guys. The next day, I walk across the park to the place Sammy tells me. Sure enough, the guy's waiting.

I pick up some papers on my own and get to rolling. Sammy says the way to start is dealing stick by stick. I know a little something about this, from back in my shoe-shine days at the Roseland. Back then, though, I would move a couple of sticks a night, at best, because most people already had a place to get reefer, and they came to the parties already stocked. If I'd been caught with my five or ten sticks at a time back then, it woulda been nothing.

Cops would figure it was my own stock to smoke. I was small-time.

This is the big time.

I walk into the Braddock bar with fifty slender sticks up my sleeve. First thing I do is take note of my friends in the room. People I've smoked with. I walk up to some musicians, members of the band that played at the Cotton Club last night.

"Hey, Red," they say. "What's shaking?" We slap some skin.

I chat with them for a minute. Sit down around the table. A few glasses of bourbon make their way around, and I don't turn one down.

After a bit, I ask them. "Anyone need a stick?"

"You selling?" one of them asks me.

"If you're buying." I pull five sticks out.

They all but cheer me, falling over themselves to hand me the cash. "Thanks, Red."

It's easy as breathing. They all know me. Already trust me. I'm not a cop, and they know it for sure. I like to smoke as much as the next guy. More.

I move from table to table. Same deal. I marvel at how quickly the cash fills my pockets. Where has this gig been all my life? Before I know it, my sleeves are empty.

I've moved all fifty.

Chapter Twenty

Harlem, spring 1943

I quickly learn a hard lesson about being so well known.
Keep a low profile, Sammy had warned. Now I know why.

I hadn't done anything quiet. I'd walked right in and
made the deals I needed to. The reefer flowed freely out
of my fingers, and the cash flowed freely in. For the time
being, that was all I cared about. But a windfall like that
can't last. At least not without the wrong someone picking
up the scent.

Cops start coming around to me. Checking in. Real
casual at first, but more and more, and sometimes they frisk
me. I've been lucky. The first few times, just by chance, I'm
not carrying any reefer. All luck, no accounting for it, except

for the fact that I always sell my stock fast. That makes it harder, perhaps, for them to keep up with me.

I get good at dropping the loot when I see something suspicious. When anyone crosses the street toward me, I turn a corner, drop the pouch.

I'm carrying my stash up in my armpit, headed over to the Braddock, when a guy comes toward me. He has his head low, and when he tilts his neck in just this certain way, I get a feeling. Like I've seen the move before.

Cop!

I pick up the pace as I round the corner onto the next block. Run toward the steps of the first brownstone. It has a potted plant on the stoop. I relax my arm and let the pouch of reefers fall to the ground, over the fence. I hope the leaves of the fern or whatever will conceal the package. I keep walking at a good clip, putting space between myself and the point of the drop.

Soon enough, hands on my shoulders. "Detroit Red?"

"Some say," I answer. "What's it to you?"

The rough hands spin me around and begin frisking me but come up empty. "We're gonna get you, Detroit," he says, shoving me off. "Sooner than later."

Thing is, I believe it. They'll get me. It's only a matter of time.

Not long after that, returning home to my boarding-house room, I catch a strange whiff in the air. I stand stock-still in the middle of the room, wondering what seems off.

My bed is messily unmade, just as I left it. My side table drawer's about an inch ajar. That seems normal. But something's not quite right.

Clearly, I'm alone. It's a very small room. Four walls, one door, one window. Bathroom down the hall. And yet I have a feeling that the space has been violated.

I've heard of this. Cops finding out where you live, knowing that you sell but unable to prove it. Planting seeds, planting dope, or something worse. All so they can burst in on you in the middle of the night, "find" the stash in "your" secret hideaway, and bust you. All that. Just to get you.

Without another thought in my head, I start packing. Walk out the door of the boardinghouse and start working out in my mind where to go stay instead.

I wander the streets alone. I can't go to Small's. At this point, it wouldn't be smart to go back to the Braddock, either, where I'm so well known.

I slip into a quiet, out-of-the-way bar in the lower floor of a brownstone just off of Seventh Avenue. It's on a calm tree-lined block that looks like the sort of place nice families live. Not hustlers. Or pimps. Or numbers runners. Or ladies of the night.

The bar is full of plain ordinary folk, some looking down on their luck, some looking to celebrate. I stay quiet, slide to the back. I fold in real nice.

Over the bar hangs a calendar showing a beach view

from a faraway someplace. It has each day up until today crossed out with a thick red *X*.

I sip a glass of bourbon, staring at that thing for a long time.

May 19, 1943.

Somewhere, in the midst of all my fretting and fleeing, I turned eighteen today.

It's my birthday. And not a soul around me knows it or cares. Not even me, until just now.

It's not like I keep close track of the date. What's the point? Wake up, keep moving. That's all there is to do.

I pull some money out, thinking I might splurge on a long-distance call. I think about it for a long while as the coins sit warming in my palm. Who is going to want to hear from me?

Sophia comes down from Boston to visit me. I'm so glad to see her. A spot of bright light, a glimmer of the highest place my old self ever reached. I take her in my arms and kiss her.

"You came all this way," I say. "Let me show you Harlem."

Sophia settles against me. "So show me."

I take her to the Cotton Club, the Braddock, the Savoy. We Lindy-Hop until the blues leak out of our fingers, until the music ends and shades of sunrise streak the sky.

We meet up with Sammy at another club for a drink the next night.

"Dang," Sammy says. "She's a fine-looking woman." He sounds impressed that someone like me can keep up with a woman like her.

"That she is," I agree. I watch her glide among the tables, making for the powder room.

Sammy shakes his head. "You got stars in your eyes, Red."

"What do you mean?"

"I mean, what do you think you're doing with her?" It isn't harsh, the way he's asking. Just kinda mellow and curious.

I shrug. "Just having a good time. We go way back."

"How long?"

"Couple of years." I'm sure in that time I've been her steadiest man. She wasn't traveling all these hours to visit anyone else.

He seems a little surprised at that. "She's stuck with you all that time," he muses.

"We have an understanding."

Sammy snorts. "Yeah, I'll bet you do."

"Come on," I say. "What are you after with this?" It isn't curiosity anymore. He's goading me now.

"I just want to help you see it like it is." Sammy picks up his glass and raises it to me. "Any day now," he intones.

"What?"

"You think you have an understanding? You just watch." He tips the drink toward me, like a salute. "One of these days she's gonna up and marry some whitey. A rich one. Right out from under your nose."

"Naw," I say. "She's not the marrying kind." Anyway, Sophia doesn't need anyone else. The white men she dates are just for appearances. She's mine. Her heart lies on top of mine in my chest, and I'm not about to give it back to her.

Sammy laughs, loud and deep. "Every woman's the marrying kind. You just watch."

Sophia's on her way back to me. Like always. "Think what you want," I tell Sammy. "I've been all over the map in the time she's known me. She ain't left me once."

The cops turn up everywhere. They see me coming, and I have to skirt. Drop my parcel, hope I can pick it up later.

"Red, you're too on edge," Sammy says. "You need to relax."

They could come for me anytime. I know it. I'm watching out the window, day and night. If they can't prove it, they'll plant it. So I stay different places, moving every night. I keep a few of my things at Sammy's, but I mostly move around.

"Keep calm; keep your head," Sammy warns. "Panic's sent more than one hustler straight into the arms of the law."

He's lying back on his new houndstooth couch, watching me pace. I'm seconds away from tearing my conk out, strand by strand. It's all I can do. I can't sit down. Can't keep still. If I stop moving, that's how they'll get me. They might be outside the door right now.

"You're off the rails, man," Sammy says. He pulls a packet of white powder from his breast pocket. Waggles it in the air. "You need some perspective."

He tosses the packet onto the coffee table, where it falls next to a few playing cards, a rolled dollar bill, and one jagged slab of a broken mirror.

Sammy takes the king of clubs and uses it to scoot the powder into a neat line. He sticks the rolled dollar bill into one nostril and runs it over the line, sniffing deeply. "Yeah." He sighs. "That's a breath of good stuff right there."

He tips the dollar toward me and motions me down. "Just like that," he says. "A hundred percent better."

Anything, I think. *Anything to get outside of how I feel.*

I bend over the powder. Look at myself in the slice of cracked mirror. Close my eyes.

The high hits right away. I feel alive. Like I can fly. It's like coming home, but to a place without memory or thoughts.

Chapter Twenty-One

Harlem, June 1943

I didn't think it was going to happen, but I finally get papers in the mail about joining the army. The cops may not have caught up with me, but Uncle Sam sure has. My number is up.

I talk to some of the guys around the street about how they handled it. Some of them haven't gotten called yet. Some of them have gone ahead and served. But I'm thinking about what Shorty said—his whole theory about how the black man shouldn't have to fight this war. Not until we can dance in the same room as white folks. Not until we're less likely to get strung up by the neck in a cornfield somewhere. Lots of guys have warned me not to take Sophia out of the city for that very reason. Might be they'll find me swinging there some morning, if we venture into the wrong parts looking like a couple.

Shoot. I can't even figure a way to take Sophia back to Lansing with me. That's if I ever wanted to go, which I don't. Is this the country I'm supposed to go to war and die for? I don't think so.

My army interview date comes up fast. After listening to the guys, it seems like the best way to go is to play it crazy.

I go up in there stinking. Haven't bathed for three days. Hair all crazy. The pretty nurses take my pulse and my temperature, then they put me in a room with a guy in a uniform—some kind of doctor. There's a metal table in the center and two thin-legged metal chairs. It looks like both a room that wasn't always for this and a room that couldn't be for anything else.

I don't even wait to find out what he wants from me. I launch into talking about smoking whitey. Whitey, who's all this time been keeping us Negroes down.

I do wild eyes. It's not hard to get to this place. The U.S. Army wants to put its hands on me, yet another white government man sent in to press me into place. I picture Mom bucking her spine beneath the grip of the welfare men, who claimed to know better. I wonder if Papa fought, too, when those white men came and pushed him on the tracks. I wonder if he ever saw it coming. I wonder if he knew they'd pounce on Mom and call her crazy so they could break up our family and send her away. They were always after our land, which they never wanted us to have in the first place.

I bet he saw it coming. How could he not? They burned our house, and yet he kept on doing the same thing, pushing his agenda, talking his big talk. He knew it would just fan the flames. He wanted to fan them. Might as well have lain right down on the tracks himself.

Yeah, he saw it coming. Just like I see it coming. Fresh and white and spit-shined, glossy and tempting. Solid paycheck. See the world. A chance to shoot and kill. Nice threads, to boot.

I've seen those servicemen in the bars and the nightclubs, working it on all the girls who want that kind of a man. What kind of a man? The kind that goes where he's told to. The cookie-cutter kind. The kind that lies down when he's told to. But I'm not gonna lie down for anyone.

Harlem, 1944

The best hustle in Harlem always has been, and always will be, the numbers racket. Everyone plays numbers. The big cheeses who own the various blocks and districts make a killing off it every single day.

As a known hustler, it's also the easiest game in town to get away with—no contraband for the cops to find if they frisk you. I admit, I've always had a hankering to get into this racket, but now I have an opening. One small-time runner we know—goes by Stone—just got drafted. He's already gone, reporting for duty somewhere upstate.

Sammy orchestrates a reintroduction for me with Stone's boss, one of the biggest numbers runners in Harlem: West Indian Archie. We wait around outside of Small's Paradise one afternoon while Archie's inside.

"Hey, Archie," Sammy says, when he finally emerges. "What's happening?" They slap skin.

Archie notices me lurking alongside. Sammy says, "Say, do you know my pal Detroit Red? He's the cat I was telling you about."

"This is him?"

Sammy nods. "The prodigy, yeah. He's a real entrepreneur, if you catch me."

I'm nervous as Archie studies me. "Sammy says you managed to escape the draft without running."

"Yes."

"That ain't easy. You must be pretty resourceful."

"I do all right." Sammy warned me to play it cool. Archie doesn't like it when people try to suck up to him too hard.

"All right?" Archie laughs. "Yeah, sounds like it." He claps me on the shoulder like he's proud of me. A small surge of gladness rises in my chest.

"I remember you, anyway," he says. "You used to wait tables here."

"Yeah, that's me." I glance at Sammy, who tilts his head,

giving me the OK to continue. "I hear you have a spot open for a runner."

"I might." Archie looks me up and down. A quality inspection. I stand tall—taller than him. Six foot four and counting. I don't know if I'll ever stop growing. Living in Harlem, I've had to tone down my flashy zoots, and it's just as well; those old fancy ones don't fit me anymore anyway.

"If it turns out you do, maybe you'll keep me in mind for the position," I say.

Archie's dark eyes study me awhile longer. "I might."

Sammy turns and starts walking away. Maybe I'm supposed to follow, now that I've said my piece and all. I nod to Archie and start after him.

"Leaving so soon?" He smiles, out of a face that's both warm and stern. Instinctively I know: you don't cross Archie. You obey. And he'll take care of you.

Archie puts out his hand and we shake. "You're with me now," he says softly as I fall into step alongside him. I feel like I've crossed into some promised land.

You can't write the numbers down, Archie teaches me. A thousand numbers, in a particular order, and you have to hold it all in your head. Not just anyone can do it. Got to remember everyone's numbers, everyone's bet, what everyone owes and is owed. Some runners use betting slips to keep track, but that's risky. If there's no paper trail, you can't be caught.

Most bookies can't do it that way; it's a lot to remember.

But I can, and Archie's pleased with me. I might even be his favorite. "We're gonna have a lot of fun, Detroit," he tells me. "With skills like that, you're going places."

When he claps me on the shoulder, I feel full. He swings through my area more often than he visits the others, just to chat. "You're my biggest earner. There'll be opportunities ahead for you if you keep up the good work."

I'm keeping it up. Archie has high expectations, but I can rise. Expectation. Opportunity. Between Archie's nice words and Sammy's powder and all the cash rolling in, I'm feeling good.

My mind is like an adding machine. *Cha-ching. Cha-ching.* I see a guy coming, gotta search for it. What's his number? Did it hit today? Does he owe me? I calculate real fast. Fast enough that when he's close I can go, "Stebbins, you got my fifteen bucks, or what?"

"Yeah, Red. Yeah. I get paid today, man. I'll be back with it." Meanwhile he's skirting across the sidewalk. Like I don't know what that means.

I follow him. Swagger close. "Hold on."

He doesn't hold. Dodges me, trying to get up on the curb and away.

I mirror him.

My moves are smooth. Always have been. I'm smart enough to see what's coming, and clever enough to turn it my way. All my skills make me perfect for this. The street dance. The hustle.

*   *   *

It's a hot-as-hell day. The kind when the streets seem to be melting—the blacktop actually sticks to my shoes as I'm walking back to my pad from dropping the bets off to Archie.

"Police shot a black serviceman," a guy tells me. "In uniform. Never did nothing!"

It starts to get a little heated. A little crazy. People running every which way. Not a purposeful kind of stride, but looking like they're on their way to nowhere.

People begin rioting against white-owned businesses, and I'm in the middle of it. Around me, folks are screaming and looting and smashing glass and all kinds of craziness. I skirt it, stay above it, but it scares me.

A soldier. A man who's willing to give his life fighting for what's right doesn't deserve to have his life taken. But that's how it goes. All the time.

So many brown bodies. So much strange fruit.

I slip past the riots, back to the safety of my own pad. Sniff a little powder. Smoke a little reefer. Anything to block out the noise from the street below.

When someone innocent gets struck down, we all look sharper for a day or two. If it can happen to someone like that, it can happen to any of us. Anytime. The cops can say, "It's you we want," and they only have to pull the trigger to seal the deal.

You have to stay on your toes. That's why every hustler I know carries a piece now. I'm going to start carrying one, too.

Chapter Twenty-Two

Harlem, 1945

Sammy pounds on the bathroom door. "Red! You gotta go, man. Gotta go!"

There's a more distant banging now, too. West Indian Archie, out in the hallway, thumping on Sammy's front door. Archie claims I lied about the fifty-cent bet I laid yesterday. I'm sure he's come here to kill me.

I picked up my winnings this morning—three hundred dollars. Archie handed over the cash, no questions asked. I go over it and over it in my mind. It seemed so normal at the time, but, in retrospect, maybe there was a bit of a frown on his face. Maybe he looked at me from a little bit of a slant. Why didn't he just *ask* me? We could have cleared up any confusion. As it was, I took the money and walked, already thinking about how to spend it. But now . . .

"Go!" Sammy shouts at me. "He's coming!"

Nowhere *to* go. Huddled here on the bathroom tile, I wonder if my life will end today, at the hands of the one who is supposed to protect me. Hustlers know: live for today because you might not get a tomorrow. But it shouldn't be over something like this.

The crack of splintering wood tells me that Archie's busted in through the door of Sammy's pad.

"Hey, man," Sammy shouts. "You didn't have to do that."

I leap to my feet. This is why I carry a piece—so when someone busts in on me, I can at least defend myself. My hand scrambles to my pocket, but the gun is not there. I forgot—I had to ditch it over the bar when the cop searched me earlier.

I press my hand against the bathroom door, which is little more than a painted piece of plywood, with no lock. I'm dead.

"Where is he?" Archie demands.

My eye flies to the narrow bathroom window. We're on the fourth floor. Too high to jump, but there's a small ledge on the window and the living-room fire escape is just a few feet over. With my long legs, I think I can make it.

"Where's who?" Sammy's voice trembles. "You don't gotta shoot me, man."

Archie carries a .25 caliber pistol. Stubby-looking gun, but scary enough when it's pointed at the bridge of your nose. "I want my money, Red!" he shouts. He knows I'm here. It's only a matter of time.

"What money?" Sammy says, stalling.

"What money?" Archie sneers. Then shouts, "The three hundred you tried to con off me! I wasn't born yesterday."

I dive across the toilet, toward the bathroom window, but its frame is all painted and rusty. I can't wedge it open far enough. I can get an arm out, or a leg, but not my shoulders or my head. I'm trapped.

The bathroom door bangs open. Archie barrels in, a steaming mass of sweat and fury. "Where is it?"

He glares at me, my body all jammed into the window recess. "What are you talking about?" I stay as calm as I can manage, but sweat pours off me. "That was my winnings."

"You never laid that bet," he says.

"I did so."

"Are you saying you don't have it?"

I do, in fact, have it. Right in my pocket. But I laid that bet, sure as I have a conk on my head.

"I'm saying I laid the bet!" I shout to Archie. "Like I always do. You know I did."

"I'll give you a day," Archie says. "Twenty-four hours to pony up the cash, or next time we meet, there'll be a bullet hole in you."

Archie storms out, slamming the broken door behind

him. The scent of him lingers, even after the echo of his presence fades to a dull hum.

"I thought you were a goner." Sammy blows out a breath. "How much of it did you spend? I can loan you."

"No. I got it all."

"Shit," Sammy says. "You shoulda given it to him."

"I can't hand it back," I say. "That's as good as admitting I lied. He'd have shot me."

"Are you playing him?"

"No," I insist. "I laid the bet."

"Shit," Sammy repeats. "He thinks you're trying to roll into his territory." This has happened before. Some young hotshot bookie tries to unseat the runner he works for. You stage a power play by conning the older guy out of some fake winnings, then mouth around that you one-upped the boss. Kill the boss's credibility. Suddenly everyone's laying bets with the new kid, moving up.

Does Archie think I'm a threat to him?

"It's a no-win," Sammy says. "You're finished."

I smoke some weed with Sammy to pass the time, because . . . shit. My life as I know it is over. I don't know who put it in the air, that I'm crooked. I pay my money faithfully every week. Never had a thought in my head of trying to hustle Archie. I know it's breaking the law in the strictest sense, but it's pure. With numbers, the magic is all in the luck of it, a thing that's out of my hands and everyone else's. We offer up our dreams, a penny at a time, to the chance that they might come true. Every penny I put on the numbers is a penny well spent; it buys me that moment to think: *What if?*

Nothing unites Negroes in Harlem or anywhere else like playing the numbers. Everyone, up and down the street, the ones who are doing OK right down to the ones who have to scrounge the penny out of the gutter to get a chance to play—all of us throw up our hands and plead. Like a prayer, to a God we know isn't listening. There's hope in that, even though it's little more than the desperate tossing of a coin. Desperate to believe that luck can offer us a more promising fate.

"What are you gonna do, man?" Sammy's voice floats at me.

"I don't know," I answer.

"He's gonna kill you."

"Then, I guess . . . I guess I'm gonna have to kill him first."

I can't believe it's come to this. Archie has promised me things. All the great hustles we were going to pull together. *You're going places, kid.* More stories. More wishes that are never to be. Is everything in this whole damn world a lie?

I ring up Jean and tell her I'll pick her up at eight. She and I usually celebrate numbers winnings, and if this is going to be my last ride, I'll at least go out in style. It'll be harder for Archie to find me if I'm not crouched at Sammy's like a sitting duck.

Sammy loans me his .32 pistol, since I gave mine up in the bar earlier. I stick it in my pants, because with a guy like Archie, you just never know. If he comes back around, if he has his gun on him, he might not give me another day to fix it up.

Not hanging around Harlem seems like a good idea. I'm always dodging the cops as it is, and now I'm dodging West Indian Archie on top of it. I take Jean down to a club in midtown. Billie Holiday's singing.

"We saw her together once before, didn't we?" Jean says.

"Yeah," I answer. But I don't want to think about that night. I know Billie now, from the Braddock. Everyone hangs out there, and I've been around long enough. For a second I get a bit of longing for the old days, when I used to be able to roll up in a room like that, with or without sticks for sale, and just slap skin with folks whose voices were on the hottest records selling nationwide. There was something perfect in that. It aches sometimes, that I messed it up so hard.

Jean says, "Let's go uptown," and I've had enough drinks at this point that I don't see the problem with it. We go to a bar down the road from Small's. West Indian Archie's territory for sure, but I don't figure it matters. He gave me until noon tomorrow, and, anyway, I know I'm in the right.

I feel the shiver on the back of my neck. At first I think it's just Jean, back from the ladies' room, trying to have some fun. A little whisper.

But the feeling is cold, not warm. Slowly I turn. In the doorway stands West Indian Archie.

We share a glance. Here I am, spending what he thinks is his money on a night on the town. On a girl. And he has to take a stand—anyone would. I know this.

He bears down upon me with the heat of the sun. "Detroit Red," he calls out. My goose is cooked. Why does it have to be in front of everyone?

Archie walks toward me, real deliberate steps.

"You said we would talk tomorrow," I say.

"I said you had a day to raise my money back. Not spend it."

He's making it public. There's no turning back now. Anyone who didn't know Archie was out to get me will know after this. I'm finished.

We're going to have to have a showdown.

He's going to speak at me so that everyone will hear. Then he'll walk out on the street. I'll have to follow him. No choice in the matter. All my pride at stake.

I'm carrying Sammy's gun, tucked down my back. Archie's carrying, for sure. We'll shoot it out on the street. My heart pounds. One of us will die. The other will go to prison. Life. Maybe even the chair.

So we're both dead, looking at each other across the high-top bar table.

"Go home," I tell Jean out the side of my mouth. "Just get on out of here."

She doesn't need to be told twice. She slides off the stool and melts into the crowd. She's the only thing moving. Everyone around us has stopped to stare. West Indian Archie cuts an imposing figure under normal circumstances—when he's mad like this, he seems enormous.

I am several inches taller, but I don't feel it. Archie is large with power, with age, with this conviction that I have wronged him. Which I didn't. Did I?

My brain scrambles itself. I was high when I bet. High when I collected. High now . . . and suddenly confused. Did I get my numbers wrong?

I shake myself out of the doubt. It doesn't matter. There's no going back now. For me or for Archie.

The accusation is out there. We're locked on the path to the showdown.

A sharp pain explodes across my chest. *He's shot me,* I think. But . . . no. It's just the sting of seeing the flaming, furious look stamped on his dark, familiar face. It hurts worse than a bullet. I can see behind his eyes, the intent to punish me. To make me pay.

Then, for an instant, something different flashes across his face, a regretful scowl, as if to say, *Why did it have to come to this?*

I feel the same way, looking back at him. What we have going is great and perfect; Archie's always telling me I'm the best bookie he has running. Telling me how much more

I can do. I thought he wanted me to follow him. He's proud of me. I can see it when he looks at me. He's proud of what I can do.

You can do anything you put your mind to.

For a strange second, I don't know who I'm hearing, whispering in my ear.

Two hustler friends of Archie's ease their way to the front of the crowd. They step alongside Archie, ready to come between us. It's the only chance I'm ever going to have.

I dive backward, thrashing through a cluster of surprised onlookers. I race out onto the street. It's dark and mostly still. A few passersby glide in and out of sight through the streetlight puddles. I plunge into the shadows and wait. Draw Sammy's gun into my hand.

Any second now, Archie's going to follow me out. Gun in front of him, no doubt. When he walks through the door, I will kill him. Just like that. Before he has a chance to look and see me. Before I have to read again the disappointment on his face. *Back at you, Archie. I would have followed you forever.*

I'm ready. Finger on the trigger, curled and calm. Ready.

I flinch every time the door hinges creak. Several groups of people do leave the bar, but I see no signs of Archie. Ten minutes.

Fueled by the hurt of Archie's betrayal, I'm ready to lash out and kill.

Come out and face me. But Archie doesn't appear.

Fifteen minutes. Twenty.

I back away down the street. After half a block, I lower the gun. Tuck it back in place.

Sammy's place is my refuge. Archie might come looking for me there again, but I've got no place else to go. I tuck myself down between the sofa and coffee table. Try to believe. I am Detroit Red. I am triumphant. The cops can't get me. West Indian Archie can't get me.

At least not while I'm huddled down here.

I squeeze myself as small as I can, as small as the child I once was. The only comfort I can imagine is my mother's arms, a thing I haven't wished for—let myself wish for—in such a long time. All there is now is a broken circle.

For the first time, maybe ever, the high isn't taking. I am low. So low. I'm tiny. Breathing. Fragile. And afraid.

In the strange stillness, I can feel the breath of Papa's shame. *Have you looked at yourself, my son? What has become of you?* If there is a heaven, which I doubt, I wonder if he has turned his face away. I hear his voice in my head, but the words are like ghosts. My hands pass right through; no substance. Try as I might, I cannot feel him. Haven't wanted to in so long. Maybe all the pushing down, all the forgetting, has finally worked.

Sammy comes in. "Red?" he calls. "Where you at?"

He peers down at me. Laughs. "You're losing it, man." He raps my shoulder blade with his knuckles. "Get up."

I unfold myself. Sammy's here, watching my back. It's not so bad when I'm not alone.

"You got somebody waiting on you downstairs," he says. "Said he's looking for his homeboy. Called you by name, so I figure he's legit. . . ."

I'm already looking out the window, and then I'm out the door in a hot-streak second. I pound the stairs so hard my bones rattle.

Shorty's waiting downstairs with a car. He leans against the passenger door, arms crossed, key chain twirling on two fingers. "I heard you got yourself in some trouble," he says.

I've never been so glad to see anyone in my life. We slap hands. He gives me this look, like he's not sure what he's seeing.

Shorty rounds the car as I leap into the passenger seat.

"What are you doing here?" I blurt out.

"Came to get you," he says, pulling straight into traffic without so much as a wave to the cab he cut off. Horns blare. "Can't have my best man getting clipped by some island thug."

"I appreciate it, my man." I'm looking in the rearview. Lately all I'm doing is trying to outrun one thing or another. After a point, it starts to feel like the easy way is not so easy.

I direct him back to the place I've been staying, but only halfway, because he's Shorty, and like usual he just knows where to turn.

"Grab your things," he tells me. "We gotta get you out of town."

I don't need to be told twice. I've had enough close calls in the past few days to last a lifetime. Like always, packing makes me realize how little I have. Nothing of real value except a little cash and some reefer, plus the bundle of letters I can't make myself throw away. Two duffels and a satchel; I'm ready to fly.

Shorty bundles my bags into the trunk, and we're off. I smoke some reefer out the window as we coast up the West Side Highway. *Highway* is the word for sure; I breathe the joint deeply.

I sink low in the seat, getting comfortable. Start jawing to Shorty about all the shit that's gone down the past few weeks, about all the mess he just saved me from. The New York skyline whisks by and before long fades to miniature in the rearview mirror. *Stop looking back,* I remind myself. Better to pretend my old life has already disappeared.

Chapter Twenty-Three

Headed to Boston, 1945

Boston from New York is a long damn ride. All night it feels like. Shorty rubs his eyes. He's been up for hours and hours, counting the drive down to get me and the quick turnaround.

"I can take a turn," I offer, meaning to get behind the wheel.

"I doubt it." Shorty laughs, not really like it's funny, though. "Homeboy, you're so high right now, you could float on back to Roxbury."

He's right about that. I've just been smoking reefer to while away the hours. "It'll be good to be back," I murmur, letting my eyes drift closed.

When I wake up, we're still on the road. But the light is new, a painted sunrise.

"You OK?" Shorty asks out of nowhere. In the small space of the car, his words feel big.

I stretch my arms as wide as I can, against the window and the dash.

"You talked right through your sleep," he tells me.

"Oh, yeah?" I chuckle. "What did I say?"

Shorty's quiet. There's a thing that almost never happens. Between the two of us, someone's always jawing. He must be tired down to his bones. Like me.

"Thanks for coming," I say. In the fresh light of day, I can see how it put him out. The long drive down. Finding me. The long way back.

"You're still my homeboy, ain't you?" he answers, drumming the wheel. "My namesake, too."

"What?"

"I'm Malcolm, too," he reminds me.

I pick my head up and laugh. "That's right. I forgot. That's some kinda fluke." Saying it gives me a flashback, like the words are coming out of my mouth four years ago.

"Naw," Shorty says. "Things happen for reasons, eh?"

"No reason for something like that," I say, echoing my old self. I feel like I'm living through my life in reverse.

Our shared name doesn't really matter. Neither of us is Malcolm anymore. He's Shorty. I'm Red. I wonder if they'll call me "Detroit" back in Roxbury now, or if I'll be just

"Red" again. Maybe I can be "Harlem Red." I like the sound of that.

"I was making good in Harlem," I tell Shorty. "I wouldn't ever have left." Even through my high, leaving there hurts like a giant bruise, one that covers every inch of me.

My body is tired of trying to heal. It's funny—life deals me these punches, and I always get knocked down. But I keep finding a way to get up again. Must be there's some kind of fight in me, somewhere.

"I used to have this dream," Shorty says. "Over and over again, you know?"

I nod. We're driving through a stretch of trees so thick that where the road curves up ahead, there's no way to tell what's around the corner. Boston could be right there, or it could be a hundred miles down the road. I think about the map my brothers and sisters gave me. It's buried down in the bottom of my duffel, along with their letters. I don't know where I am in the world.

"I'm with my mama," he goes. "A little kid, right? Like six or seven."

I finger the rubber crack where the window goes into the door. I wonder if everyone has that kind of dream. It never occurred to me to wonder.

"We're just in the house, you know. And there's plenty on the table. It's a good day, coming to an end, but even though it's dinnertime, the sun never goes down."

His words are rhythmic. Lulling.

"It's more perfect than it ever was in real life," he goes

on. "I forget about leaving. I look out the window, and I know that this is where I want to be forever. It's home."

Shorty glances at me. His wrist rides high on the steering wheel. We glide into the brightening sky. "You ever had a dream like that?" he asks.

I fidget. I don't know why he's telling me this. "What of it?"

"It's just a dream," he says. "I haven't had it in a while."

I'm not prepared for how great it is to be in Roxbury again. I'm riding high. My reputation precedes me—Harlem's hottest hustler, Detroit Red, is back and he's black and he's looking sharper than ever. It seemed like a backward step at first, but now I know going back was the only way to show how far I've come.

I have a fleeting thought, from nowhere, about Mr. Ostrowski. I'm not just a nigger anymore; I'm *the* nigger! I want to serve it to him for breakfast, push it right into his bloated red grinning face.

People can't get enough of me, but despite the enthusiastic reception, mostly I want to get high and lie around. I haven't slept properly in a hundred years. I've been dozing with one eye open as long as I can remember, trying to keep a step ahead of the law.

If I thought I'd felt safe at Sammy's place, it's nothing compared to how I feel to be back at Shorty's. I'm lucky enough to catch him between roommates, my old room wide open and waiting. If I get high enough, lie still enough, play the music loud enough, I can almost believe that my whole life in Harlem was a dream.

I play records through the day and into the evening. Shorty's off playing a gig somewhere or other. He's invited me to watch, but rest is what I need right now. I lie on the couch and just listen to the greatest of the greats jam on vinyl.

There's a knock at the door.

Sophia. Dressed in yellow and white, clutching a tiny pearl handbag. Wearing a smile that's everything but innocent. "I heard you were back in town."

I keep the door half closed, blocking her entry with my body. "I heard you're married now."

"He's in the army," she says. "I hardly see him."

"The war's over," I remind her.

She shrugs it off. "I still want to see you."

Yeah. Seeing her makes it all complete. Moving the needle back to the edge. Except I'm not playing the same tracks over. I'm living the B side.

"You're not going to let me in?" She pouts. Beautifully. There is nothing about her that fails to draw me. Nothing that would ever make me turn her away.

"Maybe I don't want to share anymore," I say. "Maybe I've got plenty of women."

Sophia puts her hand on the door anyway. I kick it wider and let her in. My refusal was only a game. It will always be her and me. We both know it.

She wears her smooth blond hair neatly coiled into waves, exactly like you see on the big screen. I cozy a little closer, run my fingers through those locks. I shiver. Never felt that kind of silk on anyone else. She tilts her head to look at me, and the hair falls over her eye. I lift it back behind her ear. She smiles. Red lips, white teeth. She doesn't stop me from leaning in. I take her mouth. She tastes like milk and honey liquor. Pure and sweet and potent, and, I swear, she makes me high.

"Baby," I say. "I didn't know nothing about a kiss till I met you."

She slides her arms around my neck. The low sound in her throat is something sacred. *I don't need no church*, I think. *Let me worship at the altar that is her.*

"I have to go," she says, looking over at the door. "My husband will be waiting."

"Don't lie," I whisper, right against her cheek. "This is what you came for."

She moves her hands at the base of my neck. The muscles are tight, eager. Her long, soft fingers knead them gently.

I nuzzle her throat. "Yes, baby."

"Tomorrow," she says, a little breathless. "Or the next day. He'll be gone awhile."

I don't want to wait. It's been long enough already. I lean her back against the arm of the couch. She goes easy, kissing me back.

Then her mouth breaks away. "I have to go," she says

again. But she doesn't leave right away. No one's waiting for her, at least not right this moment. But she keeps dropping the word: my husband this, my husband that.

"Stop talking about him," I snap, feeling green all over.

"I can't help it," she says. "It is what it is."

"What is it, exactly?" *Who am I to you?* is what I want to know. It's not fair. I knew her first, knew her best.

"I have to go," she says. She kisses me. In my mind, I'm not having it, but my body lets her snuggle close all the same.

The truth of the matter is she's always got to go. She's always just stopping by. The door is always going to be closing behind her, and I will always be here. All alone.

Boston, 1945

Shorty comes in from his gig, lugging his sax case and looking tired.

"Hey, homeboy," he says.

"Hey."

"It's a mess in here," he comments, looking my way. "What have you been doing?"

Same as always. Seeing Sophia in. Seeing her right back out. Reefer. "You wanna hit?"

"Naw." Shorty's been keeping his nose clean, what with all the paying gigs he's scoring now with his band.

"Come on," I say. "Party with me. It's good stuff I got here. Real good. It'll make you feel like nothing's wrong."

I'm flying high, running my mouth like there's no business.

"Naw," he says. "Clean it up out here, OK?" He goes in his room. Closes the door. I'm already on the floor. Can't get lower. But watching Shorty walk the straight and narrow—Shorty, the guy who gave me my first reefer, the cat who schooled me in everything about the life I'm living now—it's almost too much to take.

No matter how high you get, sometimes things pop out of the darkness at you. I'm asleep, or I think I'm asleep, I don't know, but then suddenly I'm not.

I'm hit with it, hard. Right out of nowhere. This heavy feeling. I sit up, gasping and screaming. The sheets are twisted around me. I wrestle them. Can't get free of it.

Shorty stumbles in. "What is it?" he's shouting. "What happened?"

"It's coming!" I shriek at him. "Get it off! Get it off!" I see flames. I see leering white faces. I see a streetcar running at me. Tracks laid with blood. I see the welfare man, Mr. What's-His-Name. Apples rolling and chickens beating their wings. I see an empty house. A field full of dandelion heads, popped off their stems. In my ears, the echo of screaming.

I guess it's my own.

"Snap out of it, man." Shorty's hands on my shoulders.

"It's just a bad high." But it's never been bad for me, ever. It's not the drugs—I know it. It's everything underneath them. Trying to rise up.

"I need a smoke, man," I plead. "Get me another smoke." His hands are on me, not letting me up.

"No, you don't," he says. "Just relax."

I fall back, a puddle of sweat. Things are still now. Around me, if not inside.

"OK," Shorty says. "You're OK."

"Um-hmm." I close my eyes. *Just breathe. Just breathe through it.* Eventually I open them. Shorty frowns down over me. He's sitting on the edge of my mattress, one leg folded underneath.

"What happened to you, homeboy?" Shorty says quietly. "You ain't the cat I knew."

The words cut through the thick fog around my head.

"You're off the rails," he continues. "Don't know how, don't know when, but you got off." He holds my arm, smooths the sweat off my brow. Looks at me, does this brotherly sort of thing where he's almost holding me.

"What's the matter, Red?" he says. "How'd you get like this?"

"I need another smoke, man," I tell him. I'm aching. I can hear him, and it hurts. I want to go past it. Past the place where he can reach me with these quiet pressing words.

"Naw," he whispers. "You been hit hard enough."

If there's more after that, I don't know it. I just drop back, away from him. Away from everything. Let what's in me already carry me high. So high, I can't be touched.

Shorty comes and goes for his lessons, rehearsals, and gigs. He's always off, every which way, sax in hand. He never says anything about the night that everything came tumbling down. I'm grateful for his silence. I don't want to go back there. I imagine he doesn't, either.

Which is why I'm surprised when he comes home one afternoon from some kind of practice session and lays into me.

"Damn it, Red." He stalks around the room picking up random crap I've tossed aside. Reefer butts and empty bottles and I don't know what all.

"What's the beef, man?"

"I didn't come get you so you could lie around the house smoking reefer all day," Shorty says.

"When'd you get so uptight?"

"'Round about the time you stopped paying rent."

I shrug, reaching for the cash in my pocket. "How much do I owe you?"

He tells me and I blanch. Like he's thrown cold water on me. "It went up that much?"

Shorty looks at me slant, the way he often looks at me now. Like he no longer likes me, like we're no longer brothers. "No. It's been that long. It adds up."

"OK, man," I tell him. I hold up my hands. I drop the attitude with him, now that I can see good and clear that I'm in the wrong. "I'll find some work."

There is always a hustle to be had. Time to get up off the couch. Time for Detroit Red to find a stake in Roxbury.

First stop, of course, is always the Roseland. Easy hustles. Tonight I just figure I'll get the lay of the land.

The music intoxicates me, like always. It's been ages since I Lindy-Hopped or danced at all. I've been running, stepping in all directions lately. The real-life hustle. Haven't needed the dance floor, I guess.

Tonight I walk the floor, letting the old Lindy ways soak back into my skin.

Plenty of pretty ladies on the floor, of course, but one in particular catches my attention. The way she moves is familiar. Lyrical and light. So familiar. Could it actually be . . . ?

"Laura?"

Haunted, hollow eyes. They widen. "It's you."

"It's you," I echo, slightly unbelieving.

"I heard you went to Harlem," she says.

"Did. I'm back now." I gaze at her, trying to get over how different she looks.

"Oh." She wears a cream-colored dress, with small shoulder caps, a low-cut front, and a short, thin, gauzy skirt. She's not quite ragged but seems to me barely clothed, at least compared to the high-necked blouses, cardigans, and long skirts she used to wear back when I knew her.

"I'm surprised to see you here." By now she should have finished college and moved into a big house on the Hill, making her own way and trying out the newest of the new fur hats, like Ella.

"You brought me down the Hill," she says. "I guess I never made it back up."

"College?" I ask.

She shakes her head. "I thought that it would be easy. That if I worked hard, I could move to bigger and better things. But the system's not made for people like us." I've never heard her sound so bitter. "You were right about a lot of things."

"What does your grandmother think of all this?" She was always so strict. I can't imagine her letting Laura come down to the Roseland every night.

"She's too old to say anything about it," Laura says. "And there's no one else to stop me. My daddy left me. Seems like everyone's always leaving."

I don't want to think about that. Don't want to feel guilty. Just want to lose myself in the music. "You wanna dance?" I ask her. "Old times' sake?"

Out on the floor, the awkwardness fades some. We blurt and babble. She's drunk and I'm high—it lets us relax, keeps the conversation light.

"What are you doing now?"

"This," she answers. "You?"

"Oh, you know." I shrug, and she nods, like it means something.

We dance easy, like we used to. But the way she looks at me is different. I've seen that look on girls before.

Laura spins close after a while, like I hoped she might, but she says nothing. My arms go around her, and we just move.

Holding her now makes me inexplicably sad. Not the way it used to, when she was a person so far out of reach, when she talked about things that seemed too high to touch.

The place she holds in my memory is a place where all things were possible. A place I had to walk away from because of the reality of life. I realize now, though, that I thought it would always be there. Laura as she was still lives in my mind. Or she did, until tonight.

Yet another long-held vision shatters. I'm running out of room to hold the pieces. My heart is full to aching.

"I missed you," Laura whispers. "Almost always."

"Me, too." I haven't thought about her in an eon. But I miss her now. Just because she's here.

"We had something, didn't we?"

Had. Had and lost. Had and threw away.

She's still so beautiful. I guess I knew she was beautiful all along, but somehow along the way, I stopped seeing her. Decided that Sophia was the kind of woman I was looking for. Looking down at Laura now, I'm not sure how that happened.

She swings in and out, so far. Our hands never release, as if she doesn't want to let go yet. Doesn't want it to be over, even though there's nothing more that can happen. We've had all we're ever going to have together. This is all that we're ever going to be.

Count Basie's beats jump through the speaker.

Our feet fly, fingers intertwined. Laura is as light to lead as ever.

It's almost like before. Almost exactly, and yet the ways it's not are more than enough to ruin any hint of perfection. Laura used to be perfect, too. Did I ruin her?

Nothing to do but just keep moving, keep stepping. Don't stop, or it'll catch you. If it catches you, it's over, the dance is done, and there's nothing left but to lie down and close your eyes. So just keep moving.

Chapter Twenty-Four

Boston, 1945

Sophia doesn't mind loaning me some coin until I get a new hustle going. "Get straight with Shorty," she says. "Don't even worry about it." So I don't. I take hold of the snaking fur stole around her shoulders and draw her close. The fur is soft and plush. Elegant. It reminds me how much Sophia has and how much I still don't. Even in the middle of our kiss, I can't forget it.

"How many of these you got?" I ask her, rubbing the fur.

"I don't know," she says. "Maybe a dozen."

To me, one looks pretty much interchangeable with the next. "They must be expensive."

"I don't know," she says. "I didn't pay for most of them."

I let go. "He buys them for you?" It bothers me to think of her wearing gifts from her husband when she's with me. It's easier to imagine she's mine and mine alone when there's no specific tie to anything else, no reminders of black and white.

"Don't pout," she purrs, pressing against me. "I got them myself."

"How, exactly?"

She tosses her hair in a familiar, delightful way. "I have very rich friends, you know. Some of them have two or three dozen furs gathering dust in a closet." She pantomimes plucking something, like fruit. "They never miss one or two."

I laugh. "You little minx," I whisper. Truly, we are a perfect match.

"My little minks," she teases, fluffing the fur at me.

"They never miss them, eh?"

"Not a bit," she purrs, leaning over me. "My sister and I have been doing it for years. You want in?"

"You have a sister?" I probably should have known that. But we don't talk about things like home and family.

"Little sister."

"She as much trouble as you?" I breathe.

Sophia laughs throatily. She leans her cheek against me. "You like my furs? Plenty more where those came from. We'd be able to carry a lot more if you came with us."

"I can't go to those fancy parties." What is she thinking?

"No, at night," she says. "While everyone is away for the holidays. Easy money."

The idea plants itself in my brain like a seed. "A lot of it?"

Sophia nods, but with her face so close to mine, we both lose interest in talking. I let her enfold me, but my mind ticks around the sprouting idea. We may have just found ourselves a new stake. A fresh hustle, with nothing up front and a whole lot of cash on the back end.

I hand Shorty a wad of cash to cover the rent. He takes it without comment. He knows better than to ask where it came from, I suppose, especially since he seems to be living on the up-and-up for the moment.

I'm ready to change that. Sophia and I stayed up late working it all out. We figure the return will be much better if we don't try to go it alone. Sophia's going to talk to her sister, and I'm going to talk to Shorty. He's my best friend and roommate; we don't have secrets. Of course I'm going to bring him in.

"Let me bend your ear about something, man."

"What's that?" he says.

"Sophia and her sister—did you know she has a sister?"

Shorty shakes his head no.

"Anyway, they have an in, casing houses in nice areas. Suburbs, outside the city."

"Casing, as in to rob the places?"

"Yeah," I confirm. "Real nice places. Furs. Jewelry and silver. Expensive things, man."

"OK . . ." He's not shutting me down.

"With the holidays coming up, some of them are going out of town. Sophia knows when. The houses will just be sitting there, empty. All that rich stuff inside."

It isn't exactly a hustle, but it's a pretty good plan. Almost impossible to resist, as far as I'm concerned.

Shorty considers. Gears turning in his head; it's almost audible. Paying gigs don't pay so well. Reeds and pads and sheet music cost money, plus he's been saving forever for a new, better saxophone. "Listen, Red," he says finally.

"I'm listening," I tell him.

"Are you?" He pins me with a look.

"Yeah, man." I don't like this new, skeptical side of Shorty. The one who looks at me with distance in his eyes, like I'm some strange foreign thing.

"If we're gonna do this, you gotta stay straight," Shorty warns me. "You can't be getting so high you fall down on the job. You know?"

"Sure, sure," I promise him, knowing I can perfectly well work high and not show it. I'm twenty years old now, and I've been doing it for years.

Unlike Sophia, her sister is dark-haired, and right away it's pretty clear that Shorty would like to get cozy with her. He fantasizes about being with a white woman, but I don't know that he ever has. It'll probably work out for him this time. These white girls like to have fun with Negro men.

Together, the four of us outline the scheme in more detail. Our plan is pretty brilliant, if I do say so. We'll go to the neighborhoods Sophia and her sister know, targeting particular houses when people are on vacation.

"Holiday ski trips and visits to the in-laws," Sophia says. "Sometimes they're gone a week or two."

"How do you know when they're away?"

"There are ways to tell," Sophia says. "We listen at parties; people talk about their plans. Ask neighbors to watch their pets."

Sophia's sister also has a job as a makeup salesgirl, door-to-door. The girls can visit nice houses that way, and if they're invited in, see who's packed to go out of town. See what they have that looks valuable.

It's foolproof.

We drive west of the city into Brookline, to an area where the streets widen and the trees thicken and the houses grow bigger and more spaced apart.

The houses are fancy. Far nicer than the homes downtown. Perfect white snow-covered lawns, with manicured bushes and trimmed trees. Holiday lights twinkle from eaves and railings and porch columns. Like diamonds. If each house holds a diamond for every light outside, we'll never have to work another day in our lives.

Sophia takes us to a dead-end street with five houses splayed around a circle. She clicks the headlights off and drives slowly.

"That one," she says, pointing one house down. "They're away until the New Year."

Shorty and I bend our heads to look through the windshield. It's a two-story brick house with black clapboard shutters and a trio of narrow cement stairs leading to the front door.

"There's a kitchen door around there." Sophia indicates the left side of the house. "It doesn't have a deadbolt."

"OK," Shorty says. He pats the pocket where he's stashed his new lock-picking tools.

I put my hand on the door handle, ready and waiting. Shorty opens his door, and the first slice of winter cuts through the car. I open my door and follow him into the dark. The little light in the car ceiling is off, so there's only the dark—and the cold. It's terribly, terribly cold. Colder than the act of breaking in and blindly robbing some fat cat during his vacation. Cold enough to numb me to any hesitation or doubt.

"Wait for me on the porch," Shorty says. "I'll let you in." He diverts off the path, feet disappearing into the drifting clouds of white. He hurries around the side of the house as I climb the front steps.

Nothing to do but stand there for a minute. I try to stomp the chill out of my shoes. Tuck my collar closer.

Glance back at the girls, sitting in the dark car. A plume of exhaust billows from the tailpipe. Gotta have a getaway plan, of course.

The door creaks open. Shorty grins at me. "Well, come on in," he says. "Nice of you to stop by."

I push past him to get into the relative warmth of the house. It's easy to tell no one's been home for a few days. The heat's off. But being inside still blocks the wind and cuts the sharpness of the weather.

We're standing in a wood-paneled foyer that's filled corner to corner with framed family photographs. I drop one handle of the loot sack off my shoulder. Straight ahead are the stairs and what looks like a hallway to the kitchen. To the left and right, various formal-looking sitting rooms full of straight-backed chairs and all manner of couches. There's a grand piano in one and a fireplace in the other. Lacy throws draped here and there. Knickknacks on the table.

"Where do we start?" Shorty asks.

"Bedrooms, probably," I suggest. "Jewelry's up there."

He leads the way upstairs. A short hall branches off to six closed doors.

The master bedroom at the end of the hall is a gold mine of jewelry and fancy knickknacks.

Shorty tears open the closet. "Whoa," he says. A soft rush of fabrics sways forth at him. He disappears into the folds.

I lift things off the end tables and dump the contents

into a bag. Gold, silver—anything that looks expensive.

Shorty emerges, wrangling an armload of fur coats. I can't help the laugh that escapes my throat. It looks like he's wrestling a leopard.

"It's going for the jugular!" I whisper-shout, like a warning.

He spits out a mouthful of sleeve. "Shut up. Let's move."

I glance out the front window. The car is still there. The girls' silhouettes are like shadow statues in the gloom.

Shorty takes the coats downstairs. I make a circuit through the other upstairs rooms. Find a little more jewelry, but nothing like the treasure trove of the master bedroom. By the time I'm back downstairs, my sack is pretty full.

I set the bag down beside the furs, which are piled by the front door.

Shorty's in the kitchen; from the clatter and clink, it sounds like he's setting the table for dinner. I poke my head in and find him gathering silverware by the handful, thrusting it into his bag.

"This is good stuff," he says without looking up. "We OK?"

"Think so." It's been about ten minutes, I would guess.

When we go back into the sitting room, Shorty glances wistfully at the grand piano by the front window.

"We don't have room for that," I quip. I'm barely certain that we have enough space for all the rest of the things we've gathered. "Let's get out of here."

Shorty goes to the piano anyway. His fingers graze the

white and black keys, dipping them such that they make only the slightest noise. He's forever sitting down at the piano in the pool hall, but it's a small, boxy thing, always out of tune. This one must be much nicer.

The glow of oncoming headlights paints the window bright. Not from our car.

Shorty rushes toward me, startled out of whatever musical interlude was playing in his head. We peek through the curtains. Far down the road, some other car glides toward us, then turns onto a cross street. The block is dark again.

"We have to go," I tell Shorty. "Right now."

We've collected about all we can carry, but we manage it in one trip. We fill our arms and stagger out the door. Sophia leaps out to open the trunk. We stuff everything in, however it fits: jewels, furs, sacks of glittery loot.

As we jump back in the car and peel off down the street, I glance through the rear window at the house. It amazes me slightly that it looks the same as it did, though it's been looted of so many valuable things. You wouldn't know, to walk past that house, what it had lost. It looks as proud, and as firm, and as fancy as ever. As whole.

But it isn't. And there's something in that. Makes it hard to look away. I can't look away, in fact. Until we turn off the street and the house disappears from view.

The girls insist that there's plenty more to be had in Brookline. So the next night, we drive back. Same area, different street. Same feel to the neighborhood, different house. Whitewashed siding. One story.

Shorty and I work well together. He goes around back, lets me in. We hit the rooms. Master. Other bedrooms. Kitchen. Sitting rooms.

Jewelry. Silverware. Art. Nice stash of liquor this time around, too.

Bing, bang, boom. We're in; we're out. Like pros.

Stuff it in the trunk, and away we go, all of us that much richer.

As Sophia chauffeurs us away from the scene, we crack open the seal on a pilfered bottle of rich man's Scotch whiskey. Take a healthy sip. I remind myself, *Don't look in the rearview.* Tonight there's no cause to linger. I'm moving forward.

My cut of the haul is over a thousand bucks. Whew. I've never seen such a wad of cash in my life. Not too shabby for ten minutes' work. Counting the drive in and out, we're looking at maybe an hour's time expended, each day. And for this kind of coin? Heck. It makes the constant rag of the street hustle look like child's play.

Sophia and I celebrate together. I can't have her in my bed as often anymore, now that her husband is around. But when she's with me, there's no mistaking the fact that we belong together.

* * *

After we've worked a bunch of houses in Brookline, we move on to Newton, another suburb. In one night, we score a watch, a fancy vacuum cleaner, silver candlesticks, earrings, a gold pendant, and other small things. Always as much as we can carry.

The watch would be especially nice, except it isn't working right. I don't usually care about the stuff we steal, except how much we can make when we sell it. But a broken watch won't fetch much coin, and anyway this watch is so nice that I'd rather not resell it.

I'll get it fixed up instead. It'll make a nice gift for one of my brothers. Philbert, I think. I won't tell him how I got it, of course, but it's an added bonus to gift him something I lifted, because that used to be our thing. I flash back to the necklace I stole for Sophia that helped me win her back all those years ago.

I imagine Philbert opening the mail pouch and pulling out this piece of finery, with a note from me attached. He'll be surprised. He'll be delighted. He'll realize he can stop sending me lectures by mail about coming home and putting my life right. He'll see that I'm doing just fine.

Boston, January 1946

The jewelry shop is a reasonably high-end joint, its name stenciled on the windows. Inside is not the sort of dim lighting you hope for when you want to move something hot, but I was careful to dress nice enough to look like the watch is mine.

The clerk looks me over. He takes the watch and folds it into a soft cloth. "You can pick it up in two days," he tells me.

I come back when he said to. "I left a watch day before yesterday," I tell him.

"I remember you," the jeweler says. He reaches beneath the counter and extracts the soft-cloth bundle. "It's this one, isn't it?" He unwraps it slowly.

"Yeah, that's it."

"All right." He carefully smooths the cloth beneath it. "This is a very nice piece," he adds, perhaps a bit loudly.

"Were you able to fix it?"

"Yes," he says. "But the repair it needed was very . . . particular." He looks at me, almost like he's trying to tell me something.

My heart speeds up for no good reason that I can figure. "But you fixed it?"

He nods. "It'll be twenty-two dollars."

I pull out the cash and hand it to him. He quickly stuffs the money into his breast pocket. Strange that he doesn't turn to the cash register. I get a sinking feeling in my belly. Like an elevator ride.

The jeweler slides the watch toward me by pushing the soft cloth across the counter. Then he looks to his right.

My gaze follows. Out of the shadows steps a cop.

I don't know how I didn't sense his presence before now. It fills the room, takes away all the breathable air.

The officer walks forward, cautiously approaching me. He says, "Come with me."

I think about the gun at my waist. Close calls aside, I've never had to shoot anyone. Is this the moment? The cop has a gun, too. It's holstered, but it's there. And he's bound to be a quick draw.

The shop door opens just then. Some random guy walks in. We all look at him. Me. The cop. The jeweler. The new customer pauses, like he knows he just walked into something. He turns around and walks out.

The split-second distraction sets me in motion. My mind flashes through the options.

Pull the gun? Get shot.

Make a run for it? Get shot.

Lie down for the law? Get fucked.

It's no kind of decision. The kind of moment when all the horrors converge, and all you can do is stand there. I'm not even twenty-one yet, and my life is about to be over.

I raise my hands, exposing the gun tucked in my belt. The cop's gaze drops straight to it, and he reaches out in one quick motion and scoops it away from me.

"Put your hands forward," he says. I do it.

The cuffs come down cold on my wrists. My gaze falls on the short, dangling chain between them. Locked. Bound. Caught.

Chapter Twenty-Five

Massachusetts, 1946

It's hard to believe it's real. The bars and the stench of desperation, the dried sweat of the hundreds who've sat here before me. This unwelcome sobriety.

Lying here, I go over it and over it in my mind. There's nothing else to do.

Thinking: *I should have shot the cop.*

Thinking: *I wouldn't have made it in time. I was cornered.*

Thinking: *I should have shot him anyway. I should have died trying.*

Death would be better than where I am now. Anything would be.

It was a stupid move, I can see now. Going back for the watch. Sometimes after you make your bed, you just gotta lie in it. I was trying to rewrite a song, replay a note. Something impossible.

What's worse is they got my friends, too. Rounded up Shorty because he's my roommate. Sophia, because of a note in my pocket with her name on it. Her sister from something after that.

I lie on the narrow cot, sober as I've been in what feels like a hundred years. I'm going absolutely mad with it. Crazy. Itching out of my skin.

It's not just the arrest that's haunting me. It's every bad thing that's ever happened, bubbling to the surface. No high to help me rise above it. Any of it.

Shorty and I are being charged the same, so they bring us into the courtroom together. We enter through the side doors, into a wood-paneled room—real institutional feeling, with a high seat for the judge, two long tables facing him, and several rows of chairs behind.

They walk us to the tables. Shorty looks a mess. I've never seen him this way, wild-eyed and flailing, like a cornered animal. Shorty's always been so steady. He's always been ahead of me, above. But we're the same now. Our chains look very much the same.

Seeing how scared he looks makes me feel more scared. Maybe more scared than I've ever been. As scared as when

I was staring down Archie—more so, because there's no reefer high to buffer me from the fear.

They read out the charges: Carrying firearms. Larceny. Breaking and entering. Possession of stolen goods.

The lawyers take turns talking to the judge. Shorty and I sit quietly.

I'm shocked when they bring out the girls, not as defendants but as witnesses against us. My court-appointed lawyer says they'll be facing charges, too, but what they say about us might help them get lighter sentences.

Sophia takes the stand. I try to catch her eye, but she won't look at me. She sits up there, working her lacy handkerchief as if it's prayer beads. A good Christian girl, who got caught up with some big, bad darkies. She pleads misunderstanding. Fat tears roll. The jury leans forward, fingers on their lips. Horrified at the very thought.

She breaks down crying, talking about how we had taken advantage of her and confused her. How I had tricked her into telling me what I needed to know to rob those houses.

Every word is like a knife to me. It's like watching a motion picture, something you know is just made up, and yet you believe it. With every word, I feel the prison walls closing tighter around us.

"She's lying," I tell the lawyer. "She's my girl. She's my partner."

"You had no business being with white women," the

lawyer answers. "You'll do the ten years. Just count yourself lucky they aren't claiming rape, or it'd be life."

"It wasn't like that," I snap.

"Doesn't matter." The lawyer shrugs. "You were with them."

Some kind of free lawyer. He's not even really on our side. The whole court's out to get us. No reason we should have to do ten years. I know enough guys who've gone up for burglary—the usual sentence is five, six years tops. Sometimes you even get out early.

I glance at Sophia's husband, seated in the third row of the gallery, his steaming-hot glare pointed right at me.

I don't need anyone to paint the picture for me. Shorty and I are going to rot in jail, and not just because of what we stole.

We're Negroes from Roxbury. Sophia and her sister are white girls from the Hill. Oil and water. Fire and ice.

There might not be a rope, but it's a lynching all the same. I hear it in my ear, like a whisper. I try to brush it away with my hand, like a fly, but I've already heard it.

All this time, I've loved Sophia. Felt proud of her. I've wanted to squire her around. Wanted everyone to see. Now it all seems empty.

I thought Sophia loved me. But she chose her words carefully up there, never admitting that we had so much as slept together. She sold me out, sure enough. I've seen her cry in real life, and it doesn't look anything like what she was doing in court. After all we've been through. All the times we found each other in the midst of the crazy city. All the times we fell into each other's arms. Suddenly it means nothing. What made me think that Sophia was so much better than the other girls I'd known?

"Eight to ten years for each count," the judge announces. "Sentences to be served concurrently."

Concurrently, not back to back. That's a good thing. The only thing to hold on to in this whole mess. I close my eyes. I'm not relieved. Not even a little bit. Just resigned.

Shorty wails and collapses against the table. His mother reaches forward and tries to console him, but the bailiffs step in between them. Ella's there, too, reaching out for me, but I don't want to be touched. Can't be.

Charlestown Prison, 1946

22843.

It's stamped on my clothes. On my plate. On my bucket. It's sprawled in giant type across every sheet of notes they write about me. I'm made to answer to it, when they call. Like a dog on a leash. Prisoner 22843.

They might as well have written it on my skin, like they did to the Jews in their camps during the war. The prison guards are no better than Nazis. No better than slaveholders. We are the hated people, too. Chained. Degraded. Dragged through the mud. Crushed beneath their boots. Spat upon.

I wish I had fought now. But not against the Nazi stain. Shorty was right, all that time, about where our fight was. How did I not see it sooner?

Shorty's with me, but he hasn't forgiven me for how we ended up here. I thought we were sewn together, Shorty and me, after all we'd been through. I was wrong. The watch got us caught, and the watch was my fault, plus I got him into the burglaries in the first place, which makes it all my fault, which makes him hate me in a deep, seam-tearing way. He keeps to himself at the other side of any room I happen to be in with him.

Everywhere, rows of black prisoners. I wonder what Mr. Ostrowski, from all those years ago, would think of me. I'm just a nigger for sure now, just as he said. Fallen all the way down. No prospects.

I pace the cell. Seven feet by nine feet. A prison.

I get it now. The word echoes in my head. *Prison. Prison.* All the other words don't do it justice. *Big house. Upstate. Up the river. Behind bars.* You don't feel it like you do in that one closed-in, ever-so-suffocating word. *Prison.*

We have to eat with the stench of our own shit around us. I can't even tell what kind of food we're eating. The stink is stronger than anything. Once a day they empty the pots—once a day! And there's no place to wash, which just adds to the horror.

Stinks is a weak word to describe it. The full, gagging reek of a hundred shit buckets, each covered by a cloth that does nothing to stem the odor.

Prison.

The metal is a kind of cold I'd never felt before. A solid kind of cold. The bars don't begin to warm under my grip, not like a subway handle or a railing. I knew from the first touch: they're always going to be cold.

I was never meant to be held in a box. No matter who tried to put me in one: schoolmarms with their rulers, cops with their nightsticks. The prison guards now. Same difference. I don't bend.

I throw my supper tray. "I don't need this!" I shout. "I don't need this!" ·

Rough hands grab me, hold me down. I buck against it. I will not be broken. I will not stand in a row with my head down.

Some guard's knee pushes my cheek into the floor. All the grit of the jail digs into me from below. From above, I feel his joint creaking. Feels like I'm taking all of his weight on my face bones.

There's weight on the rest of me as well. I can't move a muscle anywhere. "Calm down," a voice says, like I can control how calm I feel when I'm being hog-tied like an animal and caged in preparation for slaughter.

When I am trussed, immobile, they lever me to my feet. I can shuffle, inch by inch, down the corridor. I wouldn't voluntarily walk anywhere they choose to lead me, but I have no choice, being tied like this. Two guards on either side, holding my arms. A guy in front with his hand on my chains, tugging me so that I have to either fall down or tiptoe hop. I choose to fall down, but they don't carry me. They kick and nudge and beat me, then they stand me back up. It's not a real choice. To fall is to ask them to beat me. To hop is to do their bidding, but it ultimately saves my skin.

They slide the food tray under the gap in my cell door. I pick it up and throw it back at them, watch the unidentifiable mush splash against the bars, messing the clean pressed uniform cloth and white ruddy cheeks.

"Two-two-eight-four-three," they bark. "You are out of line. You are going in the hole."

I am in the hole already. They imply a deeper hole, a deeper shame, but my shame cannot go any deeper. All that is left of me, beyond the shame, is fury.

I pound the bars. I kick. I scream. No one comes. No one cares.

Solitary.

They plunge me into darkness, someplace deep. I hear the creak of hinges, the rattle of my cage, but I can't see beyond my eyes, though they are open.

The hunger that arcs through me is an epic, longing kind. Food cannot satisfy it, certainly not the slop they slide me, so I do not eat. I throw the paltry offering back in their faces, again and again, until I am desperate, diving for the soggy crusts of bread they have resorted to.

I've eaten crusts of bread before, but they were always served with love. They never tasted so miserable. I curl into a ball on the rock-cold floor and cry for Mom. The word doesn't pass my lips, but it ricochets through me until I am rocked raw and split open.

I wake, my body like ice. Weep myself senseless.

No human should have to suffer in this place. In this lonely hellhole, there's not even a chance to get warm.

Chapter Twenty-Six

Charlestown Prison, 1947

The guys who work in the kitchens sneak us matchbooks full of nutmeg. You can buy them for a penny. If you mix the nutmeg in your water glass and drink it, you get a bit of a blurry high. Like a touch of reefer, maybe. Enough to take the edge off.

It's not the high I'm used to, it's not the one I'm craving, but it's the best there is.

The nutmeg helps keep me calm enough to go on living my life in this cage. It steadies me. It's slightly less miserable now to be out of my cell, out of solitary, and talking to a few people from time to time.

They put me to work in the license-plate shop. My station is by the conveyor belt where the pressed plates go to be painted. It's a fairly simple business. First some guys roll in these big tin sheets. Real thin but sturdy. They take them one by one and put them through the plate press, changing the numbers as they go. The big press's lid comes down on a hinge like a steam iron. Its rounding metal blades slice the edges of the tin to the right size and shape, while the letter and number forms punch the license number into the center.

Then they flip the fresh plates onto our belt. They come sliding down toward us, one by one, all metallic and plain. We paint the whole surface green. Then they dry. A little ways down the line, other guys run a roller over the raised part, the letters and numbers, turning them white. In a small white strip at the top, we punch MASS 47 to show the year of registration.

As I learn the ropes of the license-plate shop, I study the other guys, trying to see how and what they do. They chatter up and down the line, sometimes laughing and joking, sometimes spitting bitter debates. Politics. Religion. The plight of the black man in America.

We have Christians, Muslims, and atheists among us. For the Christians, everything is all about Jesus and the Bible. The Muslims have their own country, it sounds like. Something called the Nation of Islam. Their leader is a guy named Elijah Muhammad, a name that sounds familiar. "*The Honorable* Elijah Muhammad," one of them is always correcting the others. The atheists try to shoot down everyone's theories.

It amazes me how, despite their big talk, they all work through the system. Keep their heads down. Doing their part. Doing as they're told. I can barely sit still for it, especially with all this religious talk. When the Christian guys talk, I recognize their stories from my childhood, though I try to close my ears. The Muslims also claim to have it all figured out. They wear their little beanies and call each other "brother." They sound like my own brothers, though some of them speak another language; I don't know what the heck they're talking about.

Day after day, their words pound, too close. I know that I have to endure this. I know that I have no choice. But today I start to feel my edges fraying.

"Elijah Muhammad is no prophet," says one of the Christian guys. "Jesus is the flesh-and-blood son of God."

"*The Honorable* Elijah Muhammad," says a Muslim guy. "Jesus was a prophet, but Allah is supreme."

"Allah is supreme," the Muslims echo.

Call him God, call him Allah; as far as I'm concerned, no deity is looking out for any of us. If he was, why would we be here?

I grab a license plate off the line. It's wet with paint, but I don't care. I pick it up, prepare to smash it into something. The conveyor belt. Other license plates. My own head. Someone else's. I raise it high, knowing the target will find itself. Bembry, the older prisoner across the line from me, happens to catch my eye.

"Young brother," he says, holding up his hand. "All you need is your words."

I sit close to Bembry on the line after that. There's a stillness, a calm, that he emanates. I like having it near me. He's tall, like me. Light, like me. And he can talk about the world without saying *God* or *Allah* every other word.

And, boy, can he talk.

Hearing him, I remember that words are a weapon. I think of the fight I staved off on the Yankee Clipper that day, with the beefy, drunken soldier I made strip. I think of the fervor in my father's voice, channeled into sermons that shook the rafters. I remember being small and looking up, wondering if the rumble could unseat the heavens.

"How'd you learn to talk like that?" I ask Bembry, finally deciding that I want to know.

"Read a book," he tells me. "You'll find all the words you ever wanted."

"What book?" I feel eager. Deep in my stomach, a kind of stirring. Something waking up in me.

Bembry looks me up and down. "Young brother, if I were you, I'd start with the dictionary."

Bembry scores me a copy of the *Oxford English Dictionary*. It's a thick, strange book and certainly full of words. Most strange is how familiar it seems. It has a different design on the cover, but it's a book I've read from before.

When my siblings and I were little, Mom used to sit us down, making us read the dictionary from *A* to *Z* to learn vocabulary. I can almost hear her voice, over my shoulder. Almost. I push the book to the other side of the room. It lives there, closed, for days and days. Why don't I just return it? Tell Bembry it isn't for me?

But I don't return it. I actually like seeing it there when I return to my cell each night.

I read the dictionary again with new understanding. Find words that I know. Words I couldn't have guessed in a million years. Words that make me chuckle and blush. Words that make me remember.

"Good," Bembry says. "Now you've read that, you can read anything that comes along." And he puts in my hand a volume called *The Souls of Black Folk* by W. E. B. Du Bois.

Reading requires stillness. I've been running so fast, so hard, so long, it actually hurts to stand still. Everything behind me continues to move forward, while I am stuck here. I can't outrun it now. The bars won't let me. I jog in place, lifting my knees in a fierce rhythm that raises my breath and sets my heart pounding, but doesn't quite drum out my rising thoughts.

*   *   *

The fierce mental churning. The quiet, solitary dark. There is nothing, *nothing*, to distract me. No reefer. No powder. No women. No drink. The nutmeg only carries me so far. It's the most maddening kind of nothing, the everything of my head.

I write to Wilfred. To Philbert. To Hilda. To Reginald. The precious minutes I can write become a golden escape. There's little I can say that's different, because I'm stuck now, but they write to me about their lives. They've found a new God, they tell me. A God who looks out for black people: Allah.

They are happy to hear about the things I've been reading. *It's what Papa would have wanted,* Hilda writes.

I reread their letters, and what I see, apart from this chorus about Allah and the Nation of Islam, is the same old story.

They are together, and I am alone.

They all come visiting. I don't see why. I have given them nothing, *nothing*, that suggests I need anyone beyond myself. It's been so long between us. They are echoes from the past that no longer attach to any actual sound. Ella. Wilfred. Hilda. Philbert. Reginald. They ride all this way, the long bus ride I took years back, to come visit me in my prison.

My brothers have grown slightly taller and thicker with age. Next to them I am a starved, scrawny prison rat. But in most ways we are the same as we were. They stand in line, facing me, while I flail about.

331

Philbert sits across from me on his visit, his usual buoyant energy rendered nervous and quiet by our surroundings. I'm pretty used to it now, but prison walls sure have a way of being intimidating. Especially when you know you don't belong there.

"You always know where I am now, eh?" I joke, recalling the letter he once wrote and how he worried about my various travels.

Philbert cracks a slight smile. "Do you still have that map?" he asks. "The one we gave you when you left?"

I don't know. I probably have it somewhere, in my things. It's probably at Ella's house, or maybe it got lost in the shuffle when the cops raided Shorty's place.

I shrug. "They didn't let me bring things in with me," I say. "Sorry."

"How about we get you another one?" Philbert says.

I put out my hands, indicating the walls around me. "What do I need a map for now?" I ask him.

He ducks his head. "Right. Well, I guess I liked knowing you were carrying something we gave you," he says. "It meant a lot to us that you kept it."

The way he says "us" makes me feel lonely. I've had this feeling before, but I fight against it. It's strange to feel so distant and so familiar at the same time.

Seven, eight years is nothing. Nothing close to enough to tear us apart. Anyway, how it is now is how it always was. I was always the one who couldn't be quite like the rest.

* * *

I don't know the name of the prisoner who dies in the middle of the night. All I know is what the guys are saying about him. Dead. Hanged by the neck. Jailhouse suicide.

They let us out in the morning, and we have no choice but to walk by the cell where it happened if we want to get outside. Away from the stench, which, strangely, isn't made any worse by death.

They don't lift the body from the cell right away. He dangles there, half hanging, half lying. Grotesque and crumpled and black and blue.

I try to close my eyes, but I can't, in the end. It's as if they know I can't, too. They want us to see. Want us to think about his ugly, twisted death as if it were our own.

He did it to himself. Bound his bedsheet in knots and strung it around his own neck. Strung himself up from the *T* of his cell bars. We all have them, the places where the vertical bars meet the horizontal ones. We all have sheets, however filthy. We could all step out. At any time.

The shame the guards would inflict on us is made complete by the fact that we don't leave. We stay. We take the punishment. We let ourselves be pressed down. . . .

Much as he hanged himself, Brother Hang was done in by forces beyond him. It hearkens back to the long-ago rope, swinging in the slight breeze. Death at the hands of the system. I've been reading about the black man in our world. It's right there in the pages of every book Bembry hands to me. Brother Hang landed inside these walls because of a system that failed him.

The guard who knocks me down and puts his foot on my face, who drags me to the hole—he didn't build these walls. He didn't invent the word *nigger,* however well he's learned to throw it. It's all so much bigger, and so built-in.

Brother Hang found a way to free himself from prison, I write to my brothers. Maybe it is the only way. This place is meant to consume me. I should just let it, and let it be done.

Reginald writes back, saying that when I am ready, he can free me from prison. *Don't smoke cigarettes. Don't take any drugs. And don't eat any more pork,* he says. *I'll show you the way free.*

I wonder what sort of escape he's planning, but at this point I'm game for anything. I clean myself up, get ready to make my escape. All the reefer, all the coke, and all the booze is far behind me. Now even the nutmeg haze fades, and I see myself. For the first time in a long time.

The mirror is little more than a sheet of metal. Whatever thin lacquer on the surface makes it reflect has grown chipped. I can't really see myself clearly. My edges are blurred, not a crisp line in sight.

Only one thing I can see, for damn clear: I'm caged. A fucking mess.

I can't get high off anything anymore. Nothing left but to be low.

I used to want to be low. Go down the Hill. Get into the

darkness. Find the base of myself and roll around. I guess I finally found the bottom.

Prison is designed to break you, but I'm already shattered. There's nothing these bars could take from me that hasn't already been taken.

I'm ready, I write Reginald. *I'm clean. Come and get me.*

Reginald's responding instructions make no sense to me. *Allah is supreme.*

I'm waiting for the escape plan, I write back.

Then I hear from my brothers that they meant religion as the escape. *Join the Nation of Islam,* they write. *Follow the Honorable Elijah Muhammad. Trust in Allah, and you will find freedom.*

They're not coming for me. The realization hits hard. The religions collide. My brothers' Allah and the voices of the black men in prison who speak the same cryptic words. My father's distant God. The Christ my mother spent so much energy appeasing.

There's nothing there for me. I like it Bembry's way— just reading. Reading. Reading.

I can't get enough of these books. I consume the written word the way I once consumed liquor or reefer. It fills me in a way that is as powerful, as spiritual, as high. There's so much to know, so much to think about and wrestle with, so much outside of myself. I *have* to get outside of myself, or I'll die inside my mind.

I'm reminded of the days when I was a good student. I would rip through an essay assignment in a matter of minutes, and Mom would be so proud.

There comes a point when my body breathes a sigh, and there's some kind of solace in this learning. A point when I stop wrapping my hands around the bars as if I could rattle them. Not a quick change. Not like the flip of a switch or anything. It's just a softening, like the last comb stroke through the hair that makes it hold the conk. The strokes before mattered, even though you couldn't feel it. One day I just notice that I'm not gripping so tight.

I can't believe how much easier it is to get through the day now that I'm no longer in a constant state of fury. I don't fight with the guards anymore. I don't get sent into solitary. I spend every moment that I can reading. When it's time to work, I go to the plate shop, and always do what I'm asked. Accept each tray of slop with a quiet "thank you." Before long, people start coming to me for advice, and even the guards look at me with respect.

I get the word that my new good behavior has earned me a transfer out of Charlestown Prison. Where I'm headed is supposed to be better, they tell me. I figure it sure can't be any worse.

The windows of the bus are layered with a thick metal mesh. It's like looking at the world through honeycomb. We are further caged behind a fencelike wall between us and the driver and the guards, with their pair of shotguns.

It's OK, though. I'm not afraid. I've been reading my books. I'm awake to the way they think now. Chaining us to the bench rails isn't enough. They have to have us in a box. They have to have us know they could shoot us. At any time.

Chapter Twenty-Seven

Norfolk Prison Colony, 1948

Norfolk Prison Colony is like a paradise compared to Charlestown. I count my lucky stars—that is, I'm reminded again that there is some luck to be had, even for a washed-up hustler like me. Heck, I'm only twenty-three.

For a second, I wonder if all the cigarettes and reefer I haven't been smoking and all the pork I haven't been eating actually add up to something. My brothers think that my new fortune is more than luck—it's a sign from Allah that I'm supposed to do something different with my life. But thinking that way puts pressure on my chest. I don't believe in signs. Only luck.

Thinking *luck* makes me think *hustle*. Think *numbers*. Think how to make a buck, and how to keep my mind busy so I don't have to entertain these thoughts.

Turns out, I haven't lost the touch.

Guys here at Norfolk get to listen to the radio. They broadcast baseball games, and Jackie Robinson is the hit of the day, the first black man in Major League Baseball. We tune in every game. Wouldn't miss it.

Cigarettes are like cash around here. It's easy enough to lay off some bets.

I lean my ear up against the radio, and I know perfectly well that it's baseball I'm listening to, but for a while I could swear I'm hearing about Joe Louis. My eyes close of their own accord, and I can feel the living-room rug beneath my knees, Philbert's breath upon my neck. I can feel the fight rise in me. Feel the hope and the energy and—

I wrench myself out of the memory. Jackie Robinson's at bat. Focus now. Focus.

The task at hand is complicated enough. Numbers to keep in my head. Every swing of the bat, I recalculate Robinson's average. By the end of the game, I've done the math problem a couple dozen times. I roll out the cartons of cigarettes and get ready to collect.

The Joe Louis matches from years ago were the most exciting, dramatic sporting events I ever heard. Why does it feel like nothing will ever raise me to such a fevered place again? I wonder if maybe I should be taking book on boxing. Jackie Robinson is the hot item of the day, but he isn't the only game in town.

But I push away the wondering when it starts to draw me too far back. If I'm going back in time, I'll focus my memories on the good days. Harlem. Numbers. Always hustling. Always stepping.

Don't let it catch me. Don't let it hold me down.

The Norfolk hustle is a cakewalk. It's as easy as taking bets from the numbers, but with a captive audience. If they don't pay up, there's no way to dodge. They have to be right here every day. They have to face me.

One guy owes me better than a pack at this point. I go down to his block to try and find him. His bed is empty.

His neighbor says, "He's in sick bay."

"That's no excuse," I answer. "He owes what he owes."

The neighbor is an old dark man. Sitting in the corner of his bunk, reading a black-bound book with a cross on the cover. A Bible.

He squints up at me. "When he's back, you'll get your payment. He's good for it."

Sure, he's always paid before, but right now that seems beside the point. I'm glaring at this guy now. "Who are you?" I say to him. "Why do you want to get into this?"

He lays the Bible aside. "I wasn't getting into it," he says. "You came looking for my neighbor, and I was telling you where he is."

He talks quiet and firm. He's exactly like a hundred old

guys I've known. The old miner on the bus. The weathered
hustlers at Small's. Some of the musicians at the Braddock.
Bembry at Charlestown. West Indian Archie, even. Familiar.
The sort of man who's everywhere. No avoiding him.
Always butting in. Trying to get his piece.

"You want to stand in for him?" I ask. "You want to take
what's coming to him?" I don't understand the words coming out of my mouth.

The old guy stands up. "If that's what has to happen,"
he says. "But I'm trying to tell you, you'll have what he owes
you. Tomorrow or the next day."

"Well, it's due today," I tell him. "Come on out, if you're
so hot to let me know how things should be." I motion him
forward with my fists up.

Nothing about what I'm doing makes sense. I threaten
guys who don't want to pay, but just so they'll pay. I
never have to actually do anything. Still, I motion him
closer.

"I've thrown a punch or two in my day," he says, rolling
up his sleeves. "Are you a fighter, son?"

Every word he speaks enrages me further. "One more
step," I taunt. "And I'll show you."

I have never been a good boxer. Why did I invite this?
I don't need this. I never imagined he'd stand up. He's a
dark, stout Christian man. He's got no beef with me. Why
would he even agree to this fight?

Guys from the area circle around us, hooting. We face
off, stepping lightly. The old guy squints at me, taking

341

me in. His hands are large and meaty. In that moment, I know it's already over. I know I'm going down.

An instant later, I know something else.

This man is my father.

I'm in the ring with him, fists raised to block any blows to my heart, before I understand.

This man is my father.

One squinted eye. A broad, dark face. A deep, dark faith behind it.

"Come on, young brother," he says. "Let's do this." There's resignation in his voice. Like it's a fight he doesn't want to have. I don't see why; he got himself into this, same as I did.

But when we're close, he lowers his arms. Looks at me, like he's seeing something in me that he hadn't seen before. "You know, I don't want to fight you."

"Put your hands up, old man," I tell him. It's not going to be over like that. I know, with every beat of my living heart, that this fight has already started. I've been in the ring with him seventeen years and counting.

"No," he says. "But you do what you have to." He comes close to me, so close I think he's going to forget the fists and throw his arms around me. I hold my breath, but he brushes past me, returning to his cell.

I'm furious and shaking. "Don't walk away." At the core of my soul is the desire to punch him. In every fight of my life, I've been knocked down. Can't get up. Can't get up. Can't land a punch to save my life. It's just an onslaught. Every fight of my entire life leaves me lying on the mat. Arms over my face. *Don't hurt me. Don't hurt me.* But they always do. I've been slammed into oblivion over and over.

It's all I can do to get up, to get up and face the next round. There's always another round. I'm not dead yet.

The old man is well away now, back at his bunk. "How could you leave like that?" I shout after him. "How could you leave me nothing but lies?" I could chase him, but I don't. Because that's the shit of it, isn't it? I'm already knee-deep in this fight, yet it can't be had. Can't ever be had.

He's not here to fight me. He's never been here, and yet he's always here. Him not being here is here. His absence is a gaping, aching hole in me.

The circle of men disperses, muttering disappointment; they were promised a fight. I'm too stunned to consider ways to salvage any cell-block pride out of my misstep. I find myself on my knees. I stare in the only direction that makes any sense—at the dark old man reclining in his cell. He gazes back at me over the lip of his Bible, open in his hands once more.

I don't look away, although I badly want to. For the first time ever, I force myself to face the truth. Papa's gone, and he took with him my belief in everything he promised.

It's no wonder I can't win a fistfight. When I was six years old, I took the biggest punch of my life and I haven't figured out how to get up yet.

*   *   *

There's so much to be angry about. Why does it keep coming back to Papa?

I'm angry at the white guards who beat us; at the white cops who put us here; at the white slaveholders who tied our ancestors down in the guts of great ships—they caused this cascade of terrible things that have led me here.

They want to write a story about me that ends behind bars. They'll say I was no good, that I always belonged here—it just took a while for it all to catch up to me.

Papa would tell a different story. Why is it I'm remembering now all the things he used to tell me? I can hear his voice so clearly, a voice that I thought I had pounded out of my head. And hearing it, I know that what I'm being told is possible is too limiting. But I am stuck here. Stuck in it. Why is he not here to help me, now that I want to try it his way?

In desperation, I write a letter to Elijah Muhammad. If there is another way, a better way, I have to find it. My family has found wisdom in Elijah Muhammad, much of which makes him sound very much like Papa. Facing the old man—in my mind at least—has made me realize something. I don't want to fight Papa any longer, to forget him. I want to remember. I want to come home.

I think it was a dream. I think it was. It must have been a dream. It's been so long since I've seen my father. In a photo. In my mind's eye. Anywhere.

He comes up to me, real graceful. His hands, so large, reach for my shoulders. They cup me, cover me, cure me of some long-held ache.

"Papa?" I whisper.

The words flow forth from him, unending. Not a sound to be heard, only the feeling of words, warm and soft like a blanket. Rough as wool at the same time. Scolding and healing. Scalding and holy. Like the touch of the brothers' distant God.

I've gone wrong.

I've done wrong.

"Papa," I whisper. "I'm sorry."

There's no punishment in dreams, maybe. I wake, sweat-cold and starving. A soul-deep hunger that I've never known how to fill.

A line of powder.

A line in the sand.

A line between the things I know and the things I can't begin to understand. The things that threaten to consume me.

I receive a return letter, signed by the Honorable Elijah Muhammad. The words pour into me, begin to fill me in a way unlike any of the words before them.

I feel new, but his words don't. They thrum inside me at a comfortable pitch, plucking strings of my soul in places I haven't tried to reach in a long time.

Up, up, you mighty race. It's not what he writes, but it's what I hear. Black is strong. Black is holy. We must rise up again. Be proud. Be wise.

After I hear from the Honorable Elijah Muhammad, Reginald's promise of escape begins to make more sense. It begins to seem that the world is not finished with me. *It does not matter who you think you have been up until now. Go forth as a child of Allah.*

It does not matter who you have been up until now. I roll these words around in my head. I have been so many things.

Son.

Brother.

Negro.

Malcolm.

Nigger.

Red.

Homeboy.

Detroit Red.

22843.

Look what has become of me. A number is all I am now. The number erases all that has gone before, stamps it null and void. In the end, I've become a nameless thing. And what this letter seems to be saying is that I can put aside the number now, too. I can rise out of this prison hole to become a man of my own choosing.

* * *

I keep my head down as the guards walk past us, shouting. But I no longer hear them. They think it's enough to make me stand in this row with the others. Think it's enough to bind us in the same coarse cloth. My body obeys. My mind rebels.

This place. These walls. They don't contain me. That is Elijah Muhammad's message to me. My mind, my soul, is greater than anything that can bind me. I was right all along: I cannot be contained.

I don't have to be 22843 anymore. I can see it now. I can look into a proper mirror, here on the wall, and see a man, a new man, clean before Allah and ready to serve. What should I call myself? My impulse is to start fresh. Be someone completely brand-new, but it isn't quite right that way. Everything before this moment matters; it all adds up to now.

"Malcolm" was my name as a child. I am no longer a child.

"Little" was once a slaveholder's name. I am no longer a slave.

I was Shorty's "homeboy" and Sammy's "Detroit Red," but now I belong to Allah. It is his voice with which I wish to be renamed now.

I listen and listen. Until I know.

I am my father's son. My way through the world has been

paved by him. His challenges, his choices. All bequeathed to me.

These things are hard to hold.

But I see my life more clearly now.

I'm not meant to be part of the things that are wrong with the world, but neither am I meant to run from them. I'm meant to fight against them. I can't hold my own in the ring, but out in the world, I do know how to fight. With words. With truth.

Everything that I've lived through has been part of my fight.

My father's God. My mother's God. My brothers' Allah. They are one. They are in me.

I am my father's son. Still, and always. He named me, and I will carry that name, just as I carry a part of him.

What I don't want is the stamp of the white world on me. That I must fight against. Throw off the shackles of past ugliness. Buck myself free. For that, too, is Papa's legacy, and something I must carry.

I bend down and sign the letter to the Honorable Elijah Muhammad:

Malcolm X.

The guards may come for me. The devil may come. The chains and the darkness. All the wrongs of the world may come. The noose. Every force that thirsts for the destruction of the black man in America.

I am my father's son. They will always come for me. But I will never succumb.

Malcolm, age fifteen, Roxbury, Massachusetts

AUTHOR'S NOTE

I am my father's child. I consider it an honor and a privilege to tell the story of his life and work, and I proudly accept responsibility for doing so, not because he is my father but because I believe that accurate information about him and his life's journey will empower others—especially those fatherless children searching for their purpose and their identity—to achieve their highest potential. When world-renowned and eventually martyred human-rights activist El-Hajj Malik El-Shabazz—Malcolm X—came walking through the front door of our home in the evenings, he was simply Daddy. I imagine that as a child, Malcolm felt the same about his dad, my grandfather, Earl Little. At the age of six, young Malcolm could not have fully understood the broader significance of his father's life and death. He knew that Papa Earl went away, and although he heard the whispers about the Ku Klux Klan's Black Legion, years would pass before all the pieces came together as a meaningful understanding of his father's martyrdom—that he was killed while serving his people. Malcolm would endure years of turmoil and discontent before understanding that Papa Earl lived and died committed to the cause of securing freedom, justice, and equality for disenfranchised African Americans.

Those were long and difficult years for Malcolm. Grief, pain, and confusion prevented him from seeing his father's footsteps, which were paved for him to follow. Had Papa Earl lived longer, Malcolm might have found a more direct path to becoming the human-rights advocate his father wanted him to be—but in that case, Malcolm almost certainly would not have become the icon the world remembers today.

This book is a work of fiction, but it is based on real people and events. You may be wondering, How much of the story is true? As a well-known public figure, my father made speeches, kept diaries, and published his autobiography, and many other books have been written about him as well. Nevertheless, not as much is widely known about Malcolm's life "before the X." I am fortunate to have inside knowledge about my father's young life, because people who knew him longer than I did—like my mother, my aunts and uncles, and my father's childhood neighbors and friends—told me wonderful stories about him.

The story contained in this novel has lived in my heart for a long time. With Kekla's help, I am very happy and proud to have brought it to life for you. Indeed, Malcolm lived in all of the places, worked all of the jobs, and engaged in most of the activities described. All but a few minor characters are based on real people Malcolm knew, though, of course, we couldn't go back in time and capture everyone's precise dialogue and actions. We have taken a few artistic liberties for the sake of cohesion, but the overall story you have read represents the true journey of Malcolm Little, the adolescent, on the road to becoming Malcolm X.

History has recorded what came next for Malcolm. He would exit prison reconciled with his parents, their teachings, and his own individual identity. He would ultimately challenge racial injustice, defending African Americans brutalized by discrimination, fighting for human rights as well as civil rights, and working to unite the black community around the world in a single struggle for freedom and independence.

The Nation of Islam (NOI) would prove to be the platform for Malcolm to grow into the extraordinary gifts that would bring him national and international acclaim. Very often discussion of Malcolm's conversion to Islam in prison omits the fact that his so-called conversion was actually a return to his roots and a reconciliation with his family's long-standing commitment to human-rights activism. Accepting Islam meant being reunited with the father he had privately resented for abandoning him, meaning that he had had to enter manhood and resolve the many challenges he confronted alone. Grounded in his faith, Malcolm emerged from Norfolk Prison Colony eager to embrace whatever service to humanity God would ask of him, as had his father and mother before him. Malcolm Little became Malcolm X because members of the Nation of Islam were encouraged to drop the names of their forebears' slaveholders.

In 1952, at age twenty-six, Malcolm X became the Nation of Islam's chief spokesman. Within seven years, he helped the NOI expand from four temples to fifty temples, increasing membership from several hundred to hundreds of thousands. Under Malcolm's tutelage regarding self-help, self-determination, and cooperative economics, the NOI owned businesses around the United States, including the largest black-owned businesses in the country, and the NOI's children attended separate schools owned and operated by the organization.

Malcolm endured a painful split from the Nation of Islam in 1964 and began preaching and organizing independently. He retained many of his followers and formed the Muslim Mosque, Incorporated, in Harlem. Malcolm made the Islamic pilgrimage, known as hajj, to the Muslim holy land of Mecca, in Saudi Arabia. There he worshipped alongside people of all ethnic groups and decided to expand his ministry beyond the black community by preaching interracial cooperation and human rights for all. He embraced the name El-Hajj Malik El-Shabazz.

Teenage Malcolm had no way of foreseeing these great accomplishments. His adolescence, marked by separation from the firm and loving guidance of his parents, was spent trying to escape from his identity as an African American as well as his family legacy. His days as Detroit Red—a time of great pain and confusion in his life—reminded him that so many others in his community continued to struggle as he once had. He strove to hold himself up as a light for those trapped in the dark places of their own hearts and circumstances, in hopes that one day they, too, would unleash their true potential and support the ongoing cause of complete liberation. The boy who shied away from Marcus Garvey's battle cry, "Up, up, you mighty race," became a young man who dedicated his life to uplifting those who were physically, emotionally, and psychologically scarred.

Malcolm encouraged African Americans to look more deeply into their past to understand themselves even better. He taught that their history began long before enslavement in America and that their roots were in the ancient civilizations of Africa, when black men and women commanded their own destinies in their own homelands. He taught that African Americans descended from priests, scholars, scientists, architects, physicists, astrologists, warriors, farmers, musicians, and the like. Malcolm X taught black people to look beyond the degradation of the second-class citizenship in which they were mired to the days of triumph and glory that once were and would be again—as soon as African Americans stood up and claimed their heritage.

Malcolm's powerful speeches motivated crowds of disenfranchised citizens and consequently disturbed the power elite. Throughout his ministry, he was falsely classified as a racist and hate-monger and was subjected to government surveillance and subversion—all designed to undermine his efforts and disillusion his followers. On the contrary, Malcolm was a young man who loved his people and challenged the injustices committed against them. Malcolm X was assassinated on February 21, 1965, at the age of thirty-nine.

My father and I have a great deal in common, including

ng a middle child and the loss of our fathers to assassination at an early age. Though he passed away when I was not quite three years old, my father's voice, his beliefs, and his lessons remained a vital part of my childhood and my evolving identity. As a result, I have grown to become a proud African-American Muslim woman. My mother, Dr. Betty Shabazz—much like my grandmother Louise Little— raised a houseful of children alone, and she taught my five sisters and me all about our father, our extended family, our ancestors, and our history. She, too, sacrificed personal freedom to the cause of securing liberty and justice for all. I will always be inspired by her admonition, "Ilyasah, just as one must drink water, one must give back."

I share this story to remind myself and others that there is hope for each one of us. No matter where we have been, no matter how many doubts we hold, and no matter what mistakes we have made, we have the ability to rise above our current circumstances—especially when we are inspired by the lessons in our past. Each one of us possesses the power to change our present condition and become the best that life offers.

I have always been proud to be my father's child. And an important part of my journey has been to accept the part of myself that is my father. It is a privilege to carry his work and his legacy forward. I will always strive to walk in his footsteps and become the best person I can, and I invite you to do the same. Thank you for reading his story.

SOME NOTES ABOUT THE CHARACTERS

Most of the characters that exist in this novel are based on real people. A few of the minor characters are composites or purely made up, and many of Malcolm's real-life friends, relatives, and associates were left out of the novel for simplicity. Below, we attempt to give a clearer picture of the people Malcolm encountered in real life and in this novel.

Malcolm and his seven siblings remained close throughout their lives. They constantly wrote letters back and forth during his time in Boston, Harlem, and prison. Many of these letters are preserved in the archives at the New York Public Library's Schomburg Center for Research in Black Culture, located in Harlem, and at the Emory University library in Atlanta. The minor characters who populate Lansing—the welfare people, the Swerlins, Mr. Ostrowski—are also real. Richie (Richard) Dixon is named in *The Autobiography of Malcolm X* as one of Malcolm's childhood friends, but in this novel he's a composite of several white boys Malcolm mentioned there.

Malcolm became close with his elder half-siblings when he moved to Boston. In real life, Ella and Malcolm did not live in her house alone. Ella was married to a man named Kenneth Collins, and they had a son, Rodnell. Ella's sister, Mary, and brother, Earl Jr., lived there, too. Ella's side of the family originated in Georgia, and even though many er relatives eventually followed her to the Boston area, Ella retained an attachment to her southern roots.

Malcolm "Shorty" Jarvis was a trumpet player in real life, and a longtime friend of Malcolm's. Shorty joined the Nation of Islam along with Malcolm in prison. He went on to gain success as a musician and even received a pardon from the commonwealth of Massachusetts in 1976. As Malcolm became well known, Shorty kept track of his friend's career, maintaining a scrapbook discovered after his death in 1998. Most of Malcolm's other acquaintances in Boston, like Fat Frankie, are made up, or composites, based on the types of friends and associates Malcolm described in his autobiography.

Laura and Sophia were real women Malcolm knew, but these are not their real names. Malcolm concealed their true identities in *The Autobiography,* and in this novel we've stuck with the names Malcolm gave them for his own storytelling purposes. His relationship with Laura might not have ended as abruptly as it's portrayed in the novel; she wrote letters to Malcolm long after they stopped seeing each other. Malcolm's intermittent affair with Sophia ended when she betrayed him by testifying against him and Shorty.

Malcolm, Shorty, Sophia, her sister, a third woman, and two other men formed the burglary ring that led to their arrest in 1946. It is not certain who came up with the original plan for these thefts, but the group of accomplices did get caught after Malcolm took a stolen watch to get repaired.

Many of the characters that Malcolm meets in Harlem are based on real people. Sammy McKnight, nicknamed "Sammy the Pimp," ran with Malcolm in Harlem during the time Malcolm considered himself most lost and most reckless. West Indian Archie was a Harlem numbers runner famous for his excellent memory. He never wrote down the numbers but memorized them and later wrote them in a ledger he kept at home. When Malcolm ran numbers for him, he used betting slips like most numbers runners to keep track of the bets. Malcolm's final, disputed claim called Archie's memory into question, which could have unseated Archie and allowed Malcolm to take over his turf.

In this novel, Malcolm refers to meeting famous jazz artists like Duke Ellington, Lionel Hampton, Ella Fitzgerald, and Billie Holiday. He mentions them in passing in his autobiography as well, and he became quite good friends with many musicians and entertainers who were well known at the time or would become famous later. As cool as that sounds, most of these characters were too peripheral to Malcolm's life to fit into the novel.

Other minor characters in the novel are also based on real people Malcolm mentions in his writings, like Charlie Small of Small's Paradise and the prisoner John Bembry. A few characters who are completely fictional include the old miner on the bus, the pair of Garveyites who talk to Malcolm in Small's, and the old dark man in prison who Malcolm confronts near the end of the book.

TIMELINE

May 19, 1925: Malcolm is born in Omaha, Nebraska.

1929: Malcolm's family moves to Lansing, Michigan.

October 1929: The stock market crashes, plunging the nation into the Great Depression.

November 8, 1929: The Black Legion/Ku Klux Klan burns down the Littles' house because they live on land that's supposed to be reserved for white people.

September 1931: Earl Little dies—most likely killed by members of the Black Legion—leaving his family struggling to make ends meet during the Great Depression.

January 1939: Louise Little is committed to Kalamazoo State Hospital. Siblings are split up and sent to live with family friends in Lansing.

Late 1939 or early 1940: Malcolm's half-sister Ella visits Lansing.

Summer 1940: Malcolm visits Ella in Boston.

February 1941: Malcolm moves to Boston.

December 7, 1941: Japanese forces attack Pearl Harbor; the next day, the United States enters World War II.

Early 1942: Malcolm works on the train, effectively moves to Harlem.

October 1942: Malcolm is fired from the train job and officially moves to Harlem.

Late 1942: Malcolm visits his family in Lansing.

June 1, 1943: Malcolm reports to his local draft board in New York and is dismissed with a 4-F ("unfit for military service") classification.

January 1945: Malcolm visits his family in Lansing.

October 1945: After trouble in Harlem, Malcolm moves back to Boston.

December 1945: Malcolm, Shorty, and friends rob houses in Brookline and other wealthy Boston suburbs.

January 1946: Malcolm is arrested while trying to have a stolen watch repaired.

February 26, 1946: Malcolm and Shorty stand trial in Middlesex County Court.

February 1946–March 1948: Malcolm serves time at Charlestown Prison and the Massachusetts Reformatory in Concord.

March 1948: Malcolm is transferred to the Norfolk Prison Colony in Massachusetts.

1948: Via letters and visits, Malcolm's siblings begin urging him to convert to Islam.

August 1952: Malcolm is released from prison. He moves to Detroit and becomes a minister in the Nation of Islam, working alongside his mentor, Elijah Muhammad.

1954: Malcolm becomes head of the NOI's Temple No. 7 in Harlem.

January 1958: Malcolm marries Betty Dean Sanders (Betty X), a registered nurse.

March 1964: Malcolm splits with the Nation of Islam and forms his own entity, the Organization of Afro-American Unity.

March 12–May 21, 1964: Malcolm makes hajj, his pilgrimage to Mecca.

February 21, 1965: Malcolm is assassinated while speaking to followers at the Audubon Ballroom in Harlem.

MALCOLM'S FAMILY TREE

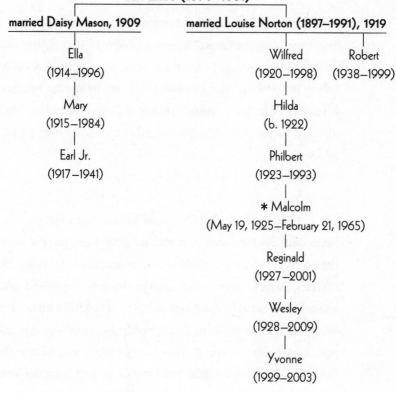

Earl Little (1890–1931)

married Daisy Mason, 1909

Ella
(1914–1996)

Mary
(1915–1984)

Earl Jr.
(1917–1941)

married Louise Norton (1897–1991), 1919

Wilfred
(1920–1998)

Robert
(1938–1999)

Hilda
(b. 1922)

Philbert
(1923–1993)

* Malcolm
(May 19, 1925–February 21, 1965)

Reginald
(1927–2001)

Wesley
(1928–2009)

Yvonne
(1929–2003)

* Malcolm Little

(Malcolm X / El-Hajj Malik El-Shabazz)

married Betty Dean Sanders (1934–1997), 1958

Attallah
(b. 1958)

Qubilah
(b. 1960)

Ilyasah
(b. 1962)

Gamilah
(b. 1964)

Malikah and Malaak
(b. 1965)

HISTORICAL CONTEXT: 1925 TO 1965

Malcolm's life spanned an extremely tumultuous time, encompassing the Great Depression, World War II, and the civil-rights movement—four decades that were especially trying for a black man in America. Long before he became a subject of history himself, Malcolm's day-to-day life was affected by the historical and social circumstances in which he lived.

1920s: Black Activism and White Supremacy

Malcolm's parents were activists who held key positions in the Universal Negro Improvement Association, founded by Marcus Garvey. Garvey's teachings about achievement and economic prosperity for black people spread from his native West Indies throughout the Caribbean, into the United States and around the world through the work of people like Earl and Louise Little. His famous outcry, "Up, up, you mighty race, you can accomplish what you will!" inspired black people everywhere. This great wave of Negro activism continued through the 1920s, with organizations like the National Association for the Advancement of Colored People (NAACP) fighting legal battles against school segregation, lynchings, and a myriad of social injustices.

White supremacist groups like the Ku Klux Klan made a point of making life very difficult for black activists like the Littles. When Earl Little purchased land inside the Lansing city limits—land designated for white residents only—and moved his family there, the Black Legion, a splinter group of the Ku Klux Klan, retaliated by burning down the house in the night. Earl and his family barely escaped alive, and moved from Lansing to East Lansing. Such racial violence was far too common in that era, especially against black activists.

Malcolm witnessed firsthand the deeply ingrained racism that characterized America in those days. His father's murder was a type of lynching—a senseless killing of a black person for a so-called crime that often was not a crime at all, like speaking one's mind about social injustices. Lynching victims were typically hanged, but the term "lynching" did not necessarily mean hanging; it meant a killing that occurred outside of the justice system. Such vigilante justice, with no trial and no due process, was technically illegal, yet when the victims were black people, these laws were not enforced.

By the 1920s, lynchings had become such a common and accepted practice throughout the central and southern United States that white people gathered over picnics to witness the hangings. Many whites held so little respect for black life that they took pictures and even created postcards of the lynched bodies. "Strange Fruit," a song written by Lewis Allen and famously recorded by Billie Holiday, chronicles the horrors of lynching culture by comparing the dead to dangling pieces of fruit.

The haunting words and melody gave voice to the distress and fear that black people already carried inside them.

1930s: The Great Depression

After Earl was killed, Louise Little worked for eight additional years to support her family, but due to the Great Depression, jobs were scarce. The stock market crash of October 1929 had caused an economic crisis that plunged much of the nation into poverty, joblessness, and despair for nearly a decade.

Because of the same prejudice that led to white supremacist actions, the Great Depression disproportionately affected black families. White workers received preference in most jobs, especially the best-paying ones. Louise Little, like many fair-skinned black people, attempted what was known as "passing": she applied to whites-only jobs and let the employers assume she was white. People like Malcolm's favorite teacher, Mr. Ostrowski, reinforced the prevailing social attitude that black people could only hold low-wage menial jobs.

Many poor families survived the Depression by relying on government welfare. The Littles received some welfare assistance at times, but Louise's pride—and the Little family values—prevented her from borrowing on credit or taking all of the welfare offerings available. State welfare workers insisted that Louise give up the children, but she held her own for nearly ten years, until the government forcefully intervened and committed her to a mental institution—not a unique occurrence for strong, independent women at the time.

1940s: World War II

Malcolm arrived in Boston shortly before the United States entered World War II. On a grand, global scale, this war was ostensibly about making the world safe for freedom, democracy, and equality—three things that black people in America were systematically denied. Black men who served in the military were often relegated to low-grade, unpleasant tasks like kitchen work, cleaning, and hard labor. Black infantry served in segregated units, routinely sent to form the front lines in dangerous battle conditions. Young black men (along with whites) ages eighteen to twenty-two could be drafted into military service, but some employed clever tricks to avoid serving. Common draft-evasion tactics included taking pills that created an arrhythmia, or irregular heartbeat, or faking other disabilities and health issues. Malcolm's approach—acting crazy—also worked for some draftees. Black men who stayed on the home front benefited from new job opportunities, since so many white workers were also forced to leave their jobs to enlist.

Still, nearly a million blacks willingly served in the armed forces during World War II. Those who survived returned home to a nation beset by segregation, lynchings, poverty, and struggle. Over the next two decades, their anger and resentment toward this injustice would help fuel the civil-rights movement, in which Malcolm himself would eventually play a pivotal role.

1950s: Imprisonment and Awakening

When Malcolm went to prison in 1946, he became just one among a vast population of despairing, often hopeless, black prisoners. The living conditions in Charlestown Prison—dark, cramped cells with no plumbing—left them feeling degraded and dehumanized. Poor treatment of prisoners and the disproportionate imprisonment and sentencing of blacks are phenomena that continue today.

Many prisoners turned to faith to sustain them through their sentences. The Nation of Islam, an American sect of Islam founded in 1931, specifically recruited black prisoners to join its ranks. Islam itself is a faith tradition that dates back to the early seventh century. The Qur'an (sometimes spelled "Koran") is the Islamic holy book of scripture, a series of poetic verses revealed to the Prophet Muhammad around the year 610. Followers of Islam, called Muslims (or "those who submit to God"), commit to enacting the five pillars of the faith: profession of faith, daily prayer, tithing, fasting, and making a pilgrimage to Mecca, a holy site in Saudi Arabia. Islam encompasses people of all races, ethnicities, nationalities, and backgrounds. As many as two million enslaved Africans in America were Muslims who had been kidnapped from Africa's western regions. In the

1950s there were about 500 million Muslims worldwide.

The Nation of Islam combined these fundamental beliefs with a Black Nationalist agenda, limiting membership to black Americans and promoting them as a chosen people, deserving of their own land and government. Elijah Muhammad, their leader, spoke eloquently about the challenges facing blacks, and the NOI as a whole worked to empower them. Throughout the country, segregation laws grated on black people, creating day-to-day challenges and reinforcing the notion of white supremacy. The Nation of Islam taught that segregation could work just fine if black citizens could be allowed to govern themselves and determine their own destinies rather than remaining second-class citizens subject to oppressive control by whites.

Malcolm's prison experience had taught him that society considered most black prisoners to be lost causes best shut away. Soon he realized that American society tended to treat *all* black people as criminals and lost causes. The Nation of Islam fought against this reality, a mission that resonated with Malcolm because it echoed the teachings of Marcus Garvey and of his father, which he knew so well.

The social and political consciousness that Malcolm gained in prison mirrored the growing unrest among blacks nationwide. After nearly two centuries of enslavement, degradation, poverty, oppression, and injustice, black Americans felt their anger and frustration once again coming to a head. This fight was not exactly new—Malcolm knew from the long lessons of history his mother had taught him that black people had been fighting for freedom and equality all along—but the struggle gained new momentum through the 1950s.

1960s: Civil-Rights Movement

Between about 1957 and 1965, black Americans staged repeated public demonstrations in favor of justice and equality. Common tactics employed by blacks, along with many white supporters, in this movement for civil rights included public marches and protests, boycotts, sit-ins, and voter registration drives. The most effective acts, sit-ins and boycotts, created economic turmoil for white businesses that refused to serve black citizens. Equally powerful was the movement's decision to respond to violence with nonviolent resistance. White authorities publicly attacked black protesters, who refused to fight back. These conflicts, when captured on film and video, revealed the extent of the brutal hatred and racial violence black citizens had been enduring for centuries.

Similar organizing activities continued through 1968 and beyond. The United States became involved in the Vietnam War in 1960 and did not withdraw until 1972. The familiar anti-enlistment conflict among blacks ("Why should we fight abroad to protect rights we don't have yet at home?") helped fuel civil-rights organizing, particularly late in the decade.

Although Malcolm's ministry as a leader in the Nation of Islam occurred concurrently with the civil-rights movement, he is often considered a peripheral figure because his organizing took place in the urban North, while the heart of the movement was widely considered to be in the segregated South. In reality, Malcolm's work and words had a direct and profound impact on black Americans nationwide, especially the youngest, most disenfranchised blacks.

While other civil-rights activists focused on changing segregation laws and mobilizing the middle and working classes, Malcolm focused on raising the attention of the most overlooked, downgraded members of society— using himself as a model for the potential to turn one's life around. He didn't agree with many other civil-rights leaders that nonviolent protest was a sufficient reaction to the brutalization of black communities. Instead, he argued that all people had the right to self-defense and self-determination. The intense, powerful rhetoric Malcolm used to talk about the needs of his people spoke directly and coherently to this target population, but confused and frightened many others. Malcolm never minded this controversy; he went ahead and said what needed to be said, and history has shown that he consistently spoke difficult but necessary truths.

FURTHER READING

Malcolm X's Life and Work

The Autobiography of Malcolm X by Malcolm X, with the assistance of Alex Haley (New York: Random House/ Ballantine, 1992).

By Any Means Necessary by Malcolm X, a collection of his speeches and writings (New York: Pathfinder, 1992).

Malcolm X: By Any Means Necessary by Walter Dean Myers (New York: Scholastic, 1993).

Malcolm X: Make It Plain by William Strickland (New York: Viking, 1994).

Black History

The African Origin of Civilization – Myth or Reality by Cheik Anta Diop (New York: Lawrence Hill Books, 1974).

The Fire Next Time by James Baldwin (New York: Vintage, 1993).

Freedom's Children: Young Civil Rights Activists Tell Their Own Stories by Ellen Levine (New York: Putnam, 1993).

From Slavery to Freedom: A History of African Americans by John Hope Franklin and Evelyn Brooks Higginbotham, 9th ed. (New York: McGraw-Hill, 2011).

Great Speeches by African Americans, edited by James Daley (Mineola, NY: Dover, 2006).

Nat Turner by Terry Bisson (New York: Chelsea House Publishers, 1988).

The New Jim Crow: Mass Incarceration in the Age of Colorblindness by Michelle Alexander (New York: New Press, 2010).

Selected Writings and Speeches of Marcus Garvey, edited by Bob Blaisdell (Mineola, NY: Dover, 2004).

Historical Fiction

Fire in the Streets by Kekla Magoon (New York: Aladdin, 2012).

Invisible Man by Ralph Ellison (New York: Vintage, 1995).

Native Son by Richard Wright (New York: Harper Perennial, 1987).

The Road to Memphis by Mildred D. Taylor (New York: Puffin, 1992).

The Rock and the River by Kekla Magoon (New York: Aladdin, 2009).

A Wreath for Emmett Till by Marilyn Nelson (Boston: Houghton Mifflin, 2005).

ACKNOWLEDGMENTS

I'd like to express gratitude first and foremost to God the Almighty, and to the many people who aided me in the process of bringing this story to life: As always, I'm grateful for the strength and support of my family, who share my commitment to imparting Malcolm's legacy to future generations. My mother, for keeping my father's presence alive in our home. My sisters, Attallah, Qubilah, Gamilah, Malikah, and Malaak, as well as my nephews and niece: Malcolm, Malik, and Bettih-Bahiyah—eternal love and strength to you. The Little family members who shared many stories, including my father's siblings, particularly my favorite aunt, Hilda Little. My cousin Steve and Deborah Little-Jones and Rodnell Collins for taking my e-mails, telephone calls, and late-night text messages, and Sheryl Little and LeAsah and Shahara Little-Brown, for sharing memories and photographs.

Much gratitude to my agent, Jason Anthony of the Lippincott Massie McQuilkin Agency, and Kekla's agent, Michelle Humphrey of the Martha Kaplan Agency, for their work in bringing us together. Thanks especially to Andrea Tompa for her keen editorial eye, along with Jon Bresman and everyone at Candlewick who helped transform this book from an idea into a reality. And most important, to Kekla Magoon, for helping to shape the story of my father's adolescence into this book.

QUESTIONS TO CONSIDER

1. Instead of telling the story in chronological order, the authors move back and forth through time. What effect does this have on the story?

2. Early in the story, Malcolm says "I am my father's son. But to be my father's son means that they will always come for me" (page 5). What do you think Malcolm means? How does this statement foreshadow everything that happens to him?

3. Malcolm buys a bus ticket to Boston, and in that moment he realizes "it takes less than a minute to buy a new life" (page 8). How did that one action change Malcolm's life?

4. Malcolm refers to the influence Marcus Garvey had on both of his parents. What did Garvey stand for, and how can his influence be seen in the way Malcolm, himself, thinks?

5. In Chapter 3, Mr. Ostrowski says Malcolm "has a lot going for him" but tells him to aim for "a realistic goal for a nigger" (page 51). What effect does this conversation have on Malcolm, and how does it influence his future actions?

6. Upon Malcolm's arrival in Boston, his half-sister Ella wants him to experience the city before he gets a job. How does this change Malcolm?

7. Shorty tells Malcolm: "In this world, everything's a hustle. . . . If it doesn't look like a hustle, you got to look at it from another angle" (page 114). Why does hustling appeal to Malcolm so much?

8. Everyone seems willing to offer Malcolm credit at first. How does this become a problem for him later on?

9. Malcolm reasons that "Negroes don't need improvement. Real Negroes don't sit around and talk about how things should be and what they should have. Real Negroes go out and get some of their own" (page 253). Why does he feel this way?

10. Malcolm feels that it is inevitable that he will go to jail and claims "the whole court is out to get [him]" (page 322). Whom does Malcolm blame for his troubles and why?

11. 22843. With these numbers, Malcolm begins to look at his life in a new way. How does Malcolm see the world through these numbers?

12. After hearing and seeing Bembry in prison, Malcolm remembers that "words are a weapon" (page 331). What do these words mean to Malcolm, and how does he begin to change?

13. What impact does Elijah Muhammad have on Malcolm? How do his words change Malcolm?

14. The words "Up, up, you mighty race" resonate with Malcolm. How does he use these words to create a new life for himself and his people?

15. At the end of the story, Ilyasah Shabazz has added notes to explain many of the events that take place in this novel. Why did she choose to combine fiction and facts? What effect does this have on the story she has told?